ALSO BY BR

THE LOST LEVEL SERIES
The Lost Level • Return to the Lost Level • Hole In the World

THE LEVI STOLTZFUS SERIES
Dark Hollow • Ghost Walk • A Gathering of Crows
Last of the Albatwitches • Invisible Monsters

THE EARTHWORM GODS SERIES
Earthworm Gods • Earthworm Gods II: Deluge
Earthworm Gods: Selected Scenes From the End of the World

THE RISING SERIES
The Rising • City of the Dead
The Rising: Selected Scenes From the End of the World
The Rising: Deliverance

THE LABYRINTH SERIES
The Seven • Submerged

THE CLICKERS SERIES (with J.F. Gonzalez)
Clickers II: The Next Wave • Clickers III: Dagon Rising
Clickers vs. Zombies • Clickers Forever

THE ROGAN SERIES (with Steven Shrewsbury)
King of the Bastards • Throne of the Bastards
Curse of the Bastards

NON-SERIES

Alone • *An Occurrence in Crazy Bear Valley* • *The Cage* • *Castaways*
The Complex • *The Damned Highway* (with Nick Mamatas)
Darkness on the Edge of Town • *Dead Sea* • *Entombed* • *Ghoul*
The Girl on the Glider • *Jack's Magic Beans* • *Kill Whitey*
Liber Nigrum Scientia Secreta (with J.F. Gonzalez) • *Pressure*
School's Out • *Scratch* • *Shades* (with Geoff Cooper)
Silverwood: The Door (with Richard Chizmar, Stephen Kozeniewski, Michelle Garza, and Melissa Lason)
Take The Long Way Home • *Tequila's Sunrise* • *Terminal*
Thor: Metal Gods (with Aaron Stewart-Ahn, Jay Edidin, and Yoon Ha Lee)
Urban Gothic • *White Fire*

COLLECTIONS

Blood on the Page: The Complete Short Fiction, Vol. 1
All Dark, All the Time: The Complete Short Fiction, Vol. 2
Love Letters From A Nihilist: The Complete Short Fiction, Vol. 3
Trigger Warnings
Where We Live and Die

TRIGGER WARNINGS

BRIAN KEENE

Trigger Warnings is a collection of essays, satire, and opinion regarding writing, the horror genre, the publishing industry, pop culture, current events, and people in the public eye. Any resemblance to persons real or imagined (with exception to satire) is purely coincidental.

Trigger Warnings © 2014-2020 by Brian Keene

Cover illustration © 2020 Kealan Patrick Burke

The material in this book was first published at Brian Keene.com between 2009 and 2014, with the following exceptions:

'Not Dead Yet' is original to this collection; 'Cold Warriors – An Examination of George Miller's Mad Max 2: The Road Warrior' first published in *Cinema Futura*, edited by Mark Morris, PS Publishing 2010; 'Seminal Screams' (all four installments) first published in *Shroud Magazine*, Shroud Publishing, 2010-2011; 'Deliverance: On Zombies and Writer's Block and Such' first published (in a different form) in *The Rising: Deliverance*, Thunderstorm Books, 2010; 'Roots' first delivered as the keynote speech at Anthocon, 2011; 'Ghoul: The Author's Perspective' first published in *Brian Keene's Ghoul Collector's Edition Screenplay & Storyboard*, Moderncine, 2012; 'On Writing Full-Time' first delivered as the keynote speech at Borderlands Boot Camp, 2013; 'How Long, Oh Lord, How Long: Hunter S. Thompson and Horror' first published in the lettered edition of *The Damned Highway*, Thunderstorm Books, 2013; 'Why I Still Do This Shit' first delivered as the keynote speech at C3 Writer's Conference, 2013; 'Children Playing with Guns' first published in *The Battle Royale Slam Book*, Haikasoru, 2014; 'Grand-Master Award Acceptance Speech' first delivered at World Horror Convention 2014

ISBN: 9798651133420

CONTENTS

I Am Not Dean Koontz	1
The Strange Case Of The American Reader	4
Vacation	7
Signing In Hell	10
Scream For Me M. Night: Random Thoughts On Iron Maiden And The Happening	15
Love And Worms	21
On Self-Promotion	23
Unsinkable	25
F-Bombs Away	28
The Magus At 41	30
What I Learned At Context 21	34
The More They Say "Change", The More Things Stay The Same	36
Hwa, Or, What To Do With A Sick Dog	39
The Day After: "We The People…"	42
John Urbancik: A New Blurb	47
Cold Warriors — An Examination Of George Miller's "Mad Max 2: The Road Warrior"	48
3 AM Thoughts	52
Days Of Our Lives	54
King Quest (Parts 1 & 2)	57
Stoker Season	61
Seminal Screams: Introduction	63
Seminal Screams: "Among Madmen" By Jim Starlin And Daina Graziunas	67
Seminal Screams: "The House On The Borderland" By William Hope Hodgson	71
Seminal Screams: "The Drive-In" By Joe R. Lansdale	75
Dystopian Tuesday, Or, In The Year 2025	79
Self-Help Books I Intend To Write	82

How Neil Gaiman Broke My Heart And Allowed Me To Win A Debate With J.F. Gonzalez	84
The Dorchester Wars	86
Farewell Teddy Garnett	121
Deliverance: On Zombies And Writer's Block And Such	125
Thoughts On Awards	129
Things They Don't Teach You In Writing Class	132
The End Of Borders	134
Roots	138
The Good Years	149
The Apathy Of Autumn	152
"Dead Air", Or, A Rant About Online Piracy	159
"Ghoul": The Author's Perspective	163
Thoughts On Being Prolific	166
Some Thoughts On Gender, Genre, And Reading	168
Writing, Relationships, And "Dark Hollow"	172
On Ideas And Making Them Yours	175
How To Write 80,000 Words In A Weekend	179
A Grim, Bleak, And Nihilistic Happy Place	184
"What If Nobody Likes It?"	187
Autumn And The Cabal: Musings On Friendship, Time, Writing, And Costs	191
More Than Man's Best Friend	197
Sometimes Writing Doesn't Involve Writing	201
Win A Date With Nickolaus Pacione	204
Self-Publishing: One Year Later	209
The Magus At 45	211
The Centre Cannot Hold	213
Twenty-Five Years In Four Colors	216
On Marriage Equality	219
Twenty-Four Hours After Kindle	221
Today's Tom Sawyer	224
On The House	227
To All The Girls I've Loved Before	230
On Writing Full-Time	234
How Long, Oh Lord, How Long: Hunter S. Thompson And Horror	247

On Professionalism, Elitism, And Things More Important	251
More On Professionalism And Elitism	260
Why I Still Do This Shit	263
How Paul Campion Became The Frank Darabont To My Stephen King	270
Crawling From The Wreckage	272
The Sound Of One Man Giving Up	274
Nickolaus Pacione: Concert Promoter	276
Miss Manners Guide To Being Nominated For A Bram Stoker Award	280
On Rape And Repugnance	282
Children Playing With Guns	289
Grand-Master Award Acceptance Speech	295
What Was I Thinking?	300
Not Dead Yet	304
About the Author	307

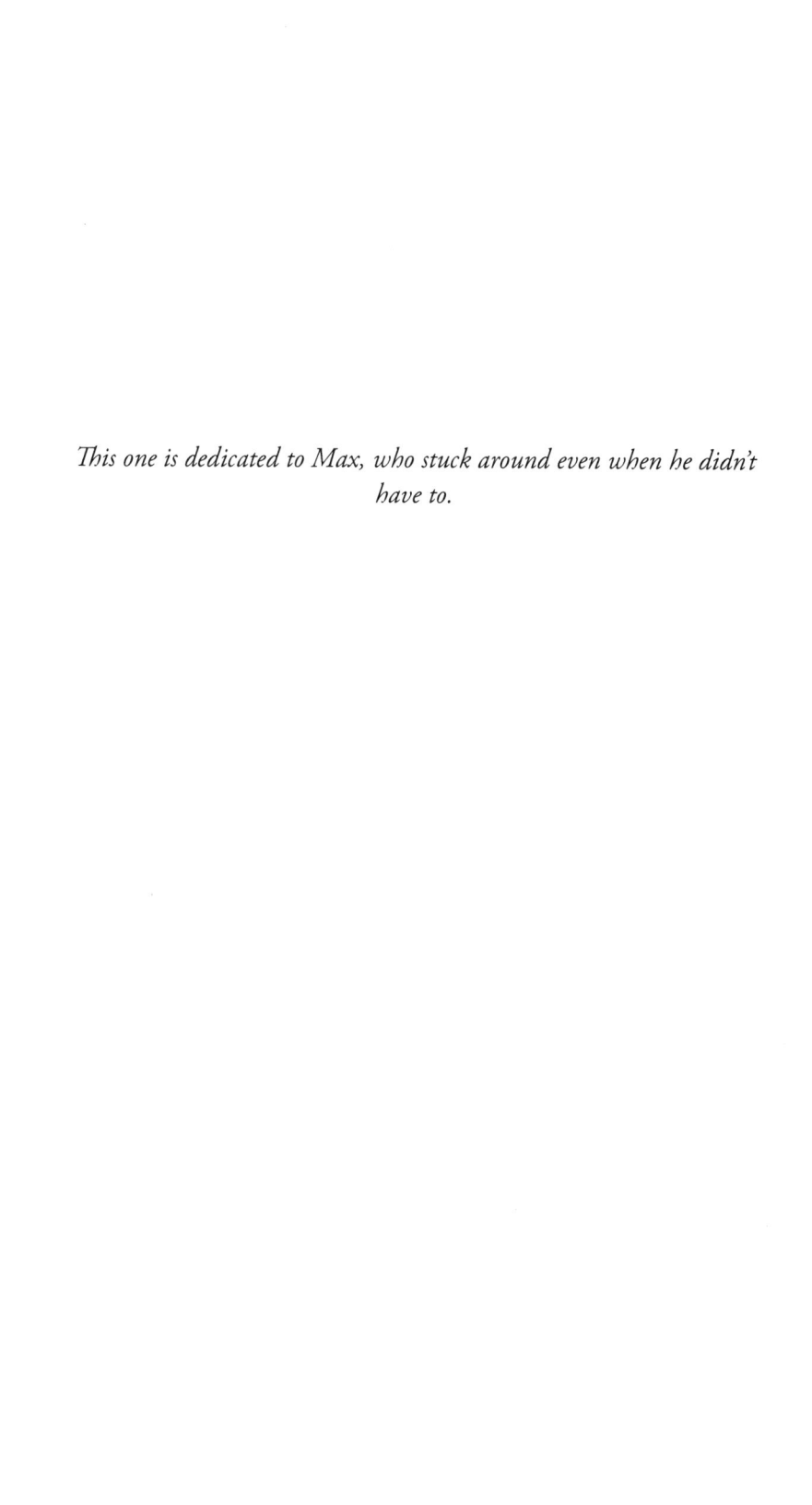

This one is dedicated to Max, who stuck around even when he didn't have to.

I AM NOT DEAN KOONTZ

When Bryan Smith published his first horror novel, *House of Blood*, many people were convinced that he was really nothing more than a pseudonym for Stephen King (the theory being that Bryan Smith was also the name of the driver who ran over Stephen King with his van, and this was King's way of exacting revenge). One London-based newspaper even ran an article speculating as much. This freaked Bryan out at the time, and when he asked me for advice, I told him, "Run with it, dumb ass! Embrace the controversy. It will help sell books." And he did, for about a month, until he had to go out on the road and do book signings. It was then obvious to everyone that Bryan was indeed a real, flesh-and-blood person.

One of my publishers (Cemetery Dance) says there's a new rumor going around. They've been getting emails from fans about it. According to the rumor, 'Brian Keene' is a pseudonym for Dean Koontz. Apparently, because we both have ties to Central Pennsylvania, we are one and the same.

Well, hell. If we apply this logic, then Stephen King can't be Bryan Smith, because he is actually Rick Hautala (they both come from Maine). Nick Mamatas must be Harlan Ellison, because neither of them suffer fools gladly. It also means that Joe R. Lansdale and Bev Vincent are one and the same (they come from Texas) and Tim Lebbon is really Simon Clark (both are Welsh, talk funny and have very little hair on top of their heads. Or maybe Simon isn't Welsh. Who knows? They all talk funny over there. They say, "Cheers" but it sounds like "Chairs." "Logger" means "Lager." Getting "pissed" means getting drunk instead of getting angry). Brian Hodge plus Tom Piccirilli equals Barry Hoffman (all from Colorado). And... ready for this? Jeff Strand. Jeff Vandermeer. Same first name. Both of them reside in Florida. Obviously, they are the same person.

I am not Dean Koontz. But I know Dean. He's a nice guy. And I did, in fact, take his dog, Trixie, for a walk once. My best friend and fellow author Geoff 'Coop' Cooper was with me. We tried using the dog to pick up girls. True story.

Us: "Hey, you know who we got here? Dean Koontz's dog."

California Girl: "Who?"

Us: "Dean Koontz! *Twilight Eyes*? *Strangers*? Motherfucking *Watchers*?"

California Girl: "Are those movies or bands?"

Us: "Neither. They're books."

California Girl: "Oh, I don't read books. Nobody does anymore."

Us: "Well, then get the hell out of here with your illiterate self."

Needless to say, our efforts were less than successful. In the end, we returned Trixie to her owners. End of story.

But I am not Dean Koontz. If I was Dean Koontz, then that means that I would have written *Star Quest* (published in 1968) at the age of one.

So stop being silly.

THE STRANGE CASE OF THE AMERICAN READER

Zogby and Random House have released a thirteen-page poll supposedly detailing the book buying and reading habits of the American public. The data is supposed to be used to better market books and please consumers. The report was posted online as a free PDF.

I've read it three times now, and I still don't know what to make of it. Some of the answers the respondents gave are so infuriatingly bizarre that I'm tempted to stop writing books altogether, lest these people somehow infect the ranks of my loyal readers.

Example: For question number twelve, respondents were asked, "Do you read e-books electronically or do you print them out to read?"

That's a pretty simple question, right? I mean, it doesn't require a PHD to answer that one. If you read e-books, chances are you know whether you read them electronically or print them out, right?

Wrong. Sixty-one percent of the poll's participants responded, "Not sure."

Think about that for a moment…sixty-fucking-one-fucking-percent aren't sure whether they read their e-books electronically or whether they print them out. And one poor bastard, according to the results, was apparently unsure if he or she had ever purchased an e-book.

Even more vexing than the participants' responses were some of the questions that Zogby and Random House thought were relevant to the discussion. Keep in mind that Random House is the world's biggest publisher. Everyone pretty much agrees that the publishing industry is in trouble. You'd think that Random House would have a vested interest in discovering ways to increase sales again.

I'm not sure how results like the ones for question number twenty-six can be used in this endeavor. Question number twenty-six includes, quote: "Respondents who identify themselves as residents of the planet earth (62%)..."

What? Who the fuck did Zogby poll, exactly? Did Whitley Strieber hook them up with a few Gray aliens? Did a research team descend upon the Mos Eisley cantina and interview Hammerhead and Greedo? Did we learn that Skrulls like the works of Louisa May Alcott while Martians prefer Joel Olsteen's drivel? And if only 62% of the respondents identified themselves as residents of the Planet Earth, where the hell did the other 38% come from? Is there a Barnes and Noble on Europa? Are David Icke's Reptilians logging onto Amazon.com from the other side of the galaxy and leaving one-star reviews?

The thing I found most perplexing was the poll's repeated references to the ephemeral 'American Dream'. I'm aware that most of my younger readers probably don't even know what that is, and that's okay, kids, because it doesn't exist. It was a lie told to our grandparents and our parents and repeated to us. And even if it did exist, my generation have pretty much squandered it away. For the sake of argument, the American Dream was defined as life, liberty, and the pursuit of happiness. That's all fine and dandy. That's a lofty and valid and worthwhile goal (even if we don't have it anymore). But answer me this. How does life, liberty, and the pursuit of happiness factor in to whether or not you purchase a Stephen King novel? Can someone explain that to me? And didn't Hunter S. Thompson prove that the American Dream was a burned-out slab of concrete in Las Vegas? Perhaps a better question would have been, "How much has the price of gasoline impacted your book purchases?"

One thing the poll does seem to echo is that horror, as a genre label, is in a decline again. Some people still insist that's not true, but bookstore chain buyers have stated publicly that the genre has reached its saturation point, and many editors and publishers are confirming the same thing in private. I happen to agree with that assessment. Indeed, I predicted it about a year and a half ago, and a lot of my peers wailed and gnashed their teeth and said I was being an asshole again. Many of those same peers are now strangely absent or self-publishing their latest horror novel because they couldn't find anyone to buy it.

And many of my peers who secretly agreed with me began writing in other genres (fantasy, crime-suspense, etc.) and are doing quite well. Speaking of which, I need to get back to work on this comic book.

But never mind that, eh? We've got worse things to worry about. Apparently, according to Zogby and Random House, the American readership is composed primarily of extraterrestrials who are too stupid to know how they read their e-books.

VACATION

So, for the Fourth of July weekend (for our foreign readers, Fourth of July is a holiday in which Americans celebrate the independence of their country by blowing shit up and driving really far in their cars, which is harder to do than you might think because many states have outlawed fireworks and you can't drive that far when unleaded gasoline is almost five dollars a gallon).

But I digress. Okay, let's start over.

So, for the Fourth of July weekend, my wife and I decided to take our son to meet his great-grandparents. At three-and-a-half months old, he sleeps from 7pm to around 5am, so on Thursday, we loaded him into the car at 7pm and drove seven and a half hours to a remote location in West Virginia. He didn't cry once. That was bright spot number one.

We spent most of Friday being preached at. Examples: "It is your parental responsibility to raise that child in a God-fearing church" and "Prayers are stored in Heaven and pulled out for rainy days." I refrained from telling them I'm an agnostic, and my wife refrained from having an aneurysm each time she was told that her Catholic faith is the wrong faith.

I shouldn't complain. I love my grandparents and it was very important to me that my son get to spend as much time with them as possible. And I know they mean well. They're in the 80's and set in their ways. But there's only so much God I can take.

Seeing the looks on their faces when they played with the baby instead of preaching was bright spot number two.

Friday night involved more preaching.

Saturday morning, I saw three bucks, two doe, and a little baby fawn that let me get within eight feet of it. That was bright spot number three.

Saturday afternoon involved more preaching. Then, for a special treat, we read the Bible. Out loud. For an hour.

Saturday evening, we took Turtle to meet my cousin and his wife. That was bright spot number four.

Sunday involved preaching because that is what you do on Sunday. Then I dug up some white pine saplings to plant here at home and we took Turtle to visit his great, great aunt. That was bright spot number five.

Then we drove seven and a half hours home through a blinding rainstorm and stopped at two different gas stations in two different states who were both out of gas. I also got in a fight with a tractor trailer driver.

Then we got home at midnight and found out that while we were gone, my cat, Max, got into a fight with a raccoon, skunk, or possum, and a pipe burst in our basement, flooding the entire house and emptying our well. There is five feet of water in my basement, I can't take a shower, I probably need a new hot water heater and a new well pump, and to top it all off, my cat has an ugly scratch on his back and lost a claw and I can't take him to the vet because I have to wait for the insurance adjuster and a team of ninja plumbers.

I'll be damned if I can find a bright spot in that.

This week, I'd intended to turn in a short story called "Halves", finish a weird-western novella called *An Occurrence In*

Crazy-Bear Valley, finish the second issue of *Dead of Night: Devil Slayer*, and get cracking on something for Joe R. Lansdale. I'd also intended to answer some of these emails, because they are backing up.

But instead, I now need a vacation from my vacation.

SIGNING IN HELL

My peers had quite the weekend. They're all back from the Chicago Comic Con, Hypericon, or a big party in North Carolina at author Drew Williams' house. They're Blogging their savage tales of adventure and debauchery and good times at these events, and telling me things like, "Oh, you should have been there, Brian. Too bad you and J.F. Gonzalez had that book signing to go to on Saturday."

Yep, too-fucking-bad.

There are two things that I take great pride in regarding this business.

1) I take care of my readers.
2) I take care of my booksellers.

Seriously, we're in this war together (and believe me, brothers and sisters, these days, it is indeed a war). You support me. I support you. Thus has it always been. Thus shall it always be. Amen.

Politically, I'm mostly a Libertarian who leans left on social issues. But if there's one thing I'm a big fan of, it's capitalism—when capitalism puts money in my pockets. Be it an illicit batch of moonshine or my latest horror novel, I get behind my product. I like it to do well, because when it does well, then I do well. So do the booksellers who sell it.

This weekend, like everyone else, I could have gone to the conventions in Chicago or Nashville, or to the party in North Carolina, but I didn't. Instead, I decided to help a bookseller make some money—and thus, make myself some money and make a group of my readers happy. In fact, I could have also visited an old Navy buddy whom I haven't seen in almost twenty years, but again, I decided to forgo that in lieu of this signing.

The manager of the Borders on Lancaster's Park Drive contacted J.F. "Jesus" Gonzalez and I several months ago, and asked us to come do a book signing at her store. We happily agreed. We provided her with a list of the books we'd like to sign, including title, ISBN, publisher, and price-point. I also said, "Local readers already have *City of the Dead, Ghoul,* and the rest of my backlist. We probably won't sell many of those. Instead, make sure you have plenty of copies of *Dark Hollow, Kill Whitey,* and *The Rising: Selected Scenes from the End of the World* on hand. Those are what people will be looking for." She confirmed that indeed, she would do this.

So when I showed up half-an-hour early on Saturday, you can imagine my surprise when I saw a tiny little table up front with exactly one copy of *Dark Hollow,* four copies of *Ghoul,* and six copies of *The New Fear: The Best of Hail Saten Vol. 3.* That was it. That was all they had. And there were even less copies of books by Jesus—one copy of *Clickers,* one copy of *Survivor,* one copy of *Bully,* and four copies of *The Beloved.*

"Okay," I said to myself. "They just haven't put the rest of the books out yet."

I walked around the store, looking for the manager so I could check in. Before I found the manager, the crew from Reel Splatter Films found me instead. They'd shown up to get copies of *The Rising: Selected Scenes from the End of the World.* The first thing young filmmaker Mike Lombardo asked me was, "Dude, where the hell are your books?"

We checked the horror section, and I found one copy of *The Rising*, one copy of *Dead Sea*, and one copy of *The Conqueror Worms*. I took those up to the table. I now had twelve books to sign and sell.

Then I noticed a second, even smaller table next to ours. The nametag on the table indicated it was for author Jacquelyn Sylvan. They'd hidden her across from Jesus and me, near the magazine section. They had six copies of her books. Now, I was absolutely convinced that they must have more books in the back. Jacquelyn writes romance novels, and you can easily sell those to walk-through traffic. It was impossible that the store would only have six of her books on hand.

Eventually, I found some store employees. I introduced myself and told them I was there for the signing. It turns out they didn't know about the signing, despite the fact that they had posters up in the store advertising it, and a table up front with our names on it and a few books. An employee then told me to wait up at the table and "they" would be along shortly. I assumed that "they" meant the manager, so I did as I was told. I sat down at the table. The employees then asked me what I was doing.

I said, "You told me to wait here."

They said, "Yes, but that's where the author will sit. You have to stand in line."

"I am the author."

They blinked at me. "What was your name again?"

"Do I look like a Jacquelyn? Do I look like my last name is Gonzalez?"

"Who are they, again?"

It was at that moment that I seriously considered buying the few meager copies of my books that they had in stock, declaring a sell-out, and just blowing off the whole fucking thing. But I couldn't do that to Jesus, and I couldn't do it to my fans.

At this point, there were approximately fifty people in line. I judged that about half of them were there for Jesus and me, and the other half were there for Jacquelyn. I tried to keep them entertained while I waited. Jesus was running late. Jacquelyn arrived, quickly sold her few copies, and hightailed it out of there. She stopped by to say hi on her way out. Nice woman. If you dig romance, check her books out.

Finally, Jesus showed up, and he was less-than-pleased when he saw the books on the table.

"Where are the rest of them?" he asked.

"This is all they have."

"Are you sure?"

I told him I would check again. I found another employee and said, quote: "Hi. My name is Brian Keene. I was supposed to sign books here today, along with JF Gonzalez. Do you know if you have any more of our books in the back room?"

She blinked at me and then said, "They are probably on the shelf. Did you look on the shelf?"

"Yes, and I only found three. None of them were the new books."

"I can check. What was the name?"

"Keene and Gonzalez."

She typed—and I am not making this up—'Keene Gonzalez' into the computer. First name: Keene. Last name: Gonzalez. Then she said, "We don't have any authors named Keene Gonzalez."

I tried very hard not to shout at her. "Try Brian Keene and JF Gonzalez."

She did. The computer told her that they had twenty-one copies of *Dead Sea* and twenty-two copies of *Shapeshifter* in the store. I asked her if she could go get them out of the back room.

"Oh, they aren't back there. We must have sold them all yesterday. Or else we sent them back. It takes the computer a day to catch up."

I returned to the table, broken and defeated and in an ugly and savage mood, seriously contemplating giving the crowd of fans hanging out at the table permission to run riot throughout the store.

So, my apologies to the folks who drove all the way from Virginia, and the nice couple from Keene, New Hampshire, and the guy who made the trek from Delaware, and all of the Reel Splatter crew, and everyone else who showed up at the bookstore on Saturday with the actual expectation of being able to purchase books (which was not an unreasonable expectation—bookstores should indeed sell books) and get them signed. I apologize for the inept, ignorant, and totally rude staff, and I whole-heartedly encourage you to run riot inside that store should you ever have the misfortune to set foot inside it again.

Then, after you've run riot inside the Lancaster Borders, head across the river to the Borders in York or the Borders Express in Camp Hill, where they have actual Brian Keene sections, and have copies of the new books on the shelf, and have copies of all of Jesus's books, too. Give them your money and support, because they support me and you.

And before someone suggests it, no, I am not disparaging Borders as a whole. Some of my best friends manage Borders stores. I sign at more Borders stores each year than I do any other. I worked at a Borders for a summer (when it was still a Waldenbooks). And I have never, ever done a three hour signing where I've sold less than thirty copies. Usually it is quite more. The store makes money. I make money. The fans are happy. When it works, it works well. I could have done that on Saturday, if I'd had the books to sell.

You couldn't pay me to sign there again.

SCREAM FOR ME M. NIGHT: RANDOM THOUGHTS ON IRON MAIDEN AND THE HAPPENING

We begin with a special shout-out to reader Rich, who recognized me in the beer line at last night's Iron Maiden concert. Nice talking to you, dude. Thanks for the good words. Hope you dig *Devil Slayer*. And sorry if I seemed incoherent. My sometime assistants Tomo and Dave "Meteornotes" Thomas were force-feeding me beer all afternoon.

My brain is fuzzy this morning. I am reminded once again why, at age forty, one cannot bang one's head all night long, and sing along with every song, and jump up and down like a lunatic, and still expect to feel like he's twenty the next morning. My ears are ringing badly, and talking is akin to gargling with ground glass.

Therefore, rather than properly reviewing both, here are some random thoughts on M. Night Shyamalan's *The Happening* and Iron Maiden's Baltimore show.

And this is your obligatory spoiler warning.

I take pride in being one of M. Night Shyamalan's most strident supporters. I enjoy his films. I watch them repeatedly, studying them for nuance and subtlety and subtext. I thought The Sixth

Sense was a fine ghost story. I thought *Unbreakable* was the perfect love letter to anyone who has ever read comic books and wished they happened in real life. *Signs* was an intriguing take on faith, belief and spirituality. *The Village* was brilliant, and remains one of my top twenty favorite horror films of all time. Hell, I even liked *The Lady in the Water* and its clever examination of the muse.

I realize this puts me in a minority, but I don't care. As far as I'm concerned, the man can't make a bad film. Plus, we Central Pennsylvania horror-meisters have to stick together.

I wanted to enjoy *The Happening*.

I did not.

The Happening might very well be one of the worst horror films I have ever seen. This is a shame, because it had the potential to be one of his finest works. All of the ingredients were there. An intriguing premise. A suspenseful plot. Beautiful cinematography. And Mark Wahlberg (joke all you want, but it is my sincere belief that Mark Wahlberg is this generation's Bruce Willis. He's a perfectly capable journeyman actor who almost always delivers a good performance).

Taken on their own, these parts should add up to box-office success. Instead, they create a turgid, listless mess.

One day, the plants decide to kill off all the human beings. They do this by creating a special type of pollen which, when inhaled, makes us kill ourselves. Unlike other M. Night movies, there is no surprise twist ending, so that's pretty much it.

However, rather than having the plot reveal this to the viewer, it is conveyed by a number of secondary characters who exist only to explain to the viewer what is happening on-screen. Seriously. There's a guy who owns a greenhouse and a National Guard private, and both of them are given lines that tell us nothing about their characters and everything about what's happening in the film. Worse—these lines are shoehorned in at awkward and totally inappropriate places:

Mark Wahlberg: "Would you like a hamburger or a hot dog?"

Greenhouse Guy: "Say, Mark, did you know that plants can create enzymes when threatened, and that those enzymes can impact the behavior of other living creatures?"

Mark Wahlberg: "So, you want a hamburger, then?"

The script is flawed. The realistic dialogue that earmarks so many of M. Night's other films is missing here, replaced by random gibberish and lines that exist only to advance the characters to the next scene.

Characters behave in decidedly unrealistic ways. "Let's all hang out in the middle of a barley field and talk about how the plants are trying to kill us." "Let's all hang out under this tree and talk about how the plants are trying to kill us." Mark Wahlberg's character never thinks to loot a gun from the nearest abandoned home (this is Pennsylvania after all, and everyone owns a gun), and thus, every peril they face throughout the rest of the film (breaking into a fortified house, trying to hitch a ride, looking for food, etc.) happens as a result.

The Happening's greatest flaw is Zooey Deschanel, who is to acting what Osama bin Laden is to world peace. Until yesterday, I had never seen Miss Deschanel in a film (at least, that I remember). I know now to avoid anything she's connected with. Her character is supposed to be tragic and flawed and sympathetic. Instead, after her first three minutes on-screen, you're begging the nearest oak tree to kill her off.

In short, there ain't much happening in *The Happening*. Everyone is allowed to produce at least one dud, however. Indeed, my critics would say I've produced quite a few. And I'll still eagerly await M. Night's next film.

* * *

After the movie, I met up with Tomo, Meteornotes, and Mrs. Meteornotes, and we went to the Iron Maiden show. It was, to the best of my knowledge, a sold out venue.

Before the concert started, we entertained ourselves by drinking beer and sending text messages to the stadium. The stadium then flashes the text messages on the big screen for all the concert-goers to see. There were lots of, "Keesha, will u marry me? Bob" and "GO ORIOLES!" and "U R 2 sexy, Jill".

We soon grew annoyed with these, so we decided to send our own.

Meteornotes sent, "GIANT CARNIVOROUS BEES ARE ATTACKING THE STADIUM!"

I sent, "Brian Keene's GHOST WALK – In Stores August 1".

And Tomo sent "Nickolaus Pacione, will you marry me? Luv Ron Dickie"

The opening act was Iron Maiden bassist Steve Harris's daughter. Meh. She was less than spectacular. Her music sounds like every generic metal song from every generic 80's movie (think of the band playing on the boardwalk in *Lost Boys* or the band playing the prom in *Better Off Dead*). She is, however, very easy on the eyes. I dunno. Maybe I need to buy her disc and give it a listen. Maybe the studio stuff sounds better than it did live.

Iron Maiden took the stage at 8:42pm. There was no preamble. No hint that it was about to occur. I was busy texting with Richard Christy and Coop and almost missed it. One minute, lights. The next minute, BOOM.

The stage set is simply awe-inspiring. Most of it is from the *Powerslave* tour, but it's been updated a bit. There were, of course, lots of pyrotechnics and explosions and fireworks and cannons shooting flames and giant mummies and giant cyborgs. Bruce Dickinson made five or six different costume changes— The Trooper, The Rhyme of the Ancient Mariner, etc. The songs were all classics—nothing past *Fear of the Dark*. The encore was especially wonderful. I was pleasantly surprised to hear several tracks off *Seventh Son of A Seventh Son* (which I personally think is Maiden's greatest disc ever—and their most underrated).

80s metal acts are the popular concert ticket right now, and they all know it, and that's why we're being treated to reunions of everybody from Van Halen and Dio-era Black Sabbath to Cinderella and Poison. Their core audience—us—are now the primary American consumers. It's a license to print money. But unlike many of those 80s bands, who have reunited for that very reason, Iron Maiden are clearly having fun. They are having a ball, playing songs and listening to the crowd sing along with every note—at times, actually drowning out the band. Their mood is infectious. Most pleasing is the phenomena I've noticed at other shows like Queensryche and Anthrax—metal becoming a multi-generational event, with parents taking their kids, and the kids being just as enthusiastic as we ever were, knowing and loving songs that we were listening to behind the shop class long before they were even born.

Final verdict: a wonderful concert, and easily worth the $85 ticket price. See it, if it comes to your town.

Oh, and I guess I'd be remiss if I left this part out. I got to punch somebody in the head during the concert, too. You know those guys who go to concerts and hop around the stadium, taking empty seats until they get kicked out by an usher, and then they move on to the next empty seat? And usually, they do this while standing right in front of you and blocking your view? Yeah, those guys. The only thing more loathsome than those guys are people who talk on their cell phones during a movie.

Anyway, one of those guys ended up in our row, which had no empty seats (since we were down front). This guy didn't care. He proceeded to stand in front of me. He was so close that my penis was quite literally lodged between his butt cheeks. Further, he kept throwing the devil horns and jostling my beer.

Tomo leaned over to me and said, "I want to go get a beer, but I know you won't behave yourself."

I said, "I will too behave. Watch this."

I then sang along with the chorus of "Number of the Beast" and threw the devil horns right into the back of homeboy's head. Once. Twice. Three times. He got the message and left, and didn't bother us again. And Tomo went and fetched some beers.

Great fucking show.

LOVE AND WORMS

Oddly enough, several people have recently asked about *Love and Worms*, and wondered what happened to it.

If you're new, perhaps an explanation is in order. *Love and Worms* is an unfinished novel that I've been working on sporadically for about fifteen years. I started it long before I ever began getting published. I re-started it after I began getting published. I scrapped it and re-started it after I began writing for a living. I lost it in a hard drive crash. I re-started it again. And so on and so on.

Love and Worms is about a serial killer who attends his twenty year high school reunion and reconnects with his childhood sweetheart. He also has to deal with his homicidal pet tapeworm, who is not happy with this turn of events. *Love and Worms* wants to be a 300,000 word manuscript in an era when it's career suicide to try and sell a 300,000 word manuscript to New York publishing. Hell, at that length, I'd even have a hard time selling it to a small press. But that's what it'll take to tell the story correctly.

I still work on it, when the mood arises. In fact, I just worked on it two weeks ago. Despite this, no progress has been made and I'm beginning to doubt you will ever see it, because I don't think there's any way I'll ever finish it.

Here's why:

Pretend you're a disc jockey. Pretend you have to mix Motley Crue's "Too Young To Fall In Love", Guns n Roses' "14 Years", Prince's "Take Me With You", Simple Minds' "Don't You (Forget About Me)", and The Scorpions' "Still Loving You". Not only do you have to mix them—you have to mix them into one cohesive song.

While you're doing this, pretend that it's taken you fifteen years to mix the fucking thing. A lot changes in fifteen years. Pretend that you've abused your body during that time with drugs, sex, alcohol, and exciting adventures both before and after you became a professional writer, and can no longer remember what it was like to feel like your protagonist. When you try, you don't even get a little twinge. Just a vague recollection.

And then, while you're doing all of that, pretend that all of the characters in the book suddenly resurface in real life, and absolutely none of them are as you remembered, so you can't even draw on that for inspiration, and thus, it further fucks up the mix.

Then, pretend that once—just once—after about ten years into this thing, you thought you had the mix right, but then your iPod crashed and you hadn't backed anything up, and all of that work was lost.

And then pretend that there are people who show up at the club every weekend to hear you spin. Pretend that when you tell them about the mix you're trying to make, they all tell you that instead of wanting to hear that unique and eclectic mix, they just want to hear more straightforward zombie songs.

That's what it's like, writing *Love and Worms*.

And that's why I'll probably never finish it.

ON SELF-PROMOTION

Yes, I know I said there wouldn't be many new Blog posts this week because my best friends and fellow authors Mike Oliveri and Michael T. Huyck were in town to visit me and Geoff Cooper. However, Mike and Mikey went to Gettysburg today, and Coop was studying, and I had a bit of free time this evening. I was lurking on an online message board, and I posted this in response to a question about new authors and self promotion, and thought it was worth a repost here:

Obviously, I'm a big believer in self-promotion. Do I think it's solely the author's domain? No. The majority of promotion should fall first and foremost on the publisher.

Of course, we know better, don't we? Publishers have tight budgets, and although they will indeed spend money to promote you, they don't seem to do that until you're making them money (or at least that's been my general experience). This is especially true in the mass market realm.

So yes, promotion is important. But I think far too many new writers focus way too much on that aspect of the business and forget about what comes first…

…the writing.

Before you worry about promotion, you have to write something *worth* promoting. Especially if you're doing this to "get your name out there". Especially given this current economy. Money is tight. Readers are still willing to take a chance on a new author, but one chance and one chance only. If that new author doesn't give them something worth coming back for, chances are they won't.

There's nothing wrong with getting up on the soapbox and shouting, "Hear me, world, for I have written something and I want you to read it!" After all, no writer in their right mind wants their work to go unread. However, before you get up on the soapbox, make sure that what you have to share is your absolute best. Make sure it shines, and that you've given it everything you have. Make sure that you've devoted just as much time and energy to its creation as you have to its promotion.

UNSINKABLE

This past weekend, I attended a reunion for the sailors (like myself) who served aboard the U.S.S. Austin, LPD-4. I had a great time, but ever since I left the reunion, I've been in a fugue state of conflicting emotions. I'm sad, happy, and introspective all at once.

The reunion was attended by men from all of the Austin's various deployments. Vietnam-era veterans (plank owners), crew members from the Seventies, my gang—the crew from the Eighties, and the kids who came after us, all the way up to the ship's decommissioning in 2006.

I did not know the sailors from the other eras, but I recognized my fellow crew members right away. Twenty years have passed. We've grown fat, bald, gray, infirm, and wrinkled. Yet we recognized each other right away. There were hugs, and quite a few spontaneous tears. We spoke of those who are no longer with us, or missing, and we reminisced about times past, recalling them as if they were yesterday, and laughing about them or raging about them with the same fervor we laughed and raged about them when they first happened.

Brotherhood is like that. You recognize each other right away, and although you haven't spoken in over two decades, you're instantly comfortable again, reliving the past and confiding in shared experiences that you haven't shared with anyone since.

If you've never served, you can't really understand it. Oh, you can empathize. But actual understanding is something else. The opposite is also true. If you haven't served, I can't successfully communicate to you just what these men mean to me. As a writer, that's very frustrating, because I make my living communicating with words.

But there are some things for which mere words will not suffice.

I haven't seen these guys in twenty years. Not a visit. Not an email. Not even a Christmas card. Yet there hasn't been a single day in which my thoughts didn't turn to them at some point. They are more than friends. They are my brothers.

And so are the sailors from the other eras.

We came from all walks of life. All races and regions and socio-political-economic backgrounds. We probably wouldn't have hung out with each other had we met somewhere else— college or a job or something like that.

We were total strangers, yet despite our disparate backgrounds, we all had one thing in common.

A woman.

She was a demanding lover. Like many other women, she had needs. She required us to take her on vacation around the world every year. We had to learn her intimately—all her nooks and crannies. What buttons she liked pushed, and what her turn offs were. She could be high maintenance, sometimes. She required constant makeovers—scrubbing the deck and painting the hull like they were lipstick and eyeliner. And she was not a fickle lover. Indeed, she gave herself to every man who came along. She had many lovers, but we accepted that. We were not her first. We would not be her last. Sometimes she was cruel. She took us to cold, desolate places or hot, sweltering locations. She kept us from our other loves, demanding that we put her before all others. In time, most of us grew to loathe her. We told ourselves that we couldn't wait to be free of her. That we would never see her again, or think of her once we'd escaped her clutches.

But we were wrong. She got under our skin, that ship. Without her, we would have never had each other.

She's seen better days. She's off the circuit now. Keeps to herself. Her make-up has faded, and that endless line of suitors have left their mark. She's been gutted of everything—equipment, copper wire, etc. She's spending her last days moored at a civilian dock in Philadelphia, with a bunch of civilians who don't know her history and can't see her beauty. All they see is the dollar value of her scrap.

Soon, she will make one final voyage. Brooklyn, this time. She'll be cut up. Recycled into razor blades.

But her memory will live on. It will last as long as we last.

Steel rusts. Decks crack. Ships sink.

But brotherhood is eternal.

Let's not wait another twenty years, guys.

F.T.N.

F-BOMBS AWAY

Recently, it has come to my attention that some of my readers think I curse too much. Or, rather, they think my characters curse too much.

Some pinhead left this review on Amazon.com: "I found *Ghost Walk* to be full of… foul-mouthed characters. (Practically every other word being an unlikely and misplaced cuss word of the lowest nature)."

Then, another pinhead left this review on B&N.com (sic): "Actually, it's… pretty foul, especially when he has characters call Diety filthy names. I won't be reading him again — or recommending him to others. He should be ashamed of himself."

Now, I stopped reading Amazon and B&N customer reviews several years ago, but my assistant thought I would get a chuckle out of these two (and I did). He also thought I'd get a chuckle out of the following, sent via MySpace (once again, sic):

"Brain, why is it that you have characters who cuss? I mean not all of your characters do but some do and that's not really necessary is it? You should be more considerate than that. My son reads your books and that's great because he's 16 and getting him to read anything is like pulling teeth. And all his friends read your books too. But don't you feel bad that your teraching a generation to swear? Please try to watch that in the future and remember that there are kids reading these. You can tell the story without all the objectionable language."

You know what? You're right. There are impressionable children reading my books, and that is my responsibility, rather than the responsibility of their parents. I mean, why should we expect parents to have an active role in their children's lives? Why should we expect them to take an interest in what their child is reading, watching, or doing?

Nope. It's the responsibility of the artist.

So what I'll do is this. I'll start writing comic books instead. After all, we know that kids don't read comic books, right?

I wrote a new comic book series for Marvel Comics. It's called *Dead of Night: Devil-Slayer* and it will be in stores next Thursday. The objectionable language for the first issue is as follows:

Hell, Helluva, Fucking, Fuck, Shit, Fuck, Christ, Hell, Pissed and Piss.

In a comic book.

And if that's the biggest thing you have to worry about in little Johnny's life, consider yourself fucking lucky.

Shit…

THE MAGUS AT 41

Before we begin, I'd like to apologize to my neighbors (all of whom I suspect read this Blog) for yesterday's rather massive explosion. I honestly did not know that an open-topped, steel, fifty-five gallon drum would explode like that just by adding gasoline and a dozen aerosol cans. Suffice to say, there were more flames atop yesterday's burn barrel than there were on yesterday evening's birthday cake. You can rest assured that I did this strictly for research purposes, for I am a writer, and life is one big research project. And I think we all learned something from the incident—standing that close to such an explosion results in you losing most of your back hair and suffering first-degree burns on your arm.

So that's how I started my forty-first year on the planet. With a rather big explosion.

And today, on the second day of my forty-first year on the planet, I was reminded once again of how my wife is much smarter than me.

As you might know, I'll be busy doing Guest of Honor stuff at Context in Columbus this coming weekend. I'm hitting the road Thursday morning, along with fellow authors JF Gonzalez and Bob Ford. I'll return Sunday night.

So this evening, my wife was feeding Turtle (the public name I use for my son so that crazies don't know his real name) his oatmeal and I was making him laugh and spit it all back out, and she said, "I'm nervous about this weekend."

And I said, "I know. This is the first time I've been away this long since Turtle was born. But I left the .357 in the foyer, and the .38 is in the dresser, and the .45 is in the kitchen. Just remember to disengage the child locks before you shoot any intruders."

"That's not what I'm nervous about," my wife said in a tone that clearly communicated what she was really saying was, "You are such an idiot. I can't believe I married you when I could have married a nice investment banker instead, who didn't have such an unreliable job or weird friends."

"Then what's bothering you?"

"I'm not looking forward to teaching Turtle to sleep in the crib."

See, Turtle turned six months old recently, and he has yet to sleep in the crib by himself for an entire night. We've attempted it, certainly, but the child is blessed with his father's temperament, which means that he basically screams and rants at the top of his lungs until someone picks him up.

"Well," I said. "Why start this weekend?"

"Because you won't be here."

"Why do you have to do it when I'm not here?"

"Because you don't have the guts."

I opened my mouth to respond, but nothing came out. I searched my mind for a witty response, but none was forthcoming.

"Erm," I said.

"Ah," I followed it up with.

"Um," came next.

"Erm," I repeated again, just to round things off.

"Guts," I finally stammered. "I don't have the guts? Jesus Christ, honey!"

"What?"

"You don't tell a man—especially a forty-one year old man who's in the beginning stages of feeling his mortality—that he lacks guts. I mean, what the hell, while you're at it, why not just suggest that my penis size is inadequate?"

"I can make it longer than you can."

"So it *is* inadequate! I knew it. I knew all those women before you were lying to me!"

"Not your dick, you dick. Trust me, you've got more down there than most men do. I'm talking about the crib."

"Huh?"

"All I meant was that when we put him in the crib, I can take him crying longer than you can. As soon as he whimpers, you pick him up and soothe him."

"Well, duh. He's a baby."

"But he needs to learn to soothe himself. Do you want him to be doing this when he's five?"

I shook my head. Obviously, if Turtle was still doing this five years from now, it would seriously hamper my sex life. He needed to learn to sleep in his own room.

"I'm his Daddy," I explained. "I don't like it when he's unhappy or upset. It's my job to fix those things."

"Yes, but you have to be strong. You have to let him cry it out."

"I do."

My wife laughed at me. Turtle watched her laughing, then joined in, banging his high chair with his little fists and giggling with glee.

I frowned. "What's so funny?"

"You don't have the guts," she repeated.

"I do so."

"Coop's wife told me that you told her and Coop that he cried for an hour and forty-five minutes the other night."

"He did!"

"It was fifteen minutes."

Now it was my turn to laugh. "I think you're wrong."

"How would you even know how long he cried? You were only in there for three minutes. Then you ran outside in tears because you said you couldn't take it."

I mumbled, "It sure felt like and hour and forty-five minutes."

"My point is," my wife said, "it might be best to do this while you're not home."

I reluctantly agreed that she was right. Then we played with Turtle for an hour or so. Then I kissed them both goodnight and went out to my office to work.

I am blessed with a beautiful wife who is much smarter than me, and a wonderful child who is blessed with his mother's good looks and intelligence. And I still get paid to make up stories about monsters and heroes and get paid good money for it.

Forty-one is gonna be magic.

I am still the Magus.

And my penis is still massive…

WHAT I LEARNED AT CONTEXT 21

6:00am on a Sunday morning in Columbus, Ohio. Two-hundred drunken authors and their fans are snoring it up and sleeping it off. But not me, and not Kealan Patrick Burke.

I am sitting here typing, and wishing I had some way of contacting my old Navy buddy Paul, who lives here in Columbus. Sadly, my cell phone fell into a toilet yesterday, and his number, along with everyone else's' numbers, are now also in the toilet. Everyone else that's here at the con—Gary Braunbeck, Nick Mamatas, Tim Waggoner, Michael Laimo, Lawrence Connolly, JF Gonzalez, and all the others—may rest easy this morning, safe from my notorious pre-dawn drunken prank calls.

They are asleep.

I am awake.

And so is Kealan Patrick Burke.

Here is what I learned this weekend:

1. I still have the absolute best readers in the god-damned world. Seriously. You guys rock, and it is such a pleasure to write for you.

2. Kealan Patrick Burke is not human. Kealan Patrick Burke has the stamina and constitution of Sam Adams, Jim Beam, and Jack Daniels all rolled into one. Understand me when I say this.

I come from a long line of Irish drinkers. Like Hunter S. Thompson, I am blessed with an almost super-human liver that allows me to ingest enormous quantities of alcohol with no real wear and tear on my body. I can and have drank such notorious drinkers as Tim Lebbon and Carlton Mellick III under the table, and then remained standing to go sign books or deliver a reading. But Kealan Patrick Burke has broken me. Kealan Patrick Burke could pour vodka into the Boston Harbor, drink the whole fucking thing in one gulp, and then wash it down with a tanker truckload of Harp lager. Kealan Patrick Burke inhales alcohol the way you and I inhale air.

I am sitting here, nearly forty-eight hours after drinking with Kealan, barely able to function because my liver feels like Wrath James White and Joe Lansdale have been using it as a punching bag.

But somewhere, out there in the darkness, Kealan is on the prowl, thirsty, dangerous, and probably writing.

Your livers are not safe…

THE MORE THEY SAY "CHANGE", THE MORE THINGS STAY THE SAME

My friend Willis just called. Willis isn't his real name. I'm not allowed to tell you his real name. Willis and I served in the military together. I got out and became a writer. He stayed in and graduated to a special branch who do things that you're not supposed to ever know about. Occasionally, Willis gets drunk and tells me about them anyway.

"Hey," I said. "I was just thinking about you."

"Why's that?"

"I'm heading back to Langley next month. The CIA wants me, JF Gonzalez, F. Paul Wilson, Tom Monteleone, and Chet Williamson to come down for the day."

"Sweet Jesus," Willis moaned. "What hope can a bunch of horror writers offer our country?"

"I don't know," I admitted, "but we get a nice luncheon on taxpayer dollars, so it's all good."

"Never mind that. What are you doing right now? Are you writing?"

"No. It's hospital week. I'm sitting here drinking whiskey and watching this travesty that network news calls a Presidential debate."

"What do you mean?" Willis asked.

"Remember when we were kids? Presidential candidates actually stood behind podiums and debated the issues. Not anymore. First there was the Faith forum, and now it's the Service forum. I could give a shit about either. How about a 'What The Fuck Are We Going To Do About Iraq' forum, or a 'I'm Real Tired Of Paying Five Bucks For A Gallon Of Gas' forum?"

Willis paused. In the background, I heard Turkish flute music playing. Willis travels to bizarre and colorful locales, and phone calls from him are like a telecommuting game of Where's Waldo.

"Keene…" he spoke slowly. "Are you saying that you expect the candidates of our two major parties and the mainstream media to actually talk about real, substantive issues, rather than distracting us with polarizing, team-building nonsense?"

"I am, but it's the whiskey talking. I should know better by now."

"It doesn't matter," Willis said. "But you can't put what I'm about to tell you on your Hail Saten Blog."

"I won't," I said, and I wasn't lying, because my old Hail Saten Blog has been gone for almost a year.

Willis got mad a while back because I published one of our conversations in *The New Fear: The Best of Hail Saten Vol. 3*. In it, he predicted World War Three by Christmas of 2006. He was wrong. That doesn't happen very often, but when it does, I like to catch him on it.

More times than not, Willis is right. Willis has an occupation that allows him insight into world affairs.

"Did you watch the news today?" he asked.

"I always do. You know that. I'm a news junkie."

"Who are you voting for?"

"Obama, but with deep, deep reservations. In truth, I don't agree with either of them, but the Patriot Act and the wars are my primary concern, and I have to think he'll do away with them all. I mean, both Obama and McCain are probably globalist tools, but Obama is the least like Bush, so I'm voting for him."

"Don't bother," Willis said. "If you watched the news, then you know that Bush authorized us to start conducting cross-border raids into Pakistan."

"So?"

"So we know where bin Laden is. We're bringing him out in late-October, right before the election."

"If you know where he is, why not go in and get him now?"

"Orders are to wait. It's a trick out of the old Reagan play book. If we capture him at the end of October, we salvage Bush's legacy, and people vote McCain in November."

"Why you cynical bastard," I shouted. "Do you really think the American people are so blindly ignorant that they'll fall for that old trick?"

"Of course they will, Keene. As long as they have American Idol and Wal Mart and Christian contemporary hip hop and fast food, they'll do whatever we want them to."

I hung up on Willis. He'd obviously been drinking again and was full of bad craziness. I have enough bad craziness in my life, and I recently decided to excise some of it.

"Ridiculous," I snorted, and then turned back to the television. "An October surprise…"

On TV, John McCain and Barack Obama were talking about things that don't impact the average American, and were deftly not talking about how they would specifically fix the economy or the housing crisis or the war. Each time they were asked to explain how they'd fix these things, their eyes would glaze over with talking points, and they'd shout "Change!"

The more things change, the more they stay the same.

So I popped in a *Doctor Who* DVD and watched that instead.

HWA, OR, WHAT TO DO WITH A SICK DOG

New writers often ask me, "Should I join the HWA?"

I used to be a member of HWA (Horror Writers Association). I joined as a young, impressionable horror writer, during the Somtow/Kramer administration. I soon learned that pretty much nothing got done because of bickering egos and in-fighting, and that the organization was little more than a life-support system for the Bram Stoker Awards.

So I quit.

Richard Laymon convinced me and a whole bunch of other folks to re-join after he became President. When Dick passed away, I stayed in and watched all of the hard work he'd put into the organization crumble because of bickering egos and in-fighting. HWA once again became little more than a life-support system for the Bram Stoker Awards.

So I quit again.

Last year, I was talked into rejoining. I was told it was a better organization—that things had changed. That it was more focused. More professional. They needed veterans like myself (because yeah, ten years later, I was now a veteran) to join the organization and provide guidance and advice and wisdom to the newer writers.

So I did. I've been back four months, and I'm here to tell you, children—ain't a damn thing changed. It's still bickering egos and in-fighting, and it still all revolves around the Bram Stoker Awards.

The really sad part is that there are some wonderful veteran members—folks like Ellen Datlow and Rocky Wood (and until recently, Lee Thomas and Nick Mamatas, who have now, like me, quit), who still have sound advice and lots of wisdom to offer. Unfortunately, they are either ignored, shouted down, or pushed aside by those with an ego to assuage and attention to seek.

So, my advice and guidance and wisdom are as follows:

ADVICE FOR NEW WRITERS:

Don't join HWA. DON'T DO IT! The organization offers absolutely nothing that you can't get for free elsewhere online: mentoring, a message board, a newsletter, and the chance to submit to anthologies. That's it. That's all you get. And you can find each of those (indeed, you can find much better versions of each of those) elsewhere. And it won't cost you $65. So, instead of joining HWA, take that $65 and buy yourself subscriptions to *Cemetery Dance, Shroud, Rue Morgue, Fangoria, Publisher's Weekly*, and *Locus*. Between them, you'll get all the industry news you need. Then attend either a Borderlands Boot Camp or a professional convention such as World Horror or BFS or Necon. You'll get much more guidance and advice and help at one of these. There will be better networking opportunities. Your career will be better served. (Note: Depending on where you are in your career, you may want to join the International Thriller Writers, although it is not an organization for beginners).

ADVICE FOR ANYONE CONSIDERING RUNNING FOR OFFICE IN HWA:

The only way to fix the organization is to destroy it. Seriously. At this point, the cancer has advanced too far. It has metastasized. Soon, the organization will be nothing more than a giant tumor, swelling and pulsing and spilling poison all over the world. HWA is a slavering, rabid dog—a mad beast on the loose in the forest, flecks of foam dripping from its jaws while worms burrow deeper into its brain. We should shoot it in the head and put the poor thing out of its misery. Nuke it from within. We don't need Stokers. We've got the IHG awards and the Shirley Jackson awards and the BFS awards and the World Fantasy awards and a whole slew of other awards.

That's my advice. Thanks for asking.

THE DAY AFTER: "WE THE PEOPLE..."

Dear Turtle,

You won't remember this day, but history will. While you were sitting with Mommy and Daddy and chewing on the remote control, we watched the world give your generation a chance at a better life than we have had. Or at least that's what we hope.

Ideally, that should be the ultimate goal of each generation —to make things better for the next generation. That's always been the way it was in our family. Your great, great, great grandparents came to this country from Ireland because they wanted things to be better for their kids. They worked hard to make sure that happened. Your great, great grandfather fought in World War One to make the world a better place for his kids. Your great-grandfather fought during World War Two for the same ideals. Your grandfather and your Daddy also served, and while our government's ideals may have been different in those times, ours were not. Your Papaw wanted the world to be a better place for my generation, and I wanted the world to be a better place for your generation. Your Papaw busted his ass eight-to-ten hours a day, seven days a week, to give your aunt and I the things that he never had growing up. He worked hard and sacrificed. I learned those ideals from him, and have tried to do the same thing.

Your great-grandparents are part of something called The Greatest Generation. They knew hardship, son. They had World War Two and the Great Depression and hard, lean times. Your grandparents are part of something called The Boomer Generation. They also knew hardship. They had Vietnam and Kent State and a man named Richard Nixon who shit all over the ideals that make this country great.

There is another group of people who have known strife, son. And that group are people of color. And although they were a part of all three of these generations, and although they shared in our struggles and fought for the same things we fought for, they had their own share of personal hardships and strife, as well. And those hardships dwarfed ours in comparison. People of color have had to struggle even harder in this country. And even though the Greatest Generation fought to make this world a better place, it really only held true for half of the population. People of color didn't enjoy the same freedoms that the rest of us did. The Boomer Generation worked to change that, and perhaps they succeeded somewhat. But the divisions still remained. Those divisions ran through our country like echoes. Ghosts of the past.

It should not have been that way. But it was. And that's not the only thing that has been wrong, son. You see, Mommy and Daddy are part of something called Generation X and Generation Y. We had no hard, lean times. We were spoiled brats, for the most part. Because of the sacrifices of the two generations that came before us, we were fat and content. Our greatest hardships were David Lee Roth quitting Van Halen and Kurt Cobain deep-throating a shotgun. And so, for the last twenty years, we've had a procession of crooks shit all over this nation's ideals in a way that makes Nixon seem positively benign. Somewhere along the line, the representatives of the Greatest Generation and the Boomer Generation have forgotten about their duty to the generations to come. For twenty years, BOTH parties, represented by the Bush dynasty and the Clinton dynasty, have made things progressively worse. And my generation let them get away with it because, unlike our parents and our grandparents, we simply didn't care. We had no strife. Unlike the previous generations, we've had no hard, lean times.

Until 9/11.

On 9/11, we understandably and justifiably lost our shit. On 9/11, our generation realized that we were part of this planet, whether we liked it or not, and that there were more important things in life than Britney's latest meltdown or the Superbowl or funny LOL Cat pictures. 9/11 ushered in those hard, lean times, and it's eerie how much they resemble the hardships of your grandparents and great-grandparent's generations. War. Economic chaos. Social unrest. The world has become an ugly place.

Well, we finally got involved, son. My generation woke up after 9/11 and Hurricane Katrina and the Patriot Act and the $700 Billion Dollar Bailout and realized that we're in our thirties and forties now, and that we pretty much run this country. Our generation—we the People—white, black, brown, moderate, liberal, Christian, atheist—joined together today in order to hopefully form a more perfect Union. We elected one of our own, a forty-seven year old man of color, to run the country, and in doing so, we made history.

And maybe—just maybe—we actually finally put to rest some of the mistakes of the previous generations. Maybe we can lay to rest those ghosts of the past, and put away those old divisions. Maybe we can finally draw a curtain on the racist bullshit that has fucked this country up since day one. Maybe we can stop looking at the color of a person's skin, or their sexual orientation, or their religious beliefs, or which political party they are registered to. Maybe we can finally move beyond ideology and dogma and talking points. Maybe we can forget about Republicans and Democrats, Liberals and Conservatives, Religious Right and Atheist Left, African-American and White, Gay or Straight, Man or Woman, Steelers fan or Redskins fan—maybe we can move beyond all that crap and really start to make a difference. It might not be forty acres and a mule. Indeed, it might be the start of something better.

It's our generation's first shot at this, and I'm sure we'll stumble. Maybe if we work together, we won't completely blow it. We'd better not, because sometimes I wonder if this isn't our last chance to get it right.

Daddy loves you, kiddo. He loves you and your brother very much, and he really hopes that this is the start of something better for you both. He hopes that by the time you're both his age, you'll live in a world where the air is cleaner, and global poverty is something you read about in a history book, and people can marry whomever they want regardless of their gender, and we won't see each other in terms of the color of our skin, and if you get sick a doctor will be able to help you, and that if your country ever calls on you to go to war it will be right and just, fighting for this country's ideals, fighting to make this world a better place for your kids, rather than on the whim of a pack of criminals who have dishonored every generation of Americans who have worked hard and struggled to uphold the dream.

And that's why Daddy voted for Barack Obama today.

And now, just a few hours later, I'm terrified that I might have been wrong. That I might have been tricked. That we might all have been tricked. I'm scared that he's nothing more than a continuation of the Bush/Clinton/Bush dynasty, that the conspiracy theorists are right and he's just another pawn of the globalists and bankers, and that he won't do anything he said he'd do, and that Washington will return to politics as usual. But despite these fears, I voted for him because I hope.

In a minute, I'm going to post this, because I bet there are other parents out there right now who are feeling the same thing, and that's my job—to put into words what other people are feeling. After I do that, I'm going to tip-toe into the bedroom and kiss you and Mommy both goodnight. And for the first time in a very long time, kiddo, Daddy will feel something when he goes to sleep.

And that something is called Hope.

We the People… in order to form a more perfect Union.

I hope.

I hope…

Time will tell.

I hope.

JOHN URBANCIK: A NEW BLURB

John Urbancik is a dark fantasy writer of some note. He is also one of my closest friends, and as such, knows how overwhelmed I am with requests for cover blurbs. But despite knowing this, he still asked me for one, and this is what I gave him:

"John Urbancik is a drunken, bumbling oaf who often molests sheep and other small mammals when he should be writing. He once pissed in my mother's petunia patch, and on two occasions he has stripped naked, lathered himself in a noxious mixture of bacon grease and the ashes of burned William W. Johnstone novels, and then ran howling through the streets. He is not to be trusted—especially when he's been drinking." —Brian Keene, author of *Ghost Walk* and *Kill Whitey*

COLD WARRIORS — AN EXAMINATION OF GEORGE MILLER'S "MAD MAX 2: THE ROAD WARRIOR"

My father wanted to be a cowboy when he grew up. His heroes were Roy Rogers, the Lone Ranger, *Gunsmoke's* Marshall Matt Dillon, and pretty much any character played by John Wayne or Clint Eastwood. My father and his friends were fed on a steady diet of Western movies. The plots were often the same—a group of settlers are menaced by a lawless band of thugs until a laconic, emotionally-scarred stranger arrives to save the day with his guns.

I didn't grow up wanting to be a cowboy. Instead, I grew up praying for nuclear war.

I was 14 years old in 1981, and according to all reports, the world was supposed to end at any time. We weren't sure who would be responsible. Ronald Reagan, Margaret Thatcher and Leonid Brezhnev seemed the most likely candidates. It didn't matter to my friends and I who pushed the button, as long as the button was eventually pushed. We'd been fed on a steady diet of post-apocalyptic and dystopian films, comic books, novels and cartoons—*Kamandi: Last Boy on Earth, Escape From New York, Thundarr the Barbarian, Damnation Alley, Planet of the Apes, Doomsday +1, Def-Con 4*, and of course, *Mad Max*.

Nothing mattered after that. Not getting good grades or the

pretty blonde girl who sat in front of me in history class or the school bully who used to try to take my comic books or anything else. None of it mattered to me because I was convinced that at any moment the world was going to be reduced to a radioactive slag heap infested with cannibalistic mutants and roving gangs of punk barbarians, and that was when I'd find my true calling. That was when I would rise up like the anti-heroes in those books and movies, and rule the wasteland. All of my friends had the same dream, and that summer—the summer of 1981—*Mad Max 2: The Road Warrior* fueled those dreams like a scarce drum of gasoline for a Ford Falcon GT coupe with a supercharged V-8 engine—

just like Max's legendary Pursuit Special.

That year also saw the release of another post-apocalyptic classic, *Escape from New York*, but while Kurt Russell's uniquely American Snake Plissken appealed to our patriotic sense of nationalism, it was Mel Gibson's Australian Max Rockatansky who we really aspired to be. (Well, some of us, anyway. Most kids—the ones who weren't juvenile delinquents like me and my friends, wanted to be *Star Wars*' Han Solo. I liked Han Solo well enough at the time, but personally, he didn't have enough shades of gray to appeal to my nature the way Max did).

The Road Warrior is considered by most to be the best installment of the Mad Max trilogy. The first film, 1979's *Mad Max*, depicts civilization's collapse. The third film, 1985's *Mad Max: Beyond Thunderdome*, shows us civilization rising once more from the ashes. *The Road Warrior* is what happens in-between. Most called it a nightmare. I called it a wonderland. It is *The Road Warrior's* bleak, nihilistic vision that appealed to a generation of teens growing up in the shadow of not only nuclear annihilation, but of rampant Yuppie greed reminiscent of the movie's barbaric hordes. It has also become the visual blueprint for nearly every post-apocalyptic film since then. *Mad Max 2: The Road Warrior's* iconic imagery and themes have influenced countless films, comic books, novels, video games and other media. Its bleak junkyard landscape pops up in everything from *Doomsday* and *The Book of Eli* to Disney-Pixar's *Wall-E*.

The film's plot borrows from the aforementioned Old West archetype—a laconic, hardened anti-hero emerges from the wasteland and helps a group of well-meaning settlers defend themselves against marauders, thus reclaiming his humanity (and quite often ending up with a buffoonish sidekick for comedy relief). It worked well for Clint Eastwood's Cowboy with No Name in most of his 'spaghetti Westerns' and it works just as well for Mel Gibson's Max. But instead of riding out of the sunset on a horse like The Lone Ranger and his trusty steed Silver, Max comes barreling down the highway in his dependable, fast-as-shit V-8 Pursuit Special. The settlers in this case are a group of people, led by the wise and benevolent Pappagallo, who have inhabited a functioning oil refinery. The marauders, led by a disfigured but charismatic mutant named Lord Humungus (played by the foreboding Kjell Nilsson), want the refinery—and its precious content—for themselves. The sidekick role is filled by the pilot of an auto-gyro (played to iconic stature by Bruce Spence). *Mad Max 2: The Road Warrior* even gives us a permuted version of the 'child looking for a father-figure' motif popularized by the western Shane, but in this case, it's a feral, savage little boy armed with a razor-sharp and deadly-accurate boomerang.

The movie's set-up is at once easy and recognizable, yet new. Instead of cowboys and Indians, we have survivors and mutant bikers. Instead of raiders going after cattle or grazing rights, Humungus and his marauders seek gasoline and ammunition. This seems fitting when you consider that, at the time of the film's release, America and much of the rest of the world were just recovering from a gas shortage crisis and were facing economic uncertainty, civil unrest and concerns about gun control. *Mad Max 2: The Road Warrior* was a fable for those times. Of course, we didn't know that as kids. We didn't see the rich and layered subtext. We just knew that Max was a badass motherfucker, and the man we most wanted to be when we grew up.

My father is in his sixties now. He never became a cowboy. Instead, he went to Vietnam, came home, and worked in a paper mill until his retirement. I'm forty-two, and instead of becoming the warrior of the wastelands, I became an author. I have two sons of my own. The youngest, who is two, might grow up to be an artist, judging by how much he likes to draw on the walls of our home with his crayons. My other son, who is nineteen, admires the characters of a popular Japanese anime series that leaves me feeling confused and vaguely uncomfortable. The threat of nuclear war seems distant and unreal. Russia is no longer the enemy. China will not nuke us when they can simply buy us out instead. The more realistic scenario these days is that of a dirty radiological bomb detonated in a large city by one militant extremist group or another.

The cold war is over, and that's probably for the best. I know now, with the prescience of adulthood, that the aftermath of a nuclear holocaust would be much more grim and un-survivable than the fantasy depicted in the Mad Max films.

But there are still times, late at night, when I've had too much bourbon and I find myself unsatisfied with what I do for a living, that I dream of wearing black leather and racing down a cracked and pitted highway in a supercharged V-8, armed with a sawed-off shotgun and battling punk-rock barbarians.

And I smile.

3 AM THOUGHTS

Been on a weird schedule—going to bed at 7pm. Getting up at 1am to work. Around three this morning, I was putting my tax receipts in the filing cabinet and I came across a folder full of late Nineties correspondence. There were emails and letters from Geoff Cooper, Mike Oliveri, Mikey Huyck, John Urbancik, Tim Lebbon, Tom Piccirilli, J. F. Gonzalez, Mary SanGiovanni, Weston Ochse, Rain Graves, Regina Mitchell, Ryan Harding, Gak, James Newman, and dozens more—back when we were all young and naive and full of piss and vinegar, ready to fight whoever got in our way.

I also found a bunch of correspondence from Richard Laymon, Bentley Little, Brian Hodge, Edward Lee, John Pelan and others, as well—all offering a then newbie named Brian Keene advice and support and encouragement.

Sometimes I miss those days. I miss being a newbie. When the checks are late and the books haven't shipped and negotiations break down and the signings become circuses, I envy today's writers who are just starting out. They don't have to worry about how much they're getting paid and if it will pay the mortgage or what rights they're signing away or whether or not their kid will remember them by the time they get back from the next signing/press junket.

They're free to just write.

If there's anything better in this world, I don't know what it is.

Well, okay, maybe sex, good whiskey and a fine cigar. But I'm pretty sure that writing just for the hell of it trumps even those.

DAYS OF OUR LIVES

No, not the soap opera. I'm talking about something else. Been a while since I've mused on anything personal in public. There is a reason for this. Over the last few years, it seems like every time I do a bit of public soul-searching, some wit out there says something like, "Stop fucking whining, Keene, and write us another zombie novel."

But never mind all that. These are kinder, gentler days. Being an angry young man is one thing. Being an angry old man is another. I don't want to be an angry old man. Over the last few weeks, I've been trying to bring some peace and serenity into my life because I've noticed something recently.

Time is speeding up.

It's true.

I recently heard from my childhood sweetheart (who is, to some extent, the character of Katie in *Ghoul*). She's going to be a grandmother. At first, I didn't see how this could be possible. She is two years younger than me. She couldn't be a grandmother already. She is still the girl I kissed on that raft in the pond (and in the rain, and at the Hanover YMCA, and pretty much everywhere else around York County). That person couldn't be old enough to be a grandmother because that would mean that I, too, am old enough for such an honor. And then it occurred to me that I am indeed old enough. My oldest son graduates high school next month. From here on out, I could be a grandfather.

I also recently heard from a writer whom I've always admired and looked up to. I've been reading this man's work since high school, and he's never ceased to please me. Like Dick Laymon, he's an author many of us use as a moral compass. In his email, he commented on my current output and how he used to be able to do that when he was a younger man. I admitted to him that I seem to be slowing down a bit. The days of 24-hour writing marathons are far and few between now. At 31, there were times when I could produce 15,000 words a day and still go out and party that night. Now, at 41, I have to work very hard just to do 10,000 words in 10 hours, after which I collapse in exhaustion and slip into a Kentucky bourbon fugue state and spread chaos across the Twitter-verse.

Time is speeding up. I woke up this morning and things had changed. There was someone other than a Clinton or a Bush in the White House, and Shatner wasn't playing Kirk, and Guns n Roses was no longer the greatest rock and roll band of all time, and the Beatles would never have a reunion, and nobody knew what roll 2d20 meant anymore, and Madonna looked like someone's grandmother, and while I slept, someone stole my hair and aged my friends and loved ones.

I have no memory of these changes taking place. They quite literally seem to have happened overnight. I know this isn't so, but that's how it feels. Time is speeding up, like sands through the hourglass, and so go the days of our lives. But the hourglass is now a little more than halfway empty (or halfway full, if you're one of those type of people). There is a finite amount of sand in the damn thing. Sooner or later, the grains run out. I've still got a lot of stuff to write before I die. I just seem to write it slower these days.

Anyway, that's it. That's all. Just figured I'd share my

thoughts because I'm betting that, like always, there are many of you who can identify with them. That's what we writers do. We communicate things that people can identify with. If you can dig that, cool.

And if not, go bother somebody else about shutting the fuck up and writing you that zombie novel. I'm tired and there is no time for your nonsense.

KING QUEST (PARTS 1 & 2)

2009 has been a strange year for both mainstream publishing and the small press. We've seen bookstores close and publishers fold and editors cry and authors quit and people who were sane one day turn bat-shit crazy seemingly overnight. Many of my friends, peers and colleagues have been left privately feeling demoralized and burned out and in desperate need of a recharge. I have, too.

Usually, when I feel this way, I re-read Richard Laymon's *A Writer's Tale* and all is right with the world again. But that hasn't worked this time, and I'm not sure why. My wife has suggested that it's because I don't need to be reminded of why I wanted to become a writer in the genre. What I need to be reminded of is why I became a fan of the genre.

My wife is very smart.

I want to go back to my roots. I want to be a fan again, if just for one day or one hour. I don't want to see behind the curtain and know what it takes to write a novel or what hoops and compromises one has to make—because I've been there and done that and it takes the shine off the brass ring. I don't want to know the story behind the story, if you can dig what I'm saying. I just want the story itself to matter to me again.

Stephen King is signing at a Wal-Mart in Baltimore tomorrow morning at 10am. I'm told that people are already lining up tonight. I'm going to go down there tonight and lose myself in the crowd. I'm going to be a fan again, just for one day. My sometime assistant Tomo suggested (half in jest and half serious) that I "use my mid-list fame to move to the middle of the line", but Tomo often says silly things like that because years of drinking Golden Monkey Ale have caused him to suffer from early onset Alzheimer's disease.

I'm not going down there as Brian Keene, because Brian Keene is a part of this business and for one day, I don't want to be a part of the business. I just want to enjoy the horror genre again. I want to be reminded of why I'm a fan. I don't want to be recognized. I want to blend.

It occurs to me, however, that this pilgrimage is ripe for Twitter, so I'll be Tweeting about it tonight and tomorrow morning. I'm sure that the usual suspects will pick this apart the same way they do with everything else I say and do, but you know what? That's okay. In the end, we all have to find our own way.

Me, I'm gonna rediscover my roots…

Awake again. Drinking first cup of coffee and wondering if I really need it since the last of the coffee I drank six hours ago is still floating around in my system.

So, previously on Brian Keene dot com, a mid-list horror writer, feeling demoralized by all of the corporate changes to the publishing industry, decided to go on a pilgrimage of sorts. Except that, as you know if you followed the abbreviated saga on Twitter, the roots-quest came to a sudden and jarring halt when it was discovered that several different Wal-Mart employees are too illiterate to properly read book signing instructions to customers over the phone—let alone read a book as thick as *Under the Dome*.

Or, to further simplify things: I called the Dundalk, Maryland Wal-Mart, and was told that wristbands for the Stephen King signing would be given to the first four hundred people in line at 6am Wednesday morning, and the signing itself would begin at 10am.

That seemed an odd time to me, so I asked, "Are you sure that's right?"

"Oh, yes, hon," the woman assured me. "Says so right here on this paper they gave us. The signing starts at ten in the morning."

Now, I could have checked with the King compound to verify this information was correct, but remember—I wanted to be a fan-boy and not use my powers. Still, the information I'd been given just didn't sit right with me. A signing at ten in the morning?

So I called the store back twice more and was given the same information: wristbands at 6am, signing at 10am.

So, I get there around 1am last night, take my spot in a line of about seventy-five to a hundred people, and engage in some fan-talk with other fans. And then a Wal-Mart employee comes along and hands each of us copies of a flyer—a flyer which states that bands will be given out at 10am and the signing will start at 6pm. Many in the line groan out loud. A lady behind me confirms that she was given the same information I was given.

Some people shrug.

Many grow angry.

I grow even more demoralized.

Then I leave. After all, for me, this was about the journey, not the destination, and what I've divined from the journey is unsettling.

I will allow you to fill in the irony because I am too tired to type it out in full. Consider this: a writer, concerned over the corporate changes to the industry, has his quest shat upon by the corporation responsible for several of the negative changes.

On the way home, I drove past an independent bookstore

that's been shut down. It sat dark and empty and shuttered, the sign outside hanging askew. All that was missing was a tumbleweed.

Sometimes you have to search for metaphors.

Other times metaphors jump out and smash you in the face.

STOKER SEASON

It's that time of year again. That time of year when horror writers whom I don't know, have never talked to or haven't heard from since this time last year suddenly decide that I'm their 'friend' and start lobbying me to vote for their book in the Bram Stoker Awards. Which is funny for many reasons, because a) I have not been a member of HWA for a very long time and therefore, cannot vote for shit, Stoker or otherwise, and b) when I was a member, my method was to vote against anybody who actively lobbied for the award, and c) I happen to think the word 'friend' has more meaning and connotation behind it than simply adding somebody to a Facebook or MySpace page.

During the last few long, cold winter weeks, I have once again faced down depression and death and found them not to my liking. I've just finished writing a novella called *The Girl on the Glider*. I'm back now, ready to write and take care of business, but I can't get to the business because my email inbox and Twitter feed are full of "Hey Brian, any chance I can send you a review copy of my book for consideration in the Stoker Awards?" and "Hey Brian, I see that your book *Unhappy Endings* made the preliminary Stoker ballot. I'll vote for it if you'll vote for mine."

I fucking hate Stoker season in the same way I hate organized sports, racism, beets, child abuse, the current state of hip-hop, our two-party political system, and those god-damned zombie/classic literature mash-up novels.

I have two Bram Stoker awards on my shelf, amongst other awards. I used to be proud of them. They used to mean something. But with each passing year, the Bram Stoker awards get cheapened by all of the constant whoring to the point where I consider selling those two haunted house statues on eBay and using the proceeds to buy something for my sons instead.

I've said it before and I'll say it again—if the HWA reformists are serious about repairing the now decades-long damage that the organization has suffered in the public eye, the first step should be to put the Bram Stoker awards on hiatus for at least three years. The current incarnation of HWA exists as nothing more than a life-support system for the awards. Both the organization and the awards are in desperate need of an overhaul. Imagine what the membership could accomplish if they didn't have to worry about the awards for three years?

After that, their second order of business could be issuing a public apology to Nick Mamatas and Lee Thomas…

SEMINAL SCREAMS: INTRODUCTION

Let's talk about horror fiction.

Yes, I know. You were expecting something different when you heard I was writing a column for *Shroud*. Perhaps you thought I'd be handing out beat downs to those in this industry who so richly deserve them. Maybe you thought I'd share a funny anecdote or two. Sadly, we'll be having none of that. This is a serious column with a serious subject. School is in session and Headmaster Keene is standing over your ass with a ruler in hand, ready to smack your knuckles if you don't pay attention. Which reminds me of this one time back in tenth grade, when I got sent to detention for reading Stephen King's *The Stand* in English class, when I was instead supposed to be reading something by Jane Austen. Then I got suspended for reading *The Stand* while in detention for reading *The Stand*, which was fine by me, because it meant I got to stay home, smoke a bowl, and finish reading *The Stand* while I listened to Iron Maiden albums.

And now you're saying, "Ah-ha! That's what we were expecting. See that? One paragraph in and he's already digressing."

And now I've just smacked you with that ruler because you are wrong. You are wrong because being young and Stephen King's *The Stand* are exactly what this column is about. Fully half of you are under the age of thirty. Of that half, fully three-quarters of you have never read *The Stand*. Of those three-quarters, about half of you have seen the movie and figure that's just as good as reading the book. Don't argue with the math because I know this to be true. I know this to be true because I hear it all the time—at book signings and on my message board and everywhere else I encounter your generation.

When I was young, we were introduced to horror fiction in one of two ways—kid's books (John Bellairs was our J. K. Rowling) or the comic books of the Seventies (*Man-Thing*, *Weird War*, *House of Mystery*, *Werewolf By Night*, *The Occult Files of Doctor Spektor*, etc.). From there, we graduated to Stephen King and Dean Koontz. It was King's masterful history of the horror genre, *Danse Macabre*, which introduced most of us to H.P. Lovecraft, Richard Matheson, and others who'd come before him, and it was the delay between King and Koontz titles that allowed us to discover Richard Laymon, Jack Ketchum, Joe R. Lansdale, Graham Masterton, the Splatterpunks, and many others.

These days, I'm told that your generation was introduced to horror via video games and R.L. Stine's *Goosebumps* series, and you then graduated to my books. That seems so strange to me, and also leads me to believe that I should certainly be getting paid more than I am by my publishers, but that's not the point. At book signings and on my online forum, when I ask you what else you're reading (other than my books), you shrug and mumble, "Nothing."

We're going to fix that. When I was younger, in addition to *Danse Macabre*, we had a wonderful list created by Karl Edward Wagner that spotlighted forgotten gems of horror fiction. It occurs to me that your generation has no list, and *Danse Macabre* is outdated, and somebody should really work up a new resource for all this good stuff, and since nobody else will do it I guess I'll have to, especially since *Shroud Magazine* is paying me a great deal of money to do so.

Now, I'd like to speak to the older readers out there—the folks who already know who the God of the Razor is and what lurks in that sewer in Derry, Maine. Those of you who recognize that Carnacki was the greatest Ghost Finder of all-time. Those of you who understand that Cthulhu is something more than a stuffed toy or role-playing game supplement. You might be thinking that you won't benefit from this column. You might be considering skipping over it entirely. After all, you know all this stuff already, right? There's nothing out there in the world of horror fiction that you haven't read yet. Well, you'd be wrong. How about Charles Birkin's *The Harlem Horror* or the works of William Schoell or *Scars* by Warren Ellis? You read those yet?

I didn't think so. So, yeah. You'll want to stick around for this, too, you old fart.

I'm told that *Shroud* has two distinct audiences—people who enjoy reading horror fiction and people who want to write horror fiction. The books and stories we'll be discussing will appeal to both of these groups.

If you're a fan, then these are works that you'll want to read—fiction that has inspired and informed and shaped the genre into what it is today. Like those *28 Days Later*-style zombies? I bet you'll love Jim Starlin's *Among Madmen*. Got a hankering for some good old-fashioned occultism? My friend, wait until you meet Silver John the Balladeer. Think it can't get any more hard-fucking-core than Edward Lee or Wrath James White? Then you haven't read *Echo of a Curse* by R. R. Ryan—written in 1939! Like John Carpenter's *The Thing*? Yeah? But do you know who John W. Campbell is?

If you're a writer, then these are the works that you need to read—fiction that will inspire and inform and shape your own work into what it will be in the future. You know that novel you're working on about Nazi ghosts haunting a tank? Graham Masterton beat you to it back in the Seventies. If you're writing about vampires, you've probably read Dracula—but did you also read *Salem's Lot*, *They Thirst*, *Vampyrrhic*, or *Lot Lizards*? Maybe you saw Ramsey Campbell at a convention and were told he is one of the most important living authors ever, but you're not sure why. Or maybe (and most importantly) you want to become a better writer by studying and understanding the various styles of writers that came before you. Reading is a crucial part of being a writer, and it's essential at all stages of your development and career. You should certainly read outside of your chosen genre, but it's also important to read inside your genre, as well. You may not like all of them, but you should read them anyway. Your writing will be better for having done so.

There is absolutely nothing I like better than spending an occasional evening with people who love the genre as much as I do. I enjoy sitting in my library and smoking cigars and having a few drinks and just bullshitting with each other about books. I love doing that, and I'd like the opportunity to do it with you, if you'll let me. Sadly, my wife won't allow all of you to come to my house, and I doubt you'd all fit in my library anyway. Lucky for us, *Shroud Magazine* is allowing us to meet here in this manner. Make sure you thank them. And stay tuned. This will be fun and you will learn things—or I will smack you with the ruler.

My name is Brian Keene.

Let's talk about horror fiction…

SEMINAL SCREAMS: "AMONG MADMEN" BY JIM STARLIN AND DAINA GRAZIUNAS

Welcome back. As I stated in last issue's introductory column, my intent with Seminal Screams is to introduce readers to both classics and forgotten gems within the field of horror fiction. I want to shine a spotlight on works that every genre enthusiast should read at least once in their life—the novels, novellas and short stories that have inspired, informed and shaped the genre into what it is today. I'm told that *Shroud* has two distinct audiences—people who enjoy reading horror fiction and people who want to write horror fiction. The works I discuss will appeal to both of these groups.

So, I'm sitting here smoking a Partagas Black Label and sipping a glass of Basil Hayden's on the rocks, and you're having whatever it is that you're having. Comfy? Good.

Let's talk about zombies and post-apocalyptic novels. And please note, I'm not referring to the Haitian voodoo zombies popularized by William Seabrook, Henry S. Whitehead and Philip Marceline. Nor am I talking about H.P. Lovecraft's zombie in "The Outsider". I'm referring to the undead as popularized by George A. Romero—shambling corpses who want to eat your face.

Unless you've been living on Jupiter for the last decade, you know that zombies have once again permeated pop culture, dominating books, movies, video games, comics and more. Many people say this is my fault, and I won't argue with that, but I do propose that filmmaker Danny Boyle shares at least part of the blame. When Boyle's *28 Days Later* and my own *The Rising* first came out, the zombie sub-genre was in the midst of a dry spell. Zombies had returned to the graves from which they'd once risen. Oh, there was the occasional sighting—*The Dead*, by Mark Rogers, for example, but for the most part, new zombie fiction was as uncommon as a new story from T.E.D. Klein.

Both *28 Days Later* and *The Rising* attempted to do something different with the zombie canon—an advancement beyond Romero's original ideas. In my work, I eschewed the stereotypical slow, mindless zombie in favor of possessed corpses more akin to *Evil Dead* than *Dawn of the Dead*. Danny Boyle, on the other hand, did away with the zombie as a corpse, envisioning them instead as virus-infected human beings who, while every bit as murderous and violent as traditional zombies, were still very much alive. The movie and the novel came out within a few months of each other. Both were successful. Critics and fans responded favorably. And suddenly, zombies crawled back out of their graves.

What most people don't know is that *The Rising, 28 Days Later*, and a host of other post-millennial zombie and end-of-civilization novels (including *The Walking Dead*, Simon Clark's *Blood Crazy*, Cormac McCarthy's *The Road*, Joe McKinney's *Dead City*, David Wellington's zombie trilogy, and Stephen King's *Cell*) are building on riffs first laid down not by George Romero, but by Jim Starlin and Daina Graziunas in 1990's *Among Madmen*.

The novel is set in a post-apocalyptic America where much of the population has been transformed into murderous, savage berserkers. They aren't dead. They're just insane. The cause is unclear. Many think it's a new form of schizophrenia. Others think it's a virus. A few suspect it may have been a government experiment gone awry. Whatever the cause, citizens begin slaughtering each other. Anyone can succumb to the bloodlust—children, parents, spouses, etc. Soon, the cities are overrun and the countryside consists of small fiefdoms bartering with other rural towns while protecting themselves from roving bands of raiders and crazies. One such place is the small town of Shandaken, nestled deep in the heart of the Catskills and protected by Tom Laker, a war veteran and former New York City police officer. Laker is a man on the edge—doing whatever needs to be done to protect his town from not only the berserkers in the outside world, but from his own wife, Maria, who has also fallen victim to the madness.

Among Madmen is an account of one man's personal apocalypse. Other than some early set-up, the narrative focuses solely on Shandaken and its surrounding communities, and does a remarkable job of realistically depicting what rural life might be like after civilization collapses. No detail is forgotten, be it alternative commerce, or how the local government functions in this new world, or how residents cope with dwindling supplies of alcohol and ammunition. Unlike many of the lesser post-apocalyptic novels that have followed it, *Among Madmen* is not mere survivalist porn. It's a heartfelt and moving account of a good man striving to do what's right even as the world continues to fall apart around him. Rich in characterization and multi-layered themes, *Among Madmen* should have a position of honor in any collection of post-apocalyptic fiction. There is violence and gore and enough pulp fun to satisfy even the most jaded horror fan, but the novel never lets the human drama fall to the wayside.

The novel, published in paperback by ROC, also includes over fifty illustrations by Jim Starlin, who, until his turn as co-author of this book, was best known for his work as both a writer and illustrator for Marvel and DC Comics, including the New York Times bestselling graphic novel, *The Death of Captain Marvel*. His wife and co-author, Daina Graziunas, is a visual artist. She wrote a sequel to *Among Madmen*, which was published a few years later. The sequel doesn't live up to the original, however.

Sadly, *Among Madmen* is currently out-of-print, but as of this writing, numerous used copies are available from Amazon.com, ABE Books and other online book retailers. It is also a common find in good used bookstores (sometimes it is shelved under Science Fiction and other times it is shelved under Horror). Wherever you find it, the book is well-worth seeking out, and a seminal addition to any horror library. Influential and timeless, *Among Madmen* is a thinking person's pulp novel, and there's no better combination than that.

So, you have your first reading assignment. Next time, we'll take a trip to Ireland and visit a very strange house on the borderlands...

SEMINAL SCREAMS: "THE HOUSE ON THE BORDERLAND" BY WILLIAM HOPE HODGSON

A few years ago, I was a Guest of Honor at Hypericon—a science fiction, fantasy and horror convention held annually in Nashville. It's primarily a fan con, which means that you'll often encounter drunken Jedi Knights fighting meth-crazed Klingons or Vampires or Harry Potter fans in the hotel hallways at night. I don't know about you, but whenever I run afoul of a horde of psychotic Furries, my first instinct is to open fire. Since shooting convention attendees is usually frowned upon when one is the Guest of Honor, I instead spent my time hiding out in the dealer's room. If you've never been to a convention, a dealer's room is just that—a large room where various dealers hawk their wares: t-shirts, jewelry, movies, toys, comics and books. Lots and lots of books.

On the first night of the convention, I was perusing a large stack of used books in the dealer's room when I ran into Brian Hatcher, a young, aspiring writer whose acquaintance I'd made several years before. Hatcher and I talked books while we browsed through the piles. When I came across a certain volume, my eyes lit up with nostalgia and I sighed happily.

"Are you going to buy that?" Hatcher asked me.

"No. You are."

"Me?" Hatcher flinched, no doubt calculating how much money he'd set aside for the weekend's bar tab—money which was now going to please the seemingly insane whims of a bestselling mid-list horror novelist.

"Yes," I said. "I'm not going to buy it because I've read it at least a dozen times and I own the Arkham House edition. You're going to buy it because I can tell by your expression that you've never heard of the book or the writer, and if you want to become a horror writer, then this is required reading. To become the future, you must first know the past."

Hatcher begrudgingly bought the book and then sulked away, no doubt silently cursing me for making him spend all his beer money. Keep in mind, this was a Friday night. I didn't see him again until Sunday morning, as the convention was ending.

"Where the hell were you all weekend?" I asked.

He smiled. "I was in my hotel room, reading that book. I couldn't put it down. Thanks, Brian. You were right. What a great book!"

Grinning, I nodded and tried to look wise. If my beard had been long enough, I would have stroked it.

The book was, of course, *The House on the Borderland* by William Hope Hodgson. It is one of the most important works in our genre. If you haven't read it, you need to un-fuck that right now.

First published in 1908… Hey! Stop that. I mention 1908 and immediately, you all groan and say, "God, that's like a billion years ago! Nobody wants to read that. It probably sounds like that Shakespeare and Milton crap they made us read in high school." Well, you're wrong. That's the beauty of this book. Over one hundred years later, it is still fresh and relevant and exciting and not-at-all a chore to read.

So, as I was saying before you so rudely interrupted me, first published in 1908, *The House on the Borderland* is notable for moving the genre from the gothic supernatural trappings of the late nineteenth century and into new directions, many of which are still prevalent in the field today. Indeed, I'd argue that this is the first modern horror novel. It has had a profound influence on several generations of writers—everyone from H.P. Lovecraft, Robert E. Howard, and Manly Wade Wellman to Tim Lebbon, China Mieville, and myself.

In *The House on the Borderland*, an unnamed, reclusive narrator discovers that the remote country house he lives in with his sister and dog straddles the border between our world and another dimension. That other world is populated by a giant, demonic swine-creature. After confronting the beast during an involuntary bout of astral projection, our hero finds his home here in our world under siege by similar—if smaller—swine things. The narrator and his sister manage to hold off the horde, but then he takes another involuntary out-of-body trip—this time through time itself, where he witnesses the extinction of the sun and the end of our world. Upon returning, he must face the giant creature he first encountered in that other dimension, now loosed upon our world, and also cope with a strange fungal infection that's spreading throughout the house.

If you're sitting there right now, saying, "Hey, some of those themes and situations sound familiar," you'd be right. Monsters besieging a house with people trapped inside. Sinister fungus. Astral projection. Other hellish dimensions. *The House on the Borderland* utilizes all of these and more. When you pause to consider how many other novels you've seen such scenes and situations pop up in (including my own), then you begin to understand just how influential this book has been to generations of horror and dark fantasy authors. It all starts here, kids. *The House on the Borderland* is an important, essential part of our genre's history. You can't call yourself a fan or writer unless you've read it.

Luckily, *The House on the Borderland* (as well as many of Hodgson's other seminal works) is still in print and easily available. A quick check of Amazon.com shows several inexpensive paperback editions, all new. Of all the various editions, I recommend the Gollancz trade paperback version, published as part of their Fantasy Masterworks series, as it also contains Hodgson's *The Boats of the Glen Carrig*, *The Ghost Pirates*, and *The Night Land* (each of which is also important and will be examined in future columns).

So, there's your next reading assignment. Next time, we'll head on down to Texas and visit a certain drive-in theatre…

SEMINAL SCREAMS: "THE DRIVE-IN" BY JOE R. LANSDALE

There has been quite a buzz over the last decade regarding a new genre and literary movement called Bizarro. Perhaps best typified by the books of Carlton Mellick III, Jeremy Robert Johnson, and Andersen Prunty, and television programs such as *Aqua Teen Hunger Force*, the Bizarro genre often blends elements from other genres, especially science fiction, fantasy, humor, and horror. It also features subliminal—or sometimes not-so-subliminal—social, political and religious commentary. In recent years, the Bizarro genre has gone from an underground movement to a professionally accepted literary category with designated slots at discerning bookstores and legions of rabid fans worldwide. And while it deserves such accolades, what many younger readers don't realize is that Bizarro is nothing new. It existed years before, popularized by the subversive and avant-garde work of filmmakers like Alejandro Jodorowsky and David Lynch, and in books such as Joe R. Lansdale's *The Drive-In*. Indeed, not only has *The Drive-In* informed much of today's Bizarro fiction—it also may very well be the most influential novel for an entire generation of horror writers.

Specifically, my generation.

First published in 1988, *The Drive-In* signaled a huge

paradigm shift within the horror and dark fantasy genres. Oh, scholars and critics didn't know at the time that the novel would have such a huge impact, but looking back on now, twenty-some years into the past, it's easy to see how everything changed with its release.

Perhaps the best way to illustrate this is to tell you how it impacted me the first time I read it. I remember it very clearly. The year was 1988 and I was twenty years old and finishing up a stint in the U.S. Navy. I didn't want to make a career out of the military, but I didn't want to return to my small Pennsylvanian town, either, because that seemed like a trap to me. Like everyone else I'd graduated with who'd stayed there, I figured if I went back, I'd get married, have kids, get a job at either the paper mill, the foundry, or the Harley Davidson plant, and live only for that week of vacation every year. And a few months later, that's exactly what happened. I got married, we had a kid, and I was working in the foundry. But by then, I'd read *The Drive-In*, and I knew I was meant to do something other than work in the foundry for the rest of my life.

I'd grown up reading horror, science-fiction and fantasy, of course. I'd started with the Marvel, DC, and Charlton comic books of the Seventies, and then moved on to more adult fare like Stephen King, Edgar Rice Burroughs, Arthur C. Clarke, James Herbert, and Robert E. Howard. In High School, I discovered newer authors like Jack Ketchum and Richard Laymon. It was their work, along with the works of a handful of others that made me first pick up a pencil and try my hand at writing for publication. I'd had a vague idea that I wanted to be a writer since the age of seven (after reading an issue of *The Defenders* written by Steve Gerber—another transformative moment because it was the first time I realized that somebody had actually written the words I was reading, rather than them just magically appearing on the page) but it wasn't until High School that I actually made my first attempt. Those early efforts failed miserably, and then I got distracted by girls and graduation and that aforementioned stint in the Navy.

Then came *The Drive-In*. When I finished it, I had two very distinct thoughts. The first was, "Holy shit, what a great book!" The second, and even more fervent thought was, "Holy shit, I have to do this for a living."

So I did.

And so did a lot of other writers. Joe Hill, J.F. Gonzalez, Duane Swierczynski, Tom Piccirilli, Weston Ochse, Cody Goodfellow, Kelli Owen, James A. Moore, Christopher Golden, Bryan Smith, Tim Lebbon, James Newman, and dozens of other genre authors (including the aforementioned Bizarro authors) list *The Drive-In* as one of the most seminal, transformative and defining books they've read.

That's because it is, and twenty-plus years later, you can see *The Drive-In*'s influence across a wide spectrum of popular genre fiction. Its style, voice, pacing, and gleefully genre-bending storyline bleed into everything. *The Drive-In* made us want to be writers. It made us want to do what Lansdale had done, which was create something magical.

A literary potluck of horror, science-fiction, humor, and fantasy, *The Drive-In* is best described by the book's actual synopsis (taken from the most recent edition): "Friday night at the Orbit Drive-in: a circus of noise, sex, teenage hormones, B-movie blood, and popcorn. On a cool, crisp summer night, with the Texas stars shining down like rattlesnake eyes, movie-goers for the All-Night Horror Show are trapped in the drive-in by a demonic-looking comet. Then the fun begins. If the movie-goers try to leave, their bodies dissolve into goo. Cowboys are reduced to tears. Lovers quarrel. Bikini-clad women let their stomachs sag, having lost the ambition to hold them in. The world outside the six monstrous screens fades to black while the movie-goers spiral into base humanity, resorting to fighting, murdering, crucifying, and cannibalizing to survive. Part dark comedy, part horror show, Lansdale's cult Drive-In books are as shocking and entertaining today as they were 20 years ago."

That pretty much sums it up, folks. A cast of colorful characters get trapped in an other-dimensional drive-in and have to fight an increasingly-bizarre array of monsters, as well as each other. It sounds simple, but it's not. Lansdale's characterization, pacing and social commentary are razor-sharp here, and though many writers (including my own self) have tried to mimic him at some point in their development, nobody else comes close.

The Drive-In spawned two sequels (1989's *The Drive-In 2* and 2005's *The Drive-In: The Bus Tour*), as well as an omnibus edition, a graphic novel adaptation, and a feature film (currently in development as of this writing).

As stated in previous columns, my intent with Seminal Screams is to examine the roots of horror fiction, spotlighting the most important works—books that everyone, be they horror writers or horror fans—should read at least once in their lives. *The Drive-In* goes beyond that. This is a cornerstone of the genre's history. This is part of the foundation that the last twenty years have been built on. This is important. This is essential. This is our roots. *The Drive-In* is easily available for purchase. You are required to read it before our next column.

AUTHOR'S NOTE: Unfortunately, no further columns followed. I do intend to expand these into a book-length work at some point, however.

DYSTOPIAN TUESDAY, OR, IN THE YEAR 2025

So I'm back home for two quick days. Just enough time to catch up on email and do laundry before hopping back on a plane again. The next time someone tells you that writers lead glamorous lives, punch them in the mouth and then tell them that Brian Keene says "Hi."

Had a wonderful time on the California leg of the *Clickers* tour. Thanks to Del and Sue at Dark Delicacies and Alan, Jude, and everyone else at Borderlands Books. And thanks to all of you who showed up and had us sign things. Always great meeting you guys. And extra special thanks to Ann Laymon, David Schow, Richard C. Matheson, John Skipp, Cody Goodfellow, Brian Emrich, Gene O'Neill, Rain Graves, Nick Mamatas, and Paul and Shannon Legerski for giving us homes and family away from our homes and family.

On the brutal slog back across the country yesterday, J.F. Gonzalez and I had a long talk about publishing and emergent technologies. And it was that discussion which prompted today's Blog entry.

Close your eyes. Picture a town. An average mid-sized American town. Perhaps the town of Walden, Virginia (from my new novel *Darkness on the Edge of Town*). Now picture that town in

2025—fifteen years from now. It's still the same assortment of Wal-Marts, Targets, Taco Bells, Home Depots and Bath & Body Works that cover our country like Triffids. But there is one thing that is different.

There is one thing that has changed.

There are no book stores.

There are no book stores in the year 2025. Unable to compete with digital books, the big box stores like Borders and Barnes & Noble have gone the way of Circuit City and Ames. They are extinct. The retail spaces formerly occupied by them now host internet cafes where one can drink coffee and read things on a Kindle, which is ironic when you think about it since people go into Borders and Barnes & Noble right now and do the exact same thing.

As we walk downtown, to a street populated by curio stores and antique shops and little boutique restaurants, we notice something else. The used book stores are gone, as well. There are no dusty, dimly-lit hole-in-the-wall stores piled high with moldering pulps and Ace doubles and yellowed Seventies paperbacks, because all of those formerly out of print backlist titles are now available to read for free via Google Books, a division of Google Corp, who now own everything and insert their latest toolbar into our children at birth.

That is the year 2025. According to science-fiction, in 2025 we should have jet-packs and manned flights to Jupiter. Or we will live in a giant post-apocalyptic junkyard. I propose that it will be a little bit of both scenarios. We'll have wonderful new technologies and we will revel in them, even as we wander through an apocalypse of our own making.

Or maybe I'm just exhausted and punch-drunk after a whirlwind weekend of meeting readers and signing books in stores where the owners, employees and clientele still love the feel of paper and the comfort that only a physical book can deliver—a comfort that our grandchildren might never know, because physical books will be nothing more than curious oddities

Grandpa rambles on about, much like vinyl albums, eight track and cassette tapes, movies on VHS, and American politics when you could tell the two political parties apart.

J.F. and I finished our discussion as we touched down in Baltimore. I considered expanding on that grim, book store-less future world and advancing the clock five more years to 2030, when some bastard sets off an EMP and wipes out everything, including everyone's digital libraries... but J.F. was tired and cranky and I didn't want to depress him. Instead, we drove home and listened to music on my iPod and called our wives from our cell phones, both of which came with Kindle applications.

And then I got home and found out that my wife didn't want to be married to a writer anymore.

And I can't really blame her.

I may be away for some time.

SELF-HELP BOOKS I INTEND TO WRITE

So, over the last four weeks, I've suffered a severe case of bronchitis that hovered on the edge of pneumonia and refused to go away. I also suddenly found myself in the midst of a divorce and suddenly single again at the age of forty-two, and ended up moving into a small apartment and trying to assemble pre-packaged bookshelves.

Other than a few pages on a Friday afternoon, I haven't written shit in over three weeks time, which leaves me with deadlines double-stacked. I intend to start digging my way out of that this week, now that I have an office to write in again (and thanks to Rhiannon and the staff of Seattle's Best at Borders in York, for graciously allowing me to temporarily set up shop there until I found a place).

This Blog entry is the first thing I've typed from my new office, which is... cozy. Yes, that's a nice word. Cozy. Makes me think of a fireplace and snow outside and curling up on the couch with some whiskey, a cigar and a good book by Joe R. Lansdale or Elmore Leonard.

Yesterday, I found myself in the self-help section at my local Borders, looking for divorce books specifically written for men or fathers. The closest thing the bookstore had were tomes from Tucker Max and Denis Leary, both of which I already own.

I decided that if I want to read a self-help book about divorce that's written specifically for men and fathers, I will have to write it myself. I've thought about it over the last 24 hours, and here are some of the titles I've come up with. Which one do you prefer?

1. MY FRIEND, WHISKEY: A MAN'S GUIDE TO SUCCESSFULLY COPING WITH DIVORCE
2. EMBRACING TELEVISION RE-RUNS: SOCIAL LIFE FOR DIVORCED, BALDING, PAUNCHY, FORTY-SOMETHING MID-LIST WRITERS
3. HEATHER MAY HAVE TWO MOMMIES, BUT BRIAN HAS TWO EX-WIVES
4. "NO, IT DOESN'T COME WITH A TOY": A DIVORCED DAD'S GUIDE TO KID CUISINE
5. DIVORCE, FATHERHOOD & ZOMBIES (BECAUSE ZOMBIES ARE HOT RIGHT NOW AND THAT'S MY FAULT, SO THE PUBLISHER INSISTED THAT I INCLUDE THEM IN THIS BOOK)

HOW NEIL GAIMAN BROKE MY HEART AND ALLOWED ME TO WIN A DEBATE WITH J.F. GONZALEZ

I've read just about everything Neil Gaiman has ever written. My favorites, until yesterday, were always *American Gods*, "Babycakes", "We Can Get Them For You Wholesale", *The Books of Magic*, and the prologue to *Sweeney Todd: The Demon Barber of Fleet Street* (which is a wonderful slice of meta-fiction via comics).

Yesterday, he posted a Blog entry right before attending the Oscars. The part that jumped out and broke my heart—the part that has now become my favorite thing Neil Gaiman has ever written—was this: "There are days that you just want to walk the dog in the woods, write a bit, and be with your loved ones, and this, it seems, is really one of those days, and I should have been smart enough to figure that out, and I wasn't."

I'm two months into a divorce. I don't miss my house or my office or my beehives or my trout stream or my truck, but I do miss the important things. I miss walking my dog in the woods, and writing for a bit, and then coming inside at the end of the day to be with my loved ones. Those are the important things. Those are the things that matter. I should have been smart enough to figure that out, but I wasn't.

J.F. Gonzalez recently told me that I put too much of myself out there, and I'm sure that when he reads this, my phone will ring and he'll say, "See? That's exactly what the hell I was talking about!" But isn't it an artist's job to tell the world how he sees it? To express how he feels, so that others may say, "I have felt similar emotions", and thus, reveal a truth about the human condition?

And if so, then isn't that what Neil Gaiman did yesterday? And isn't that what I'm doing now, as I type this in an apartment that doesn't feel at all like home, but with each passing day, feels more and more like a prison cell in which I'll be serving out a life sentence?

Writing is a weird gig. Sometimes, I like to fantasize that I became a plumber instead...

THE DORCHESTER WARS

AUTHOR'S NOTE: What follows are a selection of Blog posts dealing with the downfall of America's oldest paperback publisher, Dorchester Publishing/Leisure Books, and the part I played in it. This is only a sampling of what appeared, as much of this story played out elsewhere—on other Blogs and websites, in the news, radio and podcasts, *Publisher's Weekly*, *CNN*, and of course, on social media.

If you are unfamiliar with what happened, in a nutshell, because of drastic changes in both publishing and bookselling, the company found themselves in the red, and unable to pay their authors (and other creditors). At first, they attempted to switch to a digital-only publishing model, but when that didn't work, they engaged in other tactics—namely, selling books to which they no longer had the rights to, and denying the return of those rights to their individual authors, agents, or estates.

During a conference call with their biggest creditors, they announced that they were going to, quote: "operate as if they had filed bankruptcy without actually filing bankruptcy".

They intended to sell all of their intellectual property (meaning the rights to their authors' novels) to a third party, thus making themselves a nice financial windfall while simultaneously screwing their authors in the process. But they made one mistake in announcing this.

They forgot that, as one of their thirty biggest creditors, I was on the line.

After disconnecting the call, I contacted several of the biggest names in our industry—authors whom I had an immense amount of respect for, and told them what was occurring. They advised me that there was probably no chance I would ever get paid, and thus, I had to fight to get my rights back before the company could sell them. So I did. In exchange for reverting the rights to all of my books, I agreed to waive the estimated five-figures the company owed me.

But then, after reverting my rights (and doing the same for several other authors) the company continued to manufacture and sell new editions of our work, including e-books. This malfeasance was a direct violation of our agreement, and it was at that point that myself, J.F. Gonzalez, Bryan Smith, Craig Spector, and a few other authors decided to go to war and force the company out of business before anyone else could get screwed.

We organized a worldwide boycott that made international headlines. Thousands of readers, booksellers, authors, and professional writing organizations announced their support of us and joined the boycott. The company fought back. We fought harder. And eventually, all of the authors either had their rights returned or were bought out by Amazon, who paid them what Dorchester had owed, and allowed the authors to retain their rights.

In short, we won. We won through the help of our readers, our fans, and our peers.

The press commented on our victory. Life returned to normal for everyone.

And then I filed bankruptcy and suffered a heart attack.

Here is a sampling of that saga.

MID-LIST BLUES, or, I SING A NEW SONG

Unless you've been sleeping under a rock, you've no doubt heard the news that my main publisher, Leisure Books (a division of Dorchester Publishing) is immediately switching to e-book format only, with select titles to be published down the road as trade paperbacks. Or maybe not. Or… maybe so? In truth, it's hard to follow the story in the press because the story changes or contradicts itself by the day, if not the hour. The bottom line, from the perspective of some of the authors, agents and even a few of Dorchester's former employees, is that the company's solvency is in question, and this might be a last-ditch Hail Mary pass. If true, then it's sad.

There's been a persistent belief among some, over the years, that an author couldn't make money writing for Leisure. I'm living proof that this isn't true. During my decade writing for them, I managed to get a significantly higher advance with each book, and racked up a back-list of eleven titles, all of which remain in print and continue to sell well and thus, make me money. Indeed, as a mid-lister, those regular royalty and advance checks from Leisure accounted for roughly 45% of my annual income. Although many of my peers have indeed gotten raw deals in the past, I was always treated fairly well by Leisure. My checks arrived in a timely fashion. The sales staff did a remarkable job of pushing my books. I was content. I've made a decent, blue-collar income level living as a mid-list writer for the last decade. It wasn't always easy, but neither was working in a foundry or on the loading docks or any of the other decent-paying blue-collar jobs I held before I became a writer. Writing is hard fucking work, but it's also rewarding work, and I've done pretty well for myself. I never wanted to be Tom Clancy or Dan Brown or James Patterson. My heroes were always the guys like Ed Gorman and Richard Laymon and Robert Randisi, mid-listers all, and the heart and soul of the paperback trade. No, I've never been wealthy, but I've done alright every year, and Leisure accounted for almost half of that sum.

Which is why it was hard yesterday, after several days of back and forth negotiations, to choose not to continue publishing with them. I mentioned above that my checks always arrived on time and I was always treated fairly. That's true, but not so much for the last year. I don't think I'm talking out of school here, because I've seen dozens of other Leisure authors saying the same thing in public, including an official reprimand from the RWA.

Fact is, over the last year, my checks haven't been showing up on time. I'm owed a significant amount of money—money that pays for the next six months of bills. That is why, when those checks stopped arriving, you saw me start doing things like offering the Lifetime Subscriptions and writing more comic books. It was a way to keep the lights on while I waited for things to fix themselves. Understand, Leisure wasn't the only publisher to pay me late. Many others did, as well, on account of the economy. But the late payments from Leisure were significant because they were substantial. I wish I had confidence and faith that I will eventually see that money, but right now, I don't.

Sadly, given the payment issue, the confusion both in public and in private as to what the company's new business model actually entails, and the overall instability of the marketplace and industry in general, I've elected not to continue with Leisure for the foreseeable future. If they are able to turn things around and demonstrate that they can start paying authors in a timely fashion again, I'd certainly reconsider. I've enjoyed working with my editor, Don D'Auria, and I'd write for him no matter which company he's working for. But I also need to do things like eat and pay child support to two ex-wives and have an apartment to store my books in, and therefore, I've decided to take my brand elsewhere for the time being.

What this means for you, the reader, is that *Entombed* (the follow-up to *Dead Sea*), *With Teeth* (my vampire novel), *Bad Ground* (the next Levi Stoltzfus novel), and *Suburban Gothic* (the sequel to *Urban Gothic*) will not come out from Leisure as expected. All rights have reverted back to me. You'll see them, eventually. I've had a number of offers from other mass-market publishers, as well as a number of small presses. I'm currently mulling those offers over. I'm in no rush to decide, because in truth, I'm considering another possibility.

Earlier this year, we talked about self-publishing, and whether or not it's acceptable for a professional, brand-name author with a dedicated fan base to self-publish. What I didn't announce then, but am announcing now, is that I intend to experiment by self-publishing a few titles, making them available in both digital and trade paperback formats. I'm convinced that, given the size of my fan base and the demand for my books, this will be a successful venture for me. At the very least, I can pay myself on time.

Anyway, the point of this rather long-winded ramble (which it wasn't supposed to be when I started typing it) is that for the first time in over a decade, I've got a bunch of different options to choose from, and the luxury of taking my time with whatever decision I make.

And I like that.

I've just got to figure out how to get some more money in the meantime…

MORE BAD NEWS FROM LEISURE

Last week, we examined in detail the mounting troubles at Leisure Books (Dorchester) and why I'd ceased writing for them.

Now, my sources tell me that Don D'Auria, the editor who created Leisure's venerable horror line and oversaw the Western and Thriller lines, and editorial director Leah Hultenschmidt have both been let go as part of a staff reduction. Apparently, the entire editorial department is now one person: Chris Keeslar. No word on what this means for the horror line… or indeed, the company itself. But I have some speculations.

However, before we get into that, I want to comment on how much I've enjoyed working with Don these past ten years. Other authors have often asked me why I stayed with Leisure as long as I did. The answer is Don. We had a great working relationship, and I'd write for him again, no matter where he lands or what he's editing. If Don D'Auria called me and said, "Hey, I just got on at St. Martin's and I'm editing a line of NASCAR romance novels" you'd see me write a NASCAR romance novel so fast it would make your head spin. And a note to potential publishers—you hire Don, and I guarantee you that you've also acquired the Brian Keene brand. Mull that over and then give him a call. Seriously, I wish both Don and Leah the best, and I have no doubt they'll land safely.

Sadly, the same thing can't be said for Leisure – Dorchester. Now keep in mind, this is my opinion only, and should not be taken as fact, but based on what we learned last week and what we're all hearing off-the-record, I give the company six months. Maybe a year, but I think six months is more likely. I expect CEO John Prebich will either sell it off, piece by piece if necessary, or have the company file bankruptcy. One thing that is abundantly clear is that the company is gathering and holding on to assets like a squirrel preparing for winter. Just days before the announcement that they were switching to digital format, the publisher was still signing authors to contracts for multiple books without telling the authors of the digital plans.

Worse, from what I've been told, the company is apparently not filling orders to vendors, bookstores or authors. I've seen this personally over the last week. In the past, authors could call the warehouse and order a box of their books to take along to conventions, etc. Last week, the warehouse staff was informed that no orders were to be shipped—not to bookstores. Not to distributors. And not to authors or other vendors. Insiders tell me three different reasons were given for this, including that the company "was switching warehouses" and "was taking inventory." In my opinion, they're holding onto their assets so that they can either liquidate those paperbacks to a discount outlet or use them in bankruptcy proceedings. At last weekend's signings in York and Lebanon, PA, the store managers reported to me that they had trouble getting books in, and indeed, ended up with only about half of what they ordered. I'm told those shipments were fulfilled from their own warehouses, rather than via Leisure's distributor.

Most disturbing (in my opinion) is that there has still been no clear answer from the publisher as to how the recent changes will impact the book clubs, including the popular Leisure Horror Book Club, which new subscriptions were still being processed for as of last week.

It is my opinion that neither I nor my fellow authors will see any more royalty checks (checks which, as I mentioned last week, are already woefully late). Therefore, I can't see the point of doing any more signings this year. Why should I spend my own money and travel across the country to promote a book that I'm most likely never going to get paid for? I'll do the signings in LaVale, MD and Williamsburg, VA next weekend, because it's too late to cancel and I don't want to bone the bookstore managers, and I'll sign at Horrorfind, but that's it for the rest of the year. Consider the Horrorfind Weekend convention the last signing for the foreseeable future.

What's my advice to my fellow Leisure authors? Run. Get the fuck out and don't look back. It is my opinion that we are screwed. At this point, you're an absolute fool if you sign with them for anything else. Remember Zebra and Dell Abyss in the Nineties? Yeah?

This has all happened before…

BRIAN GOT BACK

I'm back from Horrorfind Weekend 12. I had a wonderful time. Thanks so much to all of you who stopped by my table over the weekend. It was great to meet and chat with you, and sign your books. A few personal highlights for me: Finally meeting Brandon and Angela, and Mark and Paula (aka Mr. and Mrs. Ruderabbit); J.F. Gonzalez and I listening to Joe Lansdale, Chet Williamson and Tom Monteleone reminisce about old times (especially a hilarious tale involving Richard Laymon, a bottle of booze and the wrong hotel); reading to an absolutely packed room with Mary SanGiovanni and Rio Youers; hearing the crowd response to *Demonstration of the Dead*; dinner on Friday night; and hanging out on Saturday night; and finally, watching new authors like Kelli Owen, Sheldon Higdon, Thomas Erb, Andersen Prunty, Kevin Lucia, and Norman Prentiss really come into their own. You kids did good.

Maelstrom, my new small press imprint through Thunderstorm Books, was announced at Horrorfind. Soon as I get permission, I'll post some of the details here, as well.

The other big news I announced at Horrorfind is that I've reached an agreement with Leisure Books/Dorchester Publishing for the return of my back-list (*The Rising, City of the Dead, The Conqueror Worms, Ghoul, Dead Sea, Dark Hollow, Ghost Walk, Castaways, Urban Gothic, Darkness of the Edge of Town* and *A Gathering of Crows*). Print rights reverted back to me today. Digital rights will revert back to me on December 31st. What this means for you, the reader, is that all of those books will be disappearing from your local bookstore very soon. The publisher can sell off their remaining stock, but can't print more copies. So if you've been waiting to purchase one, you'd better do it soon.

Also, booksellers at both Borders and Barnes & Noble tell me that all Leisure titles—horror, western romance, etc.—are being returned. I'm not sure why, nor will I speculate (though I do have my own guess). Bottom-line: get them while you can.

As for my plans for the back-list, tune in early next year.

Speaking of out-of-print back-list titles, I am very happy to announce that both *Clickers* and *Clickers II: The Next Wave* will be available soon in both digital and trade paperback. The digital editions may be available later this week, in fact.

The first half of 2010 seems to have been all about endings. The second half of this year is gonna be about beginnings. I know things look bad for the genre right now, kids, but stick with me. I have a plan.

It's always darkest right before the dawn…

MORE LEISURE UPDATES

If you thought the saga was over, you're wrong. It's just beginning. There are reports that Leisure/Dorchester is selling digital books without permission. Hard Case Crime's Charles Ardai took the Leisure Book Club to task. Then the Mystery Writers of America de-listed them. The Romance Writers of America reprimanded them, too. The Science Fiction Writers Association is also investigating. The Horror Writers Association, of course, did absolutely nothing and have remained quiet on the issue, because the Horror Writers Association is about as effective as a ball of belly button lint. It's not all bad, though. Author Bryan Smith reports that he received a check from them this week—a partial amount of the total he is owed—and the funds cleared.

PREBICH OUT AT LEISURE

Publisher's Lunch is reporting that John Prebich, the CEO of Dorchester/Leisure, has left the company. Several months ago, it was suggested to me that Mr. Prebich didn't like some of the things I'd written about Leisure on this Blog, but I'm sure he won't mind me reporting this latest development. I'll update with details as they become available.

ANTHONY IN AT LEISURE

Publisher's Weekly confirms Robert Anthony is the new CEO of Dorchester – Leisure. This follows yesterday's announcement that embattled CEO John Prebich had left the company. They're also promising to not fuck over their authors, customers, or creditors anymore.

One thing that jumped out at me is this quote: *"Dorchester added that mixed messages to media outlets and unpredicted procedural changes also contributed, undermining author confidence and leading to rumors of imminent bankruptcy."*

Those rumors of bankruptcy were repeated by Prebich himself during last August's creditor conference call (a conference call in which I participated and still have a recording and transcript of).

MEET THE NEW BOSS, SAME AS THE OLD BOSS?

Less than 24 hours after Dorchester's new CEO Robert Anthony promised to "create an atmosphere of transparency and efficiency that was heretofore lacking" and less than 24 hours after sales manager Tim DeYoung, when asked if Dorchester could win back authors like myself who had left, stated "We know people will be watching us carefully... I hope they give us another chance" new mass-market paperback copies of *A Gathering of Crows* are apparently back in print and have been made available to Amazon and other booksellers, despite the fact that:

    a) Like the rest of my back-list, copies were no longer available to booksellers.

    b) The print rights reverted back to me months ago.

    c) I won't see a dime from these new sales.

When I inquired as to how this was possible, a representative from Dorchester, who wished to remain anonymous, stated "I have no idea." I was assured the situation would be looked into ASAP.

Could this be a simple error? Possibly. Although, given the events of the last year and the company's previous track record, I'm sure you'll forgive my cynicism. I would suggest that if Mr. Anthony is sincere about his efforts to create an atmosphere of transparency and efficiency, a wonderful way to show that sincerity would be to contact me ASAP with a full explanation of how this happened and what it means. If there has been a mistake, a full accounting of how many copies have sold in the last 24 hours would also be nice. If it *is* a simple error or misunderstanding, I'll be very happy to report so here.

Pleased to meet you, Mr. Anthony. Hope you guessed my name. What's puzzling you is the nature of my game.

NOBODY KNOWS

Yesterday, I reported that Dorchester/Leisure had brought *A Gathering of Crows* back into print, despite the fact that they no longer own the rights to it. Now, apparently, despite the fact that they no longer own the rights to it either, *Darkness on the Edge of Town* is back in print, too.

Nobody at Dorchester is still sure what happened. One source inside the company, who shall remain anonymous, suggests that this may be existing stock which is now being offered for sale. The confusion, however, lies in the fact that the stock is being offered as non-returnable and pre-pay only, which would disqualify Amazon, B&N and other retailers from carrying it (except through third party sellers).

Confused? So is everybody else.

Meanwhile, the SFWA announced that they've placed Dorchester/Leisure on probation for one year, following proven instances of the company not paying authors and publishing editions of books they did not legally have the rights to.

BOYCOTT DORCHESTER

Starting in late 2009, Dorchester/Leisure began making late payments to most of their authors. Indeed, some authors report never having received payments at all, nor royalty statements verifying what, if any, monies were owed. This continued throughout much of 2010.

In mid-2010, with these payment issues still unresolved, Dorchester announced that they were switching to an all-digital format. Then they announced that those digital books would be accompanied by trade paperbacks. Due to the ongoing payment issues, many professional writer's organizations such as the SFWA and RWA placed Dorchester on probationary status.

During a late-August conference call with their creditors (for which I was present and for which I have a transcript of, just in case Dorchester wishes to dispute what follows), they revealed that the company saw a 60% decrease in book orders in mid-2009; payroll was down from 1 million to $600,000; the company had no cash flow, but also had no bank debt; the company owed six million dollars to various creditors, including $700,000 to active authors and $400,000 to inactive authors; e-books accounted for 10% of their profit; their trade paperback plan was currently on hold; they didn't think the sale of the company was possible; and that as of August 9th (2010), they considered themselves "in bankruptcy but are not actually filing for bankruptcy". Vendors and authors who were owed money for books or services from August 8th forward took precedence in being paid. All others would have to wait.

I was one of those authors. I had not been paid since late-2009. As a result, my marriage had fallen apart and ended in divorce, my bills were piling up and I was forced into financial ruin, and more than half of my annual income was perpetually "coming soon". I decided to take a gamble. I negotiated a deal with Dorchester that allowed for the immediate reversion of all of my print rights, and the reversion of all of my digital rights as of 11:59pm 12/31/10. In exchange for this, I absolved Dorchester of any further financial debts they owed me. In other words, I said, "Forget about the rest of the money you owe me. Just give me my rights back."

It was a risky gamble, and I sought the council of some of the biggest veteran authors in the genre, but it was a gamble that ultimately paid off, because it allowed me to place my back list with a more solvent publisher. We signed the deal. Dorchester went their way. I went mine. And that should have been the end of the story.

Except that it wasn't, because since then, Dorchester has repeatedly violated that agreement. Since January of this year, unauthorized digital editions of my work have been sold via Kindle, Nook, iBooks, and Sony. These digital editions were not made available for sale until well after the rights had reverted back to me. Dorchester's response, in each case, has been to blame someone else and assure me that "they are looking into it" and that I would be "financially compensated" and that "it wouldn't happen again".

Except that I haven't been financially compensated and it keeps happening again.

In the most recent case (iBooks), Dorchester blamed their vendor, Libre Digital, but provided no documentation verifying this. An employee at Apple cast doubt on this explanation. In the case of Kindle, they blamed Amazon.com. Again, an employee at Amazon cast doubt on this. The e-books were sold under the Dorchester brand. They were sold even though Dorchester does not have the rights to them. And it is Dorchester, rather than their vendors or booksellers, who are ultimately responsible.

During a 2pm conference call today with Dorchester's creditor steering committee, several literary agents confirmed that my situation is not unique, and that a number of their client-author's books have been released digitally by Dorchester even though Dorchester did not own the rights. To quote one: "We tell them to suppress it, and they do for a few weeks, and then it's back up again."

I have been patient. I have been understanding. The first time, I allowed that it could indeed be a mistake. Four times later? It is no longer a "mistake". It is theft, or at the very least, staggering incompetence. And as of this writing, I have not seen financial restitution for these unauthorized sales, nor have I received a valid explanation of how they occurred, nor have I heard what steps the company will take to prevent it from happening again.

I am not the only author who this has happened to. Nor is this the only problem. I am told that some authors are *still* awaiting payments and royalty statements. (One author told me this morning that they have not received a royalty statement or check since April of 2009, yet their books are still being sold). I'm told that some authors' requests for the reversion of their rights are being outright ignored. And I'm told that yesterday, with many authors' books about to go out of print (which would then allow the rights to revert back to the authors)

Dorchester has announced their intent to bring many of those books out as e-books, thus seizing the rights, rather than allowing those rights to revert back to the authors—authors who, quite understandably, have concerns about this, given the company's current state of affairs.

Recently, Dorchester's customers began taking them to task on their Facebook page. These customers weren't associated with any particular group or entity. There were members of the Hard Case Crime, Romance, and Horror Book Clubs, fans of horror writers, romance writers, and western writers. They complained about the unauthorized e-book sales, the unannounced changes to the book clubs, the continued non-payment of authors, the lack of promised trade paperbacks, and other concerns. Dorchester deleted these posts from their wall, and issued a statement denying any wrongdoing. When their customers responded, Dorchester deleted those posts as well. Then Dorchester emailed me. They asked me to "make a post" stating that this wasn't their fault and that they are "trying to rectify the situation" because "people have been trolling the Dorchester Facebook page and posting angry notes." That they view their customers' legitimate concerns as "trolling" is quite telling.

A few minutes ago, someone asked me why we (the authors) didn't just seek legal means. Well, I can't speak for any of the other authors involved, but I'll tell you why I haven't—because I'm broke. I'm broke because Dorchester didn't pay me what was owed, and then I gambled to get my rights back, and then they continued to fuck me. And yes, I've got a nice new deal with Deadite Press and a movie version of my novel *Ghoul* starts filming next month, but I won't see checks from either of those until a few months from now, and until then, I can't pay the rent and eat anything more than Ramen noodles, let alone hire an attorney.

The only thing I can do is what I've done throughout my entire life any time I've encountered a bully.

I can declare war.

So I'm asking you to boycott Dorchester Publishing and Leisure Books. I said above that I can't speak for my fellow authors, but I can tell you that many of them are in the same situation—or worse. If they could get their rights back, they could do as I have done and sign with a new publisher, or they could follow the trail blazed by Joe Konrath and Scott Nicholson, and self-publish their work. In either case, they could begin to make a living again.

J.F. Gonzalez, Bryan Smith, and Craig Spector will also be calling upon you to do this today. It is our sincere hope that others will join our cause.

In short, we need your help. If you care about horror, romance, or western fiction, and more importantly, if you care about the people who write horror, romance, or western fiction for a living, and if you disagree with this publisher's methods, history, and "mistakes", then please consider withholding your financial support of Dorchester Publishing and Leisure Books.

Boycott them.

If you follow them on Twitter, please unfollow them. If you like them on Facebook, please unlike them. If you receive their marketing emails, please remove yourself from their list. If you belong to one of their book clubs, please consider canceling your membership. If you are considering publishing with them, please reconsider.

Most importantly, please don't buy their books, regardless of whether it's on their website, in the $1.99 dump bin at Wal-Mart, or available on the Kindle. If you aren't sure how to identify a Dorchester book, check the spine. It should say Leisure Fiction or Dorchester Publishing.

If you are a Leisure author with a grievance against the company, please consider sharing it with the public. If you are an author with another publisher, and wish to show your solidarity, please join us. Please consider adding your voice to our call for a boycott. And after you have done so, let me know so I can add you to the roster.

And now, I'm turning it over to you…

FRIDAY FRENZY

So, yesterday we declared war. Then I walked away from the internet long enough to spend some time with my loved ones, watch a movie, and read. When I logged back in this morning, I had over 500 emails, texts, voice mails, Tweets, and FB postings waiting for me.

Obviously, it might take me a while to get back to you. Tomorrow, I'm helping my girlfriend, fellow author Mary SanGiovanni, move. Sunday, I intend to write, because I haven't had a chance to do that since the boycott started. On Monday, I'm spending time with my sons and writing some more. Meanwhile, here are a few things I thought deserved special attention:

1. Brett Savory of Chizine says "Dorchester still owes us nearly $3,000 in advertising fees! They keep fobbing us off and spinning excuses to delay payment."

2. Author Vicki Steifel confirms "Dorchester has done exactly the same thing to me—no royalties… no statements… and illegally publishing my books in On-Demand and eBook format."

3. Author Sandra Ruttan says "When I received my last royalty statement," (from Dorchester) "there were no recorded Ebook sales, although my books are available for Kindle and through other major Ebook outlets. Being curious about sales, I'd actually occasionally popped on, noted sales rankings, and compared them to my other book… Long story short is, I know there were Ebook sales sold. But they haven't been credited to my books."

4. Jana DeLeon says "I had the EXACT same problem with Dorchester last year, and here's how I solved it—publically out them for stealing because that's exactly what this is." In relation

to Jana's comment, *Smart Bitches* revealed last year that Dorchester was doing this to romance authors.

5. Jim PI (private investigator to the mid-list stars) has started a Boycott Dorchester Facebook page. He asks folks to post links to their Blog entries and news articles there.

6. A dear friend of mine, who is one of the stalwart veterans of this genre and who was getting screwed by publishers when I was still reading his stuff in high school detention, said some things to me yesterday that really rang true. I'm protecting his identity, but these two excerpts are so valid and important that I'm considering getting them tattooed on me. "*As a holding action, Dorchester's hide-the-salami ploy is admirable: Treat the authors like mushrooms (keep them in the dark and feed them a lot of shit), because every day—every minute—rights issues remain unresolved, unclear, or fogbound in bureaucratic if-come doubles-peak, the company can rake a few more Paypal pennies for digital editions they probably don't own...*" and "*People who blithely suggest that some-people-should-sue-other-people with no regard to bank or sanity have little idea of how soul-destroying Lawsuit Land can be, whether you're in the right or not. It requires that you port your creative energy toward the battle, and before you know it, ALL of your waking time is swallowed. You go to sleep thinking about it. You wake up thinking about it. And in the end, if you prevail through the miles of mind-numbing paper, you're faced against an enemy who will just throw up their hands and admit, Okay, we give. We're broke. 'Bye! Check your history. Pinnacle Books. After them, Zebra. To my certain knowledge the BEST that was achieved in those ignominious flameouts was reversion of rights—no bonuses, pending payments or grand prizes.*"

7. The boycott got lots of press, most notably from *Galleycat* and *Publisher's Weekly*. Thanks to them (and to *Smart Bitches*, as well, who I linked to above).

8. Lots of messages from lawyers and attorneys and people who know lawyers and attorneys. My own thought on that is to follow the advice of my mentor (see #6 above). But I would

point out to those calling for a class action lawsuit that such an undertaking might be difficult, given that the authors, as a collective, are at different points. For example, Bryan Smith and I were lucky enough to get our rights back. J.F. Gonzalez, Craig Spector, Mary SanGiovanni, Wrath James White, and dozens of others have not been so lucky. Some people have been paid. Others haven't. Some people have gotten royalty statements. Some haven't. Some have gotten what they consider to be incorrect royalty statements. Some can't get any sort of response at all. Some just want the reversion of their rights. Some want to be paid. See what I mean? It's a cluster-fuck. But I do like the suggestions regarding the Attorney General...

DORCHESTER BOYCOTT: FINAL THOUGHTS

Just got home from Mary's. I spent all of that three hour drive from Jersey to Pennsylvania on the phone with various media outlets and reporters. I walked in my apartment, turned on the computer, and found several hundred more emails and messages. I updated the list of professionals who have joined the Dorchester boycott. I only wish I had time to create a similar list for the thousands of readers and fans who have pledged their support, as well.

But that's what it comes down to… time.

J.F. Gonzalez and I were talking this morning, and we've decided that we've done our part. We're exhausted. It's been a long few days. Along with Bryan Smith and Craig Spector, we got this ball rolling last Thursday. We'd hoped that some of our fellow Dorchester authors would join in, and they have. I've chronicled some of their experiences. The comments section is full of more. And dozens of Dorchester authors have taken to their own Blogs to relate their own experiences—including Stacy Dittrich, whose own experience makes mine seem like a trip to Disney World.

In short, it wasn't just me or Jesus or Bryan or Craig. The problems are widespread and systemic and indicate a clear pattern of malfeasance on Dorchester Publishing's part. Thousands have joined the boycott. Most are sincere. A sad few, I suspect, are joining simply to be a part of things and get noticed (indeed, despite their public display of solidarity, some folks on this list are still following Dorchester on Twitter, etc.). But hey, you know what? To each their own. I believe that the vast majority of readers, fans, and professionals who have pledged their support will do just that.

And in the end, that's really what it comes down to—where do we go from here? I haven't spoken for anyone else throughout this, and I won't speak for anyone else now, but I'll tell you where I go from here. I'm going to get back to writing. Leading this charge has eaten up every free minute I've had for the last four days, and unfortunately, it is not paying my bills. The landlord and electric company would like their money, so I need to get back to work. But I will stand fast and firm in my conviction. I will not purchase anything published by Dorchester, not even if it's written by my best friend. It is my sincere hope that you will each do the same.

For all of the authors and other creditors impacted by this, I encourage you to continue sharing your stories on your Blogs and websites. More importantly, I encourage you to post links to those stories on the Official Dorchester Boycott Facebook Page. Each and every person who has pledged their support should be following that page (unless of course you don't have a Facebook account). Later this week, I'll post a list of attorneys and law firms who have offered their support to us, the authors. If your firm would like to be on that list, please email me. If somebody does indeed organize a class action lawsuit, I'll happily join in, but I'm not going to be the standard bearer. With that in mind, I'd like to centralize the discussion on the Facebook page and the #BoycottDorchester hash tag on Twitter, because quite honestly, I'm one guy and I can't keep up with all the email it's generating

—not if I want to write anything for the rest of the year, or spend time with my sons, or do fun things like eat and sleep.

So… the future is in your hands. You can say, "Well, that was fun" and return to business as normal, or you can stand firm and keep up the pressure. The choice is yours. Just know that myself and a lot of other former and current Dorchester authors have faith and confidence in you. Please don't let us down…

DORCHESTER RESPONDS…AND SO DO WE

Last week, I, Bryan Smith, J.F. Gonzalez, and Craig Spector called for a boycott of Dorchester Publishing. Over 200 professional authors and an estimated 10,000 consumers also joined the boycott. The boycott garnered media attention, birthed a Twitter hash-tag, and spawned a Facebook page. Most importantly, it inspired dozens of other Dorchester authors to step forward and confirm our allegations. Today, Dorchester responded via *Publisher's Weekly*. I'd like to address a few points. Quotes from the article are in italics.

"The remaking of Dorchester Publishing… had been going fairly well until earlier this month when author Brian Keene accused the company of selling e-books for which they no longer had the rights."

Going well? Their landlord and several other creditors seemed to have a different take on things during last Thursday's creditor steering committee phone conference. More importantly, it wasn't just "Brian Keene" accusing them. Dozens of authors raised similar allegations. (This is very important and we'll come back to it in a moment).

"(CEO Bob) Anthony said the call for a boycott is "truly regrettable and not necessary to get our attention, since he has our attention." According to Anthony, after being notified by Keene that some sites had been selling e-books for which Dorchester had reverted the rights back to Keene, Dorchester sent suppression notices to the vendors. After Keene reported that some sites were still selling the e-

books, Anthony said they sent another suppression letter telling the vendors they expected the e-books to be removed from sale. "We expected the vendors to act accordingly," Anthony said, adding that "we respect the right of reversion."

The time-line: In late-December 2010, I was notified that suppression letters had been sent, and that "it might take a week or two" for the digital editions to disappear from various vendors' websites. And they did. By the end of the first week of January 2011, no digital editions of my work remained available for sale in any format. Then, in late January, they were offered for sale again via Nook. I was told it was a glitch, and another suppression letter had been sent. In early February, digital editions were offered for sale again via Sony. Again, I was told it was a glitch and another suppression letter would be sent. In late February, digital editions were made available for sale again via the Kindle. Again "glitch" and "suppression". Then, earlier this month, digital editions were made available via iBooks. If you guess "glitch" and "suppression" you win a prize.

Here's the thing, Bob. This keeps happening repeatedly, despite your assurances of sending "suppression notices" and despite your expectations that your "vendors act accordingly." For three months, I've been asking for an explanation of why it keeps happening. I've yet to receive one. So despite your claim, I don't think I've had your attention. I don't think any of your authors have.

But we do now.

"...*the publisher is committed to solving the problem with Keene and treating all authors fairly. Dorchester will pass along all money to Keene on e-books that were sold after rights reverted. "We'll get him [Keene] everything that is owed to him" Keeslar said.*"

What I want you to do is to stop selling digital editions of my work that you do not have the rights to. And I've repeatedly stated, this isn't just about me. So while you are at it, here are some allegations from other authors that you can address:

1. Author Tim Waggoner: "Before Leisure's implosion, I got

all the rights to my three Leisure novels reverted to me. Imagine my surprise a couple months ago to discover that Leisure is selling e-editions of two of those novels. My agent's on the case, and we'll see what happens—though from what I've seen on other authors' blogs/message boards , Leisure hasn't been responding to agents when they call about such problems. My personal concern is simple: Leisure is profiting from selling editions of my books that they don't have the rights to."

2. Author Stacy Dittrich: "(I) never received one royalty check. The publisher claims… didn't sell enough books, but Nielsen book scan says differently. In fact, one of (my) e-books hit 1,000 and…Wait a minute! The publisher doesn't even OWN the rights to the e-books… agent kept requesting a contract but heard crickets. Digging a little deeper… the book, (that the publisher is illegally selling), is available for free. Yes, for free. I will fight this to the finish at all costs… I am using my contacts to secure an attorney who will happily file a class action suit against Dorchester publishing. I am also checking contacts at several law enforcement agencies to see if criminal charges are possible as well. Interested Dorchester authors contact me at info@stacydittrich.com so I can start compiling a list for the class action."

3. Author Mary SanGiovanni: "…I sent a formal letter to Leisure/Dorchester, asking for the rights to my two books back. They were in violation of contract, as I haven't received royalty statements in over a year for either book. I've been told by Leisure that I can't have the rights back to my books. They couched it all in nice-speak, but essentially, they're using the e-book angle to keep our books in print…"

4. Author Vicki Steifel: "Dorchester has done exactly the same thing to me—no royalties… no statements… and illegally publishing my books in On-Demand and eBook format."

5. Author Craig Spector: "Authors under contract are NOT vendors; they are a separate and distinct class unto themselves. Our books and inventory are separate and distinct. They are

NOT meant to be held hostage by creditors in the event of BK proceedings, as salvageable rights to be sold off to repay the company's debts. That was nowhere in the contract I signed; indeed, the contract I signed is, in my and my attorney's estimation, in breach, and hence null and void, and my rights—including e-rights—automatically revert back to me, the owner of the underlying rights. Both Dorchester's counsel and the independent counsel representing the "loose, informal consortium" of creditors—their words—have been consistently evasive as to where "authors" fit in this mix… Dorchester is in material breach of dozens if not hundreds of author contracts."

6. Author Jana DeLeon: who managed to get the e-book versions of her titles taken down last autumn because Dorchester didn't own the digital rights, notes that her titles "are back as mobile-phone apps—from Dorchester."

That's six, Bob. Once you've taken care of them, I have several dozen more for you. And still more are on the way. If you are sincere, then immediately make sure digital editions for which you DO NOT own the rights are suppressed, and the files are removed from your vendors' systems. Send proof of this to the rights-holders. Honor the rights reversion requests you are receiving from authors and their agents. Send royalty statements. Some authors report not having received a royalty statement since 2009.

Communicate with your authors. Last week's steering committee was told Dorchester is "paying an average of $5,000 per week toward past-due royalties", yet your authors—the people who are owed that money—were kept in the dark about this.

Until then, Bob? Fuck you.

Now, if you'll excuse me, I've had a very long day playing with my three-year old, helping my ex-wife haul topsoil, and talking J.F. Gonzalez down off the ledge. I'd like to shower, put on some pajamas, pour myself some bourbon, light a Partagas cigar, and write something for which I'll be paid.

COMMITTEE DETERMINES DORCHESTER UNABLE TO PAY

As previously reported, an unofficial committee representing Dorchester Publishing's unsecured creditors (including authors and their agents) was formed last August. Since then, the committee and its financial advisers have been monitoring the company's operations, and have had access to Dorchester's financial information and legal documents.

Today, the committee notified Dorchester of their decision to disband, because they have determined that Dorchester will be "unable to propose any meaningful repayment plan to unsecured creditors in the foreseeable future". The committee states that this leaves Dorchester's unsecured creditors (including authors and agents) free to take "any action or inaction they determine to be appropriate."

Since the initial boycott call, myself and the other authors on this list, feeling we took the appropriate action (given that Dorchester was continuing to sell our work but was unable or unwilling to pay us for it), have kept quiet. Some of our peers disagreed with our actions, and took to their Blogs and online forums to decry both us and the boycott. While we respect their varied reasons for doing so, it's worth noting that most of them took issue with our stance that Dorchester was unable to repay their authors and other unsecured creditors.

We will, of course, be curious to hear their thoughts now that the committee has confirmed what we've been saying all along…

DORCHESTER SELLING MORE ILLEGAL E-BOOKS

Earlier this year, my former publisher, Dorchester, was caught illegally selling digital editions of books they no longer had the rights to. I was not the only author whom this happened to. We called for a boycott. Amazon, B&N, Sony, and Apple were quick to remove the illegal e-books. But that hasn't stopped Dorchester, who in conjunction with for-side.com are releasing the books as iPad Apps, rather than via the iBooks store.

Last month, Dorchester's CEO Bob Anthony responded to our boycott via Publisher's Weekly. From that article: *"According to Anthony, after being notified by Keene that some sites had been selling e-books for which Dorchester had reverted the rights back to Keene, Dorchester sent suppression notices to the vendors. After Keene reported that some sites were still selling the e-books, Anthony said they sent another suppression letter telling the vendors they expected the e-books to be removed from sale. "We expected the vendors to act accordingly," Anthony said, adding that "we respect the right of reversion."*

Apparently, Mr. Anthony just forgot to send a suppression letter.

Yeah, I'm sure that's it...

DORCHESTER STIFFS LANDLORD, BUYS BOOTH INSTEAD

We all remember when Dorchester CEO Robert Anthony and editor Chris Keeslar told *Publisher's Weekly* everyone would get paid. This hasn't happened. On April 22nd, a committee representing Dorchester's largest unsecured creditors determined the company was "unable to propose any meaningful repayment plan". This means creditors, including individual authors, can file petitions of bankruptcy against the company.

Last week, Dorchester met with the committee and tried to persuade them that their intentions were good. The committee remained unimpressed and did not change their stance. One participant jokingly suggested that perhaps I was on the line, listening in, and would let the public know.

Well, I wasn't. I was in Louisiana on the set of *Ghoul*. But my associates were on the line. And one of the things from their transcribed notes was that Dorchester is behind on paying their rent. That's right. They have been habitually late with their rent for their offices at 200 Madison Avenue. This was confirmed independently. We also confirmed that despite Dorchester's assurances that everyone is getting paid, the vast majority of authors who are owed money have still not seen recompense.

So… you can't afford to pay your rent. You can't afford to pay your authors. What do you do next? Apparently, you spend thousands of dollars on a booth at BEA (Book Expo America).

BEA is a trade show for publishers, booksellers, librarians, authors, editors, agents, and anyone else who makes their living from books. Apparently, Dorchester still likes to pretend that they fall into one of those categories.

Massive kudos to Edward Champion, who happened to be on hand and reported on his exchange with them. Edward asked fair, valid questions—the type of questions that a potential client would want answered. Dorchester had no comment, other than to fall back on their increasingly tired impression of a confused deer caught in oncoming headlights.

DORCHESTER SENDS COAL INSTEAD OF CHECKS

You remember the saga of Dorchester Publishing. How they ripped off their authors and vendors, including myself, in a variety of ways, including non-payment of royalties and publishing and selling books they no longer had the rights to. The entire sordid tale is documented here, along with plenty of links to everything else. Last I reported (back in May), the new CEO promised everyone would get paid. Seven months later, dozens of authors and vendors report that hasn't happened.

But Dorchester did send a digital Christmas card to their former authors and vendors yesterday, including ones they still owe. Perhaps the most egregious example was that of former copy editor Dave Thomas whom Dorchester still owes for 17 jobs. He received a card, and promptly Tweeted "Christmas cards are now considered legitimate currency in publishing. Wonder if BoA will accept a card in lieu of my mortgage payment?"

Dorchester did not respond to my multiple inquiries, nor explain why I was one of the few who didn't get a holiday card.

DORCHESTER: OFFICE CLOSED & DISPUTES UNRESOLVED

A number of troubling reports are surfacing just one month after Dorchester closed its community Blog, was officially disqualified by the SFWA, and told *Publisher's Lunch* (via company representative Hannah Wolfson) that the recent news I had reported was nothing more than "propaganda" and that things were "business as usual".

Author John Skipp stated yesterday in an update to Kickstarter supporters: "one potential piece of bad news is that Dorchester Publications has apparently gone under for good. So we may be unable to get all the copies of *Spore* we need."

Then when a second author, who wishes to remain anonymous, reported that she'd been told Dorchester had "locked the doors and turned off the lights" but were "still selling books", I asked via Twitter, if anyone else had heard these rumors. Former Dorchester Senior Vice-President of Sales and Marketing Tim DeYoung responded with, quote: "Office is closed and remaining people are working from home."

Meanwhile, Grace Wen confirmed that the company doesn't have any editorial staff for their magazine line, either. As with the book publishing arm, employees from marketing and other departments are now doubling as editors.

One year ago, Dorchester CEO Robert Anthony stated that the company would do right by authors and resolve the disputes. At that time, I listed several author disputes. To the best of my knowledge, none of them have been fully resolved. Here is a sampling of more recent disputes from the last month:

Author Deborah Macgillivray reports: *"One of the saddest casualties of this mess is the sister of Dawn Thompson. Dawn did over a dozen books with Dorchester. The rights were refused return, as were mine, and a lot authors. Before Dawn's death, she turned the rights to her books over to her sister, Diane. Diane is disabled, living at the poverty line (which Dorchester is aware of). Last August she got a notice that one (just one) of Dawn's books had earned $4300 and a check would follow. A check never followed. This is the same thing that happened before. Chris sent a notice that $10,003 would be forwarded to her and that never came either... I won't mention the dozens of foreign rights sales... To date, over 4 years, not one dime of that has made it to Diane."*

On Facebook, author Bryan Smith reports: *"I have never received a sales statement for* Depraved. *That's the one book I've never received a* (royalty) *statement for and all the anecdotal evidence available suggests it's far and away my most popular book. Coincidence? Hmm..."*

An author who wishes to remain anonymous verifies to me that she has now sent two rights revision requests, after Dorchester continues to violate their contract with her. It has been a year since the first request was sent, and she has still not received a definitive response. Meanwhile, the company continues to sell copies of her books digitally, for which she has not received restitution.

Author Deb Stover says *"Count me among the authors who has one book still allegedly 'in print' with Dorchester."*

I have confirmation from two separate authors that they have now chosen to begin legal proceedings against Dorchester.

Both authors wish to remain anonymous, and were advised by counsel to say no more, although one did confirm to me that "the paperwork is on its way to them (Dorchester) as we speak."

Oh, and remember when Dorchester sold digital copies of my books after the rights had reverted back to me, and they assured *Publisher's Weekly* that they were, quote: *"...committed to solving the problem with Keene and treating all authors fairly. Dorchester will pass along all money to Keene on e-books that were sold after rights reverted."*

Yeah, well, I haven't seen a dime. Or a statement. And I know copies were sold. I have receipts confirming such, as well as documentation from booksellers.

I must take issue with Dorchester's claim that this is all simply "propaganda" but it does indeed seem to be "business as usual" for them.

DORCHESTER: THE END

After I reported earlier this week that Dorchester had closed its office and were still selling works to which they did not own the rights, Dorchester stated via their Facebook page that they were merely moving to a new office on Park Avenue. This turned out to be just another falsehood.

As reported by *Locus* and *Publisher's Marketplace*, John Backe (founder of The Backe Group and owner of Dorchester) filed a notice of foreclosure on the company after failing to collect on an outstanding $3.4 million loan. His intent was to sell the company (including the Dorchester Media magazine division, the Dorchester Publishing book division, registered trademarks, related internet domain names, domestic and foreign copyrights, ISBN numbers, computer equipment, intellectual property, etc.) as a single unit at public auction—including the hundreds of works for which copyright and Dorchester's ownership is disputed. Since Backe is the owner and is also personally foreclosing against the company, all auction proceeds would go to him, rather than to authors and other creditors.

The auction took place at 2pm today. It was conducted by Burton Weston of the Garfunkel, Wild, Travis law firm located in Great Neck, NY. However, Dorchester's plan to sell the company as a single unit was apparently unsuccessful. When I spoke with Burton Weston earlier this afternoon, he confirmed for me that only the Dorchester Media division was auctioned today. The Dorchester Publishing division was not, although he does expect it to be at a later date.

Let me bullet-point that for you: Dorchester still plans to auction the rights to books they do not legally own the rights to.

What follows is my opinion on what each and every author who have disputed their rights should now do. I am not a legal expert, nor do I play one on TV. This commentary is mine alone.

If you are a creditor or freelancer who disputed rights ownership as part of Dorchester's media or magazine division, you should probably find out who bought those rights at auction today. I've heard reports it was FAA Investors LLC or FAA Investments Inc., but I've been unable to verify that. I would suggest you contact the Garfunkel, Wild law firm, be very polite (because none of this is their fault and they have presumably acted in good faith), explain your situation, and ask for the contact information for the winning bidder.

If you are a novelist or author who disputed rights ownership as part of Dorchester's publishing division, follow these steps:

> 1. If Dorchester reverted your rights but are still publishing your books, or if they ignored your rights reversion request but violated your contract (non-payment, late-payment, sold editions they did not have the rights to produce or sell, etc.) the first thing you should do is make the law firm in charge of the auction—see above—aware of that dispute. You should do

this in writing. You should list the title, ISBN, etc. of each work you own the copyright to. You should also include copies (not originals) of any verifying documentation (emails, phone logs, reversion letters, etc.) Let me stress again, the Garfunkel, Wild, Travis law firm aren't the bad guys in this situation. They are acting on good faith on behalf of their client. If Dorchester hasn't revealed these disputed rights to them, then it is your responsibility to do so.

2. You should immediately notify Amazon, Barnes & Noble, Apple iBooks, and any other online bookseller who is selling digital editions of your work, that they are selling unauthorized digital editions of your work for which you own the copyright to. Each of these retailers has different methods for disputing copyright or filing a DMCA, so read those methods carefully before filing your claim. Then file it. Demand that those digital editions be removed from the website and the files suppressed. It should be noted that there is very little that can be done about already existing paperback or trade paperback editions. So don't walk into a B&N and flip out on the employees for selling copies of your books. They'll be liquidated soon enough, but digital is forever. Act now and get them removed.

3. Author Scott Nicholson offers a suggestion for those who have the time and inclination to self-publish their work digitally via Kindle, Nook, etc. He suggests that you self-publish a competing digital edition of your work and undercut Dorchester's price. I would personally suggest you follow through with #2 before doing this, however.

I'm hearing rumors that Amazon may swoop in and save the day. But that hasn't been confirmed.

In the meantime, remember former CEO John Prebich, current CEO Robert Anthony, owner John Backe, and all the other special little swine-headed snowflakes involved in this mess. Sooner or later, they will begin new ventures or land at new companies. You might consider not supporting those new ventures or businesses, and voicing your reasons why.

In the words of the immortal Hunter S. Thompson, "Selah…"

THOUGHTS ON AMAZON-DORCHESTER

Today is Independence Day here in the United States. I like the not-so-subtle irony of giving you my full thoughts on the latest Dorchester twist today of all days. And here they are, after the cut.

As noted, while I was on vacation, *Publisher's Weekly* reported that Amazon "has made a bid to acquire the assets of the company and, as part of the sale, Amazon will pay all outstanding royalties owed to Dorchester authors. Through the deal, Amazon will acquire 1,900 active titles in many of the genres in which it already publishes, including romance and westerns." The article also reiterated what I've been reporting for the last two years—that Dorchester is not paying authors, "yet they continue to pocket receipts for e-books and foreign royalties." Amazon states "We want all authors to be happy being a part of the Amazon Publishing family going forward and we have structured our bid so that we will only take on authors who want to join us. As part of this philosophy, if we win the bid, Dorchester has committed to revert all titles that are not assigned to us."

Now, as I said earlier in the week, I'm cautiously optimistic about this deal. While this move does not impact authors such as myself, Bryan Smith, J.F. Gonzalez, or others who already managed to get their rights reverted and have gone on to other publishers or begun self-publishing, it does help the vast majority of former Dorchester authors who have not been so lucky (such as Stacy Dittrich, Jack Ketchum, Edward Lee, Mary SanGiovanni, Sarah Pinborough, Robert Dunbar, and hundreds more). There are, however, some very important questions which need to be answered before those authors celebrate.

1. Amazon states they will acquire 1,900 active titles. That's only a portion of what Dorchester illegally retains the rights to. If these are mostly from the romance and western lines (of which Amazon has found success) what happens to the horror, thriller, science-fiction and other lines Dorchester still holds?

2. Amazon states they will pay all outstanding royalties owed to authors. But will this be for all authors or only for those authors who choose to publish through Amazon? And how far back will those royalties be calculated? Numerous sources state that Dorchester was misreporting royalties long before its financial plight became public knowledge. And what of authors whose work Dorchester continued to illegally sell, even after those authors had obtained the reversion of their rights? Will Amazon financially compensate them?

3. Amazon states that as part of this deal, "Dorchester has committed to revert all titles that are not assigned to us." How will this be enforced? I mean, Dorchester has committed to all sorts of things, but haven't actually followed through on those commitments. They were committed to reverting rights but they didn't. They were committed to paying authors, but they didn't. What assurances can Amazon give authors who choose not to publish with them that Dorchester will suddenly do the right thing after several years of lies and malfeasance?

These are questions that must be answered. As I said, I'm cautiously optimistic for those authors still trapped in this situation, but I don't think they should pop the champagne just yet.

Yesterday, I received my monthly royalty check and statement from Deadite Press, who have published a good portion of my Dorchester backlist. In a little over a year, I have earned more money from Deadite on those same titles than I did from Dorchester in seven years. I want my fellow authors to be able to enjoy that same independence and success, and I hope this new development eventually leads to that, regardless of whether they choose to publish through Amazon or simply obtain their rights and do something else. But I suspect this is going to get messy and it might be a while before that happens. That's why it's important that we as a community continue to stick together. In the last three years you've seen the horror and romance communities come together on this Blog and elsewhere. We need to continue with that solidarity. Authors need to continue supporting each other, and fans need to continue supporting those authors.

It's also important to remember that Dorchester is just the tip of the iceberg. There are other, bigger publishers out there who are just as capable of doing this to their authors. We need to make sure they know that, just as Dorchester found a fight on its hands, so will they all.

Happy Independence Day.

FAREWELL TEDDY GARNETT

Teddy Garnett, the main character in my novel *Earthworm Gods* and a long-time fan-favorite, was based on my grandfather, Ward Crowley, who passed away earlier this week. My family asked me to write the eulogy for his funeral service, and I thought I'd share it with you, as follows:

A few years ago, at the age of 89, my grandfather woke up one morning and decided to go deer hunting. He got his rifle out of the gun case, dressed warm, and went outside to the shed behind the house. He took a seat and stuck the barrel of his gun out the window until a deer came along. And then he shot it. When I asked him later if he preferred that method instead of walking miles and miles through the cold woods for hours on end, he leaned close and whispered, "Brian, I just can't get out there and walk those mountains like I used to." After a pause, he added, "But I still brought it down with one shot."

When I was eight years old, my grandparents took my sister and me swimming in the Greenbrier River one day, and my grandfather found this rock for me. It's a fossil. Consider for a moment—after this fossil was created, it lay there on the bottom of that river for thousands and thousand of years until my Grandfather found it. For decades, it has filled both me and my sons with wonder and delight. I've never had much luck holding on to things in my life, but I've always held on to this rock. When times got tough—and there have been times that were exceedingly tough—I could always look to this rock for hope.

In many ways, my grandfather was like this rock.

Born September 6, 1919, Ward William Crowley was one of 8 children. They lived in Greenbank. His father, Russell, was the town Sheriff, but that didn't stop Ward from getting into mischief. When he was five, he was playing in his father's new Chevy touring car along with his brother Clyde (who was 7) and Jarrett (who was 3). The car had been parked on top of a hill overlooking the family's chicken house. Somehow, they disengaged the parking brake, and the car started rolling down the hill. My grandfather and Clyde jumped free, but little Jarrett clung to the wheel and steered the car away from the chicken house. For his valiant efforts, Jarrett got bread, butter and brown sugar. My grandfather and his brother, meanwhile, got spanked with the razor strap.

This seemed to be a common theme. Another time, the two

older boys became jealous of Jarrett's bright new balloon. They tried cajoling him into popping it, but he refused. They offered him candy (which they didn't have) and other bribes, but still he refused. Eventually, Grandpa and Clyde decided to make Jarrett eat a cow patty as punishment. Their mother stepped in before the deed could be done and once again, Jarrett got bread, butter and brown sugar while Grandpa and Clyde became further acquainted with the razor strap.

Despite sibling rivalries, Ward was always someone his brothers and sisters could look to for hope and strength. He was their rock.

Eventually, he grew up and joined the Army Air Corps. He became a radioman on a B-29, and he flew countless missions all over the world, including numerous bombing raids over Japan. He flew throughout World War II, from the beginning of that terrible conflict until the very end of the war. He saw men die in the most horrible ways imaginable, but it never shook his faith. A few years ago, I had the opportunity to speak on the phone with Ace Hall, one of my grandfather's fellow crewmembers. Ace told me that my Grandfather was the guy who always gave them hope. He was their rock.

Grandpa came home on leave, after being stationed in Panama and Galapagos for 20 months, and while he was home, he met a young woman named Anna Ruth Lyall. They had one date before he had to ship back out, but they wrote to each other nearly every day. Seven months later, they were married.

They had two children, Mark and Shannon. Sadly, Mark lost his life in an automobile accident at the age of sixteen. During this tragedy, my grandmother and my mother and the rest of the family clung to two things to see them through that terrible time: the first was their faith. The second was my grandfather. He was their rock.

He retired from the Air Force in 1964 and after a stint working at Fort Deitrich, retired from Civil Service in 1975. After that, he and my Grandmother moved back here and they've lived here ever since. My grandfather was active in this community. He volunteered his time, money, blood and sweat to this very church we are gathered in. He helped build the community center in Renick. He was always available to lend a hand to his friends and neighbors. And just like he was for his children, grandchildren, great-grandchildren, nephews, and nieces, he was a playmate, mentor and advisor for several generations of youngsters.

He was this community's rock.

My grandfather lived a full and varied life—one marked by love and hope, tragedy and heartbreak, faith and charity. When things got tough, he never shirked, never backed down, never once asked for the cup to be taken from his lips. He accepted all of life's triumphs and tragedies with strength and faith and a steadfast belief that good will always triumph over evil and that love and kindness will always prevail. He was a rock, and while he is no longer with us, his memory is. Just as my sons and I have looked at this fossil with a continued sense of amazement and wonder, we can all look back on and consider my grandfather's example in the years to come, and in doing so, we will find peace and wisdom and an inner strength of our own.

After flying thousands of miles, he's taken one final flight. He passed away on the first day of squirrel season, and I'd like to think that maybe it's the first day of squirrel season in Heaven, too, and that he's with his son, Mark, and his friends Matthew and Billy and Frank, and other loved ones who arrived there before him, and that he's still bringing them down with just one shot.

I'd like to close with the words of Lt. Colonel Theodore Danielson, US Army Airborne: "Well done, faithful soldier. Be thou at peace."

DELIVERANCE: ON ZOMBIES AND WRITER'S BLOCK AND SUCH

As you're no doubt aware, I'm still recovering from my heart attack, so instead of new content, I thought I'd post the afterword to the recently released *The Rising: Deliverance*. It is edited for brevity (the complete version appears at the end of the book). You can read it without fear of spoilers. There are none (unless you haven't read *City of the Dead*). I like this afterword. I think it sheds some light on where my head was most of last year.

For a guy who keeps swearing that he's done with zombies, I sure do seem to still be writing about them a lot. In case you've been living under a rock or in a coma for the last decade, most critics and media-watchers agree that the current uber-zombie craze in pop culture (books, movies, comics, television, games, trading cards, clothing, food, philosophy, college courses, etc.) is at least partially my fault. The publication of my first novel, *The Rising*, coincided with the release of a movie called *28 Days Later*. Both *The Rising* and *28 Days Later* featured different kinds of zombies, which was okay with most people, since nobody else had done much with zombies for the decade leading up to the book and movie's releases. Both were big hits. *City of the Dead*, my sequel to *The Rising*, followed soon after, and so did a lot of other books and movies and comics. And they haven't gone away. Indeed, there seem to be more of them than ever. There are now publishing companies that publish nothing but zombie literature and authors who write about nothing but the living dead.

I had a chance to do the same. In truth, I could have probably made a very good living (i.e. a lot more money than what I make now) doing for zombies what Anne Rice and Laurell K. Hamilton did for vampires, but doing so didn't appeal to me. I didn't want to become 'The Zombie Guy'. I wanted to write about other monsters and other situations. So I did. And a lot of other people came along and wrote about zombies instead and made a lot of money doing so, while I went broke writing about things like ghouls and un-killable Russian mobsters and giant, carnivorous earthworms. In hindsight, those other authors might have been a lot smarter than me.

Occasionally, I did indeed return to writing about zombies. I tried my hand at the traditional "Romero-style" undead (with *Dead Sea*) and returned to the world of *The Rising* with a collection of thirty-two original short stories that all took place in that world, called *The Rising: Selected Scenes from the End of the World*. After that, I decided I was really burned out on them. Upon reflection, though, I wasn't so much burned out as I was written-out. I didn't want to just repeat the same story over and over again (which is the risk any author or filmmaker runs when dealing with the undead—or any other genre trope). So I proclaimed myself as 'DONE WITH ZOMBIES'. And I fucking damn well meant it, too…

…except that people kept offering me money to write about zombies one more time. It's hard to say no to money. I like money. I'm a big fan. With two ex-wives and two sons and a metric fuck-ton of debt, I have no choice but to be a big fan of money. So I've returned to zombies a few more times since then, but only when I thought I had an original idea (such as my comic series *The Last Zombie*, which deals with the aftermath of a zombie apocalypse, after the dead are all dead again) and my novel *Entombed* (which takes place in the world of *Dead Sea* and deals with bunker mentality and the psychological ramifications of surviving a zombie apocalypse). But when I pause to consider those two works, it occurs to me that the zombies are nothing more than window dressing. They appear only briefly in *Entombed*, and don't appear at all in *The Last Zombie* (except in flashbacks). So maybe I really am done with zombies, after all.

What I'm not done with, however, is characters. The Reverend Thomas Martin has always been a personal favorite character of mine (along with a handful of other character such as Adam Senft, Levi Stoltzfus, Timmy Graco, Teddy Garnett, Whitey Putin and Tony Genova). I'm quite fond of Reverend Martin, and nobody was more surprised than I was when he died in the first few chapters of *City of the Dead*. I did not see that coming.

I've written a lot of novels since then, but occasionally, I'd find my thoughts returning to Martin. I knew his story wasn't over yet, even though he was dead. I knew there was a lot more to him than what readers saw in *The Rising* and *City of the Dead*. I knew that some of the more interesting parts of his saga took place before the events in those books, and I'm glad I've finally gotten the chance to write about them.

This isn't a story about zombies. It's a story about people. And fate. And faith. And doubt. And all the other things that define us and make us human. It's a story of the things that shaped Reverend Thomas Martin before readers met him in *The Rising*. It's about the real reason he agreed to go with Jim in search of Danny. You might have enjoyed it. You might not have. But I can tell you that I enjoyed writing it. As I type this, it is mid-September 2010, and I have barely survived the Year From Hell. In the last nine months, I've gone through a second divorce, the slow death of a family member, a cancer scare, a nervous breakdown, absolute financial destitution at the hands of several publishers, the wholesale collapse (again) of the horror genre, and a host of other personal crises. On top of that, I've watched those closest to me suffer through their own personal tragedies, many of which dwarf my own, and all of which I'm powerless to prevent. As my faithful assistant Big Joe Maynard so astutely put it last week, "What did we do to piss off God this time?"

Truth time: I've been tempted to pack it all in, to quit writing and fuck off somewhere—Alaska or maybe Guam—reinvent myself under an assumed name in some remote location where nobody knows me and get a job tending bar or fishing or logging trees. There have been some days over the last nine months, when the going got especially tough, when that urge to quit was overwhelmingly strong, and you will never know how close I came to acting on it. But instead of running away, I fled to the place where it all began—the world of *The Rising*—and returned to a character that has always been near in my head and my heart—the Reverend Thomas Martin. Writing about him restored my faith in what I do and gave me hope that it's worthwhile. Seeing him again, if only for this brief novella, gave me my own form of deliverance. And I needed that.

I hope it did something for you, as well.

THOUGHTS ON AWARDS

This Blog entry is Nick Mamatas's fault. Before going further, you'll want to read the latest entry on his Livejournal. So, go do that. Then come back here. I'll wait.

Done? Okay, good. Now, I don't know the author who posted that. Perhaps she meant well. Perhaps she doesn't know any better. But Nick is absolutely right in pointing out that it is exactly this type of stance and behavior that makes many professional authors grouse about the Stoker Award (mostly in private but sometimes in public). So what follows isn't an attack on her. It is meant for the many who also perpetuate this type of nonsense.

I've got eight awards, including two Bram Stoker Awards. You know what a Bram Stoker Award is? It's a haunted house statue that the doors frequently fall off of. They are a bitch to dust around, attract chocolate fingerprint smudges from curious toddlers, and make perfectly serviceable paperweights.

That's all they are.

That's all any award is.

A material object that you put on a shelf and then have to dust around.

The physical award isn't important. What's important is why you received the award. For example, on the shelf right next to my Stokers is an award bestowed upon me by the men and women of the 509th Logistics Fuels Flight at Whitman Air Force Base (home of the B-2 Stealth Bomber). They gave me that many years ago for the Books for Troops program I used to run. To express their gratitude, these men and women pooled their money and commissioned that award, and let me tell you, it remains the single-most thing I am proud of in my fifteen-year career. The award itself is also a bitch to dust around, and it has a tendency to fall over anytime my cat or toddler jumps too hard, but the sentiment behind it means the world to me. I'm proud of that award because of why I received it.

I used to be proud of my Stokers, too, because the Stokers used to mean something. They meant that your peers—most of whom were well-read and knowledgeable and knew their roots—had judged your work to be superior. These days, not so much. The vast public perception is that the Stokers are now nothing more than a shill's game—a primary election where the majority of the candidates promote their eligibility for a paperweight instead of the Presidency, and the electorate expects and encourages this behavior by grubbing for free books and patting the backs of those who pat theirs. Knowing that, it's hard to feel the same sense of pride toward those two haunted houses as I do that award next to them.

Contrary to popular opinion, a Stoker Award will not help you sell a book or a movie. They do not mean you'll get a bigger advance or better royalty rates. They do not sell extra copies of your books. To achieve these things, one does what writers have always done to achieve them. You write, submit, negotiate, and market.

Or, if none of those things are important to you, and what you want is a perfectly serviceable paperweight that is a bitch to dust around, then instead of spending your time writing, negotiating, and marketing, just keep doing what so many writers these days seem to be doing.

Postscript: This should go without saying, but I'm obviously not implying that every single person up for a Stoker or voting in the Stokers engages in these practices. They aren't. Sadly, there are enough, however, who do, and thus, taint the entire process.

THINGS THEY DON'T TEACH YOU IN WRITING CLASS

Brian Keene's Helpful Writing Tips That No One Else Will Teach You

1. Never say, "Well, life can't get any worse." Because that is when life will invariably kick you in the teeth.

2. In the end, the only people you can really trust are your kids. All others are suspect, even your cat or dog.

3. Yes, your kids can break your heart, too, but that takes years. Your dog or cat will eat your face after just a week with no food.

4. Except for maybe the Six-Million Dollar Man's bionic dog. But the dog on the original *Battlestar Galactica*? That dog would have totally eaten Boxey's face.

5. They say that success breeds contempt, but they are misinformed. Success breeds one thing—loneliness.

6. Before you are successful, you have friends. Once you are successful, you have more friends. You will also attract sycophants.

7. Some sycophants don't mean to be sycophants. Others do. It can be very hard to tell a sycophant from a friend. They are like John Carpenter's *The Thing*.

8. Worse, some friends can become sycophants. Even your pre-success friends are not immune to this transformation. So you adopt an attitude of "Trust No One".

9. The problem with that is you can no longer tell the difference. So you end up treating your friends like sycophants and your sycophants like friends.

10. And after that, you build a wall, just like in the Pink Floyd song. Eventually, you either go insane, become an addict, kill yourself, or push back and clean fucking house.

11. If you love your kids, as I do, the first three ain't an option. So you choose number four. And after you've cleaned house, you find yourself truly alone for the first time in a very long time.

12. Success breed loneliness, but it is in that loneliness that you can finally breathe and hear yourself think, and in that silence, truly start to live.

THE END OF BORDERS

Author's Note: Much like the Dorchester segment of this book, this next section compiles and excerpts a number of things I wrote about the struggles—and ultimate doom—of Borders, one of America's biggest bookstore chains.

WHY BORDERS WENT BANKRUPT

Publishers Weekly reports "Borders Group has given in to the inevitable and filed for Chapter 11 bankruptcy protection in Bankruptcy Court for the Southern District of New York... Borders said it will close… about 200 locations, within the next several weeks."

What isn't being reported is the *real* reason why Borders (and others) are in such bad shape. For example, here's a quote from a fellow writer: "I wrote much of my first novel at Border's in Roseville, CA. Then it closed. So I went to the other Border's across town. Then I moved to L.A. and began going to the Border's in El Segundo. But their ridiculously loud music and arctic temperatures drove me out. So now I go to Starbucks. Why don't retailers make their stores more user-friendly? For example, it's a friggin lottery trying to find an electrical outlet so as to plug in one's laptop... Panera bread offers free Wi-Fi and an electrical outlet at every booth. And free coffee refills. Border's charges for the refill, which is stupid because I've already paid for the cup and the surcharge to cover the labor for filling it. If you can't give people what they want, you don't deserve to be in business."

You'll note that not once does the commenter say he went there to buy a book. Instead, he went there to write a novel, demand free coffee refills, and complain about the lack of electrical outlets and overall ambiance. Perhaps if he had purchased a fucking book upon occasion, the situation wouldn't be so dire.

Bookstores are just that: stores. If I want to watch a movie, I don't go to Best Buy and pop my DVD into one of their display models and kick back with some popcorn. I do it in the comfort of my home. If I want to write a novel and have free coffee refills, I stay the fuck home, sit at my desk and make a pot of coffee.

Bookstores should be for buying books. And Borders, B&N, and all the others shot themselves in the foot the moment they began positioning themselves as "a place to hang out" rather than "a place to spend money". But these are just my observations. As always, your mileage may vary.

BREAKING BORDERS

The internet is full of heartbreak tonight. Borders employees across the country report bounced paychecks. In some cases, this caused employees to default on rent, mortgage and utility payments. Employees from the closed stores report that cafe scavengers are now doubling their demands of entitlement. Author Michele Lee, who is also a Borders employee and whose store is one of those being closed, is offering a day-by-day Blog about the experience.

It's all so sad and infuriating. That list of closed stores

includes at least two dozen I've signed at over the last decade. These were stores full of good people who loved books and loved helping people who loved books, and now they're fucked because of a succession of barely literate corporate slugs, all apparently cloned from Wile E. Coyote, who thought selling books was like selling groceries, and a generation of slothful nu-yuppie cafe crawlers whose only sense of self-worth came from hanging out in the store—not to purchase something—but to show the world how oh-so-fucking-important they were because they were writing on their laptops or chattering on their cell-phones while their mutant hell-spawn ran rampant in the children's section.

So what's next on the horizon? Well, according to *Ecolibris*, Barnes & Noble "doesn't look too good and bankruptcy is becoming a more realistic threat".

If there is a Borders in your area that's closing, consider stopping by with bottled water or donuts for the employees. Small gestures like that would be appreciated. These people are in Hell. And for all my friends at Borders stores—both open and closing—across the country, my thoughts are with you. You have always been incredibly gracious and supportive of my work and my readers, and I hope that all of your stories have happy endings.

BORDERS FADES TO NULL

In an 11th hour move, Borders turned down a last minute offer from Books-a-Million to buy the Waldenbooks brand and sold itself to liquidation company Hilco, rather than face bankruptcy auction today. In a statement, current President Mike Edwards continued to solely blame the "electronic reader revolution" rather than all the other actual factors which led to this outcome.

All remaining stores will close by September.

I've signed at countless Borders over the last twelve years. My heart goes out to all my friends in those locations, and all the other Borders employees who were always supportive of my work.

As for the future, with Barnes and Noble unwilling to stock Deadite Press titles, I urge my readers to order my books from a good indie bookstore or purchase them online.

First Dorchester. Now this.

What a shitty age to be a writer.

Sometimes, I wish that heart attack had fucking killed me. But then I look at my youngest son and chide myself for thinking that, and punch myself in the nuts.

Which perfectly sums up how it feels to be a working author in this day and age.

ROOTS
(KEYNOTE SPEECH, ANTHOCON 2011)

Good morning. Apparently, the bar closed early last night, judging by how many of you are here this morning.

Before I begin, I'd like to thank JF Gonzalez, Shawn Bagely, Jack Haringa, Nick Mamatas, Bev Vincent, Nick Kaufmann, Robert Swartwood, Nate Southard, and Mary SanGiovanni for their help in preparing this talk.

This speech is supposed to be about the history of the horror genre. In discussing such a topic, I should start with the cave paintings of primitive man, many of which depicted things they were afraid of. Then I should go into the *Epic of Gilgamesh*, and the various stories that make up the Jewish, Christian, Hindu, and Muslim holy books. I should talk about *Beowulf*, and Lucian Samosata's *True History* (which, written in 200AD, is the story of the crew of a ship who are transported from Earth to the Moon and Venus, and details the monsters they battle and oddities they find). I should talk about 1796's *The Monk* by Matthew Gregory Lewis, and *Melmoth the Wanderer*, and of course, the contributions of Mary Shelley, Bram Stoker, Arthur Machen, and Edgar Allan Poe. But since we only have 30 minutes and since many of you are either hung over or here only to ask me if I'll ever write another zombie novel, I'm going to focus on Modern Horror—fiction written during the 20th century.

Also, we'll be laughing at people who post on the Shocklines message board.

Growing up in the Seventies and early Eighties, my generation was introduced to horror fiction in one of two ways—kid's books (John Bellairs was our J. K. Rowling) or comic books (*Man-Thing, Weird War, House of Mystery, Werewolf By Night, The Occult Files of Doctor Spektor*, etc.). From these, we graduated to Stephen King and Dean Koontz. It was King's masterful history of the horror genre, *Danse Macabre*, which introduced most of us to H.P. Lovecraft, Richard Matheson, and others who'd come before him, and it was the delay between King and Koontz titles that allowed us to discover Richard Laymon, Jack Ketchum, Joe R. Lansdale, Graham Masterton, the Splatterpunks, and many others.

These days, we see a new generation of horror writers and readers—and what's curious is their generation was not influenced by Stephen King or comic books. Their generation was introduced to horror primarily through video games and R.L. Stine's Goosebumps series, and they've now graduated to books by myself, Edward Lee, Sarah Langan, Steve Niles, Carlton Mellick, Jonathan Maberry, JF Gonzalez, and others of our generation. That seems strange to me. It makes me feel old. It also makes me feel that I should certainly be making more money than I am. But I digress.

This generation also has more competing forms of media and entertainment than any other, and as a result, they are less well read than previous generations. Admittedly, this is a generalization, but it's one that, in my experience and the experience of my peers, is true for the majority.

And that's a shame.

A horror writer should know the genre's history for several reasons. First and foremost, they should know it so as not to repeat the mistakes of its past. They should draw upon that history, letting the books and stories that have been written in the past inspire and inform and shape their own work. You know that novel you're working on about Nazi ghosts haunting a tank? Graham Masterton beat you to it back in the Seventies. If you're writing about vampires, you've probably read Dracula—but did you also read the works of Les Daniels, or *Salem's Lot, They Thirst, Vampyrrhic,* or *Lot Lizards*? Maybe you saw Ramsey Campbell at a convention and were told he is one of the most important living authors, but you're not sure why. This is unacceptable. Maybe (and most importantly) you want to become a better writer by studying and understanding the various styles of writers that came before you. The only way to do that is through reading.

Reading is a crucial part of being a writer, and it's essential at all stages of your development and career. You should certainly read outside of your chosen genre, but it's also important to read inside your genre, as well. You may not like all of them, but you should read them anyway. Your writing will be better for having done so.

This is just as important for those of you in the audience who have no desire to become a writer, and identify yourselves as fans. If you're a reader, then you need to read fiction that has inspired and informed and shaped the genre into what it is today. Like those *28 Days Later*-style zombies? I bet you'll love Jim Starlin's *Among Madmen* or Simon Clark's *Blood Crazy*. Perhaps you enjoy the exploits of occult detectives such as F. Paul Wilson's Repairman Jack, Jim Butcher's Harry Dresden, or my own Levi Stoltzfus. But have you read Manly Wade Wellman's Silver John the Balladeer stories or William Hope Hodgson's Carnacki the Ghost Finder? Think it can't get any more hard-fucking-core than Edward Lee or Wrath James White? Then you haven't read *Echo of a Curse* by R. R. Ryan—written in 1939! Like John Carpenter's *The Thing*? Yeah? But have you read John W. Campbell's *Who Goes There*?

At least once in every decade since the First World War, the public has had a renewed interest in horror fiction. For the interests of our discussion, I have broken this era of modern horror down into six waves.

That first wave, spanning from 1900 to the mid-1920s begins, more or less, with the 1901 publication of M.P. Shiel's *The Purple Cloud*. *The Purple Cloud* is a post-apocalyptic novel. In it, much of humanity are killed by a mysterious, toxic purple cloud that floats across the Earth. The survivors learn that they are pawns in a battle between the forces of "The White" (representing good) and "The Black (representing evil). The themes and ideas presented in *The Purple Cloud* are ones that have echoed in post-apocalyptic horror fiction for more than 100 years, influencing everything from Matheson's *I Am Legend* to Stephen King's *The Stand*.

That first wave of modern horror also gave us authors such as Lord Dunsany and William Hope Hodgson, and saw an increased public interest in ghost stories, particularly the work of M. R. James, Algernon Blackwood, and Edith Wharton (among others). 1923 brought us the birth of *Weird Tales*, a magazine whose long and varied history is so entwined with modern horror that it's as difficult to imagine the genre without it as it is to imagine the genre without Stephen King.

The second wave, spanning the mid-20s through the late-40s, was an important period that gave us H.P. Lovecraft, Frank Belknap Long, Robert E. Howard, Clark Ashton Smith, Shirley Jackson, and Seabury Quinn, among others, and the early works of Fritz Leiber.

The third wave, spanning the 50s and 60s gave us more mature works from Fritz Leiber, as well as the work of Anthony Boucher, Theodore Sturgeon, John Farris, Ira Levin, and five writers who are as important, if not more important, to the genre than even the works of the esteemed Mr. King—Robert Bloch, Richard Matheson, Ray Bradbury, Rod Serling, and the early works of Ramsey Campbell. These five writers were among the first to truly begin centering horror fiction in contemporary settings, rather than crumbling New England waterfront towns or sprawling Victorian mansions. Their impact and themes still inform much of today's horror fiction.

During the first three waves, horror fiction was published as either mainstream fiction, science fiction, or mystery fiction. There was no horror marketing category. That category wasn't invented until the rise of the 4th wave.

The beginning of the fourth wave—the Seventies and Eighties, brought us Stephen King, Dean Koontz, F. Paul Wilson, Thomas Monteleone, Karl Edward Wagner, Peter Straub, and others. When King became a bestseller in paperback, the marketing category of HORROR was invented. The genre waned briefly around 1979-1980 but then came back with a vengeance. The 4th wave also gave us Clive Barker, Charles L. Grant, James Herbert, TED Klein, Robert R. McCammon, Joe R. Lansdale, Jack Ketchum, Richard Laymon, Rick Hautala, Ronald Kelly, the Splatterpunks, Brian Hodge, and Poppy Z. Brite. This era also saw the early works of such current luminaries as Edward Lee and Tom Piccirilli. These were beautiful, golden years. A great time to be a fan, and a wonderful time to be a writer.

And then came the 90's...

(Author's Note: At this point in the speech, I burst into tears at the podium and then waited for the audience to stop laughing).

Some say horror died in the 90's, but this is patently untrue. Horror as a marketing category to be stamped on the spine of a book certainly died, but the stories and books and readers were still there. From 1991 to 1995, the most prominent mass market horror publishers were Zebra Books and the Dell Abyss line.

Zebra was your traditional mass-market pulp house, cranking out novels with garish covers. Dell-Abyss was a little different. Started with the mission statement of getting away from the traditional horror of King, Koontz, and Straub, Dell Abyss was to publish more cutting-edge horror, and for a while, they did. Then the whole thing came crashing down, leaving folks like Brian Hodge and Kathe Koja homeless. Meanwhile, over at Zebra, authors weren't getting paid on time. Zebra collapsed, too, which left authors like Rick Hautala and Ronald Kelly scrambling.

Does any of that sound familiar?

With the cancellation of Zebra and Dell-Abyss, other publishers began shying away from horror, as well. Or they called it something else. Unable to sell their work to mainstream publishers, horror authors turned to the small press. Likewise, readers who were unable to find horror novels in stores did the same. The 90s saw the rise of the small press, something which had always existed, way back in the 1st wave, but which really came to prominence in the 90s.

The 90s didn't kill horror. It was just a transition period. Horror fiction was still published, it just didn't reach as wide a readership. And it was also the birthing ground of the fifth wave.

My generation—the generation of the New Weird, the New Pulp, Bizarro, and typified by writers such as Sarah Langan, Joe Hill, Christopher Golden, Tim Lebbon, Jonathan Maberry, Carlton Mellick, Jeff Vandermeer, Bryan Smith, Sarah Pinborough, Weston Ochse, JF Gonzalez, Wrath James White, Tom Piccirilli, Jeffrey Thomas, and many more, including a good cross section of the folks in this room—make up the fifth wave. We rose to prominence in that last decade and in the first decade of this new century. We were the first generation to have the Internet. We bridged the gap between the fourth wave—authors who had to adapt to new technology—and your generation, the post-internet generation. As Mary SanGiovanni pointed out to me a few weeks ago, "We're the turning point generation, in a unique position to use both experience/history and technology/adaptation."

For your generation, the Internet was already there. You didn't have to bend and shape it and figure out how to use it to the advantage of your writing or reading. We did that for you.

And you do use it. You use it, and you use all of the other technology that's available. You post on Twitter and you play *Farmville* on Facebook and *Dead Island* on X-Box, and you get the *Nightmare on Elm Street* series streamed from Netflix. But what you're not doing enough of is reading.

The editors and publishers your generation are submitting to come from the fourth and fifth waves. They know the genre's history. And while good writing will always triumph over anything else in the slush pile, if you submit something that you think is original and fresh and has never been done before, and the editor can think of twenty examples of it being done before, what do you think will happen to your manuscript? I mentioned the thematic similarities between Shiel's *The Purple Cloud* and King's *The Stand*—the end of the world, humanity dying off, the eternal struggle between good and evil. And yes, the themes are similar, but *The Stand* is King's own take on those themes, as is McCammon's *Swan Song* or Graham Masterton's *Plague* or James Herbert's *Domain* or any other novel of that type.

I truly believe that in horror fiction, there is no such thing as an original idea. They've all been done before. What's original is your take on the idea, your spin on the familiar old tropes and monsters, your unique perspective and voice—your twist. Don't waste a year of your life writing *The Stand*. It's already been written. Instead, write your take on the themes presented in the book—themes that have existed in horror fiction since primitive man first started painting stories on cave walls. Themes that make up those holy books I mentioned at the beginning. Themes that were tackled in the *Epic of Gilgamesh*. Novelist and comics writer Warren Ellis often says "tell people who you are and where you are and what the world looks like today." And that's what writing horror fiction—or any type of fiction—really is. It's taking universal themes and truths that have been examined by other writers for thousands of years, and offering your own perspective on them.

My novel *Ghoul* is a coming of age novel about kids fighting monsters. There's nothing new about that. King did it. Dan Simmons did it. Jonathan Bellairs and Don Coscarelli and Joe Lansdale and dozens of others did it. But *Ghoul* is my coming of age novel. It's who I was at the age of twelve. It's where I was, and it's about what the world looked like then. And if it hadn't been that—if it had just been a retread of all those coming of age novels that came before it—it would have been rejected by my publisher, and rightfully so. Or, I would have self published it and then discerning readers would say, "There's nothing new here. It's all been done a thousand times before."

Know your genre. Know your history. Read a book.

I talked earlier about the collapse of Zebra and Dell Abyss back in the mid-90's. Last year, we saw something similar happen with the collapse of Dorchester-Leisure. The year before that, myself, JF Gonzalez, Bryan Smith, Craig Spector, and other Leisure authors saw what was coming and prepared ourselves. This was long before the whole mess went public. How did we know to do that? Was it some form of intuition or ESP? No. It was because we know the genre's history. We saw the signs, saw the similarities to the Dell Abyss situation, and each of us took steps to prepare ourselves for the worst. And, in the end, we came out okay, while many who ignored our warnings have not. We knew the genre's history, and we knew that history was about to repeat itself.

Know your genre. Know your history. Read a book.

On the Shocklines message board right now, there's a thread about Robert Bloch. I briefly explained why Bloch was so important and influential. I know that because I've read him. Here are some quotes from members of your generation, taken from that thread:

1st Poster: "Aside mentions about *Psycho* and *Yours Truly Jack The Ripper*, some funny quotes from him, his Lovecraft connection and that he often wrote stories with predictable 50s comic book twists (not that he was inspired by the comics, I presume he had more influence on them), I rarely see Bloch discussed… I would have thought the success of *Psycho* would have made the rest of his work widely read too. Did his other books sell well? I haven't read a single word of his fiction but what do you think of his stories, novels, screenplays and what on earth are the Psycho sequels like? I can't begin to imagine what would happen in them."

Let me repeat that last sentence: "I haven't read a single word of his fiction." So here we have a young man with a sincere wish to be an artist, and has some vague sense of who Robert Bloch was, but he's NEVER READ A SINGLE WORD OF BLOCH'S FICTION. He can use Wikipedia to give him enough information to post about it on Shocklines but he apparently can't be bothered to pick up a fucking book and read it.

2nd Poster: "In Bloch's version of *Psycho 2*, Norman hacks a nun to death, escapes the mental hospital dressed in her habit, and returns to the motel. Don't know what he does there, the back cover of the book didn't give that much detail and I've not actually read it."

Again, note the last sentence. "I've not actually read it."

3rd Poster: "I can't imagine Bloch's name fading entirely, but it will be interesting to see how his legacy fares, in time. I'm not certain he'll be much more than a footnote, twenty or thirty years from now. But who knows? It's not about liking his work or not liking it (I can't even guarantee that I've read him.)"

And again, note the last sentence.

Now, let me be clear. I am not making fun of these three young authors. What I'm doing is pointing out the ridiculousness of the situation. Do you see the common theme here? They can use the internet and all of the other technology available to them to discuss Bloch's career and quote the back covers of his books and pontificate about his importance, but none of them can be fucking bothered to pick up one of his books—or better yet—utilize that same technology and try reading him for themselves.

But it goes beyond that. This isn't a case of young people

who have simply not heard of Robert Bloch. That would be excusable. But as evidenced here, all three writers know that Robert Bloch is considered important. They just don't have a sense of why. Maybe that's our fault. I don't know. I know that the writers I looked up to from the fourth wave were always quick to recommend authors from waves one through three. I'd like to think our generation does the same. So, maybe it's not our fault. At the end of the day, what matters is that they know Bloch is important. They just don't know why. And I bet some of you in this room today don't know why either.

Well, the only way to get that sense of why is to read him. Know your genre. Know your history. Read a fucking book.

There's no excuse for not reading. Sure, maybe there's no bookstore left in your town. Maybe Borders closed up shop and the local used bookstore only carries inspirational fiction and *Chicken Soup for the Soul* books. But that's no excuse, because your generation has the Internet. We already tested it out and broke it in for you. It's there for you to use. There's Amazon.com and Kindle and Nook. You can read on your cellphone or iPad or even on your video game console. And, if you're old school, I'm sure you have a library nearby.

What's infuriating to me is that the public has greater access to books than at anytime in our history, and yet less people are reading. You can change that.

Where do you start? Start anywhere. When I was younger, in addition to *Danse Macabre*, we had a wonderful list created by Karl Edward Wagner that spotlighted forgotten gems of horror fiction. Your generation has no list, and *Danse Macabre* is outdated, but it's still a good source. Start there. I've been writing a regular column for *Shroud Magazine* called Seminal Screams that focuses on things that either weren't mentioned in *Danse Macabre* or have been published since its inception.

Track down some of the non-fiction of Douglas Winter, Stephen Jones, Karl Edward Wagner, John Pelan, Les Daniels, Stanley Wiater, or ST Joshi. All of them have written at length about the history of our genre, and there is a wealth of information and recommendations to be found in their work.

Ask your favorite author for recommendations. When I was a young man, if I wanted to ask Stephen King or Dean Koontz a question, I had to write them a letter and buy a stamp and wait (hope) to get a reply. These days, you can log online and talk to your favorite writers pretty much instantly. Most of them will even talk back. Ask them who they recommend. Ask them who their influences were, and who they think you should be reading. They'll be happy to tell you, because they want to share the enjoyment they get from those author's works.

I can't tell you how many teenagers and twenty-somethings have come up to me in the last ten years and thanked me for recommending Richard Laymon, Jack Ketchum, or Joe R. Lansdale. In almost every case, they say something like "I never heard of him until you mentioned him online, but wow—this stuff is APESHIT!" And that makes me happy, because they're stuff is indeed apeshit, and it should be read by everybody.

Maybe you won't care for Laymon or Ketchum or Lansdale, but you'll never know unless you try. Maybe Peter Straub will be more to your taste. Or Tim Powers. Or Melanie Tem. Or Norman Partridge. Or David Schow. Or James Moore. Or Joe Nassise. Or Chet Williamson. Or Sarah Pinborough. Or M.R. James. Or Bentley Little. Or Thomas Ligotti.

It doesn't matter where you start or who you start with. All that matters is that you start. Once you discover horror's rich history for yourself, I guarantee you that you'll never stop…

THE GOOD YEARS

My oldest son turns 21 today. He's going out with friends tonight, to do what many young men do when they turn twenty-one in this country—discover drinking.

It's hard for me to believe he is 21. I close my eyes and I can easily see white-trash cracker me, living in a trailer, rocking a mullet, working in a foundry, dreaming of one day becoming a writer, and loving that little boy with all of my heart. Fast-forward a few years. He's moved out of state with his mother, I no longer work in a foundry, and the first few strands of mullet are circling the bathtub drain, a harbinger of hair loss to come. I'm on my way to see him for the weekend when a story idea presents itself. That idea will become a book called *The Rising*.

He's a young man now, rather than the little boy who used to snuggle up in my lap and read *Teeny-Tiny Tale* and *The Lorax* and Hulk comic books. He no longer needs my advice on how to ride a bike, or catch a fish, or what to do if he likes a girl. He doesn't need me to explain what happened to Simba's Daddy in *The Lion King* or why nobody ever stays dead in the Marvel universe. These days, his concerns and questions are a young man's concerns: how to deal with the stress of college and things like that. Today, he wanted advice on drinking. I told him stick with beer or liquor and don't mix the two, make sure he has a designated driver, don't get into a car with anyone who has been drinking (no matter how hot she is), and maybe stop after four beers and see how he feels before proceeding.

Those are the things I tell him these days. I don't tell him how a parent, looking back over the great barrier reef that is time, sees nothing but the mistakes that they made—decisions that impacted the child, even if the child is unaware of it into adulthood. I don't tell him that there's no instruction manual handed out when you're a father, and that you do the best you can, and hope you don't fuck it up too badly. I don't tell him that I'm facing similar decisions with his little brother, and that I'm trying to make better choices this time, and that twenty-one years later, those choices don't get any fucking easier, but I'll ultimately make them with the same criteria that I used for him—that my boys are the most important thing in my life, and I have to watch out for them above all others.

I don't tell him these things because he doesn't need to know them yet. These are the good years for him, and I want him to enjoy them. He doesn't need me to tell him these things yet, and he wouldn't understand them if I did. He'll find them out for himself, eventually. When he becomes a father, he'll learn those lessons just as I learned them.

And that breaks my heart.

So, while he's out tonight discovering beer and puking in some nasty college bar restroom, I'm sitting here by myself with a glass of Woodford Reserve (it's okay. F. Paul Wilson says as long as I lay off the cigars, I can still enjoy a glass of whiskey once in a while. And I have lain off the cigars, because F. Paul Wilson is a doctor, and also because he created Repairman Jack, and Repairman Jack could whoop my ass, and also because I promised Joe Lansdale and Nick Kaufmann that I'd quit cigars too, because they could also both kick my ass, as well. But I digress…)

I'm sitting here alone, enjoying a rare moment of quiet

contemplation, and as the last rays of the setting sun filter through the trees outside and reflect off the whiskey in my glass, I know that I am a good father, and that being a good father is never easy, and sometimes it will cost you everything else, but there's still nothing else I'd rather be, because it is so very worth it at the end of the day.

Being a father… they are all good years.

THE APATHY OF AUTUMN

The late, great Janis Joplin once sang "Freedom's just another word for nothing left to lose." I would add that so is apathy.

Let's talk, you and I. It's been a long time since we've really done that. Oh, sure. We talk on Twitter every day, and we talk here in the comments section. And we used to chat at The Keenedom and on Facebook until the sound of white noise in those places began to overwhelm me, throbbing in my pineal gland night and day, threatening to drive me mad, and I ended up stabbing both of them with a knife so that they wouldn't bother me anymore.

But I digress. Where was I? Oh, yes. Talking to you. I'm smoking a cigar and sipping Four Roses bourbon. I'm not supposed to be doing either of those things anymore (and please don't tell Mary, F. Paul Wilson, or Joe Lansdale that I was, because I promised them I wouldn't, and they'll kick my ass). In truth, I've only had one cigar since the heart attack (upon finishing *Clickers vs. Zombies*) and only a few glasses of bourbon on my birthday, and once while Kelli Owen was visiting. But I'm having them tonight, even though I'm not supposed to, because they are what I used to have when we talked.

Do you remember? We used to talk all the time, you and

me. For many years, I had a Blog called *Hail Saten*. It started as the title for my editorial column in *Jobs In Hell* (a weekly email newsletter for writers that I used to publish when the Internet was still in its infancy and email newsletters were still rare and neat and wonderful and welcomed, and people actually paid money to receive them). A disgruntled reader (because even back in 1997, I already had those) wrote me a very angry email one day, and called me 'Saten', complete with the typo, and I thought that was delightful and began using it. The title followed me from *Jobs In Hell* to my original Blog, which is long defunct, but for many years, was a place where I talked to people. Quite often, it got very personal. Eventually, I shut the Blog down. It's one thing to have personal conversations and observations with an audience of 500 or 5,000. It's quite a different animal when that audience is 50,000 or 500,000.

Just like the bourbon and cigars, I'm not supposed to bring back *Hail Saten*—because these three things will lead to another heart attack, or so I'm told. But lately, I've had the urge to bring the Blog back anyway.

Actually, that's not correct. I first had the urge several years ago, back when my ex-wife and I were beginning to figure out that being married to a writer is one of the worst things in the world to be, and wondering what we were going to do about that, because at age 41, and over a decade making a living writing, it was gonna be awfully hard for me to find any other kind of work. I resisted the urge to bring *Hail Saten* back at that time, knowing if I did, the marriage would be doomed for certain. Instead, I wrote a book called *The Girl on the Glider*, which came out in hardcover, and will come out in digital next year, and which many people seem to think is the best thing I've ever written, and which, in reality, was simply me doing what I'm doing right now. Just with ghosts.

The second time I had the urge to bring the Blog back was in the dark months before the Dorchester War went public. Here's something important that I want you to remember, because I will come back to it a bit further down—Craig Spector, Bryan Smith, JF Gonzalez and myself decided to go public on March 24th of 2011, but I had not been paid by Dorchester since December of 2009. As I said last March: "I had not been paid since late-2009. My marriage had fallen apart, my bills were piling up, and more than half of my annual income was perpetually coming soon." It should be noted that Dorchester wasn't the only publisher who suddenly seemed to have lost their checkbook—but they were the one who owed me the most. And so, to make ends meet, I started the newsletter and the Lifetime Subscription plan, and signed with a few new publishers to get some money to stem the crushing tide of debt. Now that you know that, I'm sure you understand why the urge to bring back *Hail Saten* and unleash some righteous fury on their ass was strong. Instead, I stayed professional, joined with other professionals, and eventually, we won.

The third time the urge to re-launch *Hail Saten* struck me was around this time last year. I don't talk much about my divorce because, quite simply, it's none of your fucking business. All you really need to know is that my ex-wife and I remain absolute best friends. We speak every day, help each other out, occasionally cook for one another, are there for each other if one of us needs a shoulder or a sounding board, and most importantly, we remain an awesome team when it comes to raising our son. My ex-wife is an incredible mother and a wonderful human being, and I am very glad to have her as a friend, and extremely grateful that she is in my son's life. And, post-divorce, we are both very happy in life, and thus, our son and everyone else around us is happy, too.

Except… that wasn't good enough for some people. There was a loose-knit group—I won't name them here because, quite frankly, they aren't worth it—who spent much of last year making me and Mary's lives miserable. They each had their own individual axes to grind with me, and when the divorce happened, they saw their opportunity. "Finally, a weak chink in the armor! Attack!" And attack they did.

Mary and I said nothing about it in public because, again, it's nobody's fucking business. Mostly, they attacked Mary, saying how terrible she was for having the audacity to fall in love with a recently divorced man with whom she'd been friends with for the last twelve years. And they didn't care about how their bullshit impacted her or my ex or my kids or my friends or anybody else in my life. All they cared about was getting to me. And they almost did. Almost… Yeah, the urge to bring back *Hail Saten* at that moment was borderline uncontrollable. But I prevailed. I prevailed, and after that, the urge went away…

…until yesterday.

Yesterday, an old friend and trusted mentor told me that he was worried that—in the eyes of the public—I was starting to appear apathetic. Now, he knew I wasn't apathetic. He knew it had been a long, strange summer, and that I was finally just finding my feet again. But he thought the public might not see that. I always listen to this friend's advice. He has always been right, and he's forgotten more about this business than I will ever learn. So yeah, let's talk about apathy. Let's talk about it in a way we haven't talked for quite some time, you and me. Let's *Hail Saten* the shit out of it, so that everybody is on the same page.

As I said, it has been a long, strange summer. Many things happened between April and September. We were victorious against Dorchester. Some folks got paid. Others got their rights reverted. I signed with Deadite Press, and was able to start earning a living again for the first time in two years. Things were good. Well, okay, yeah—there was the hurricane and the tropical storm and the fact that I was living inside a disaster area for a while, and was pretty much on my own after the National Guard blew through.

But these are minor trivialities, right? For the first time in a very long time, I had some breathing room. I had some freedom. I had nothing left to lose.

Then I had the heart attack.

Remember those books I mentioned before? The ones I contracted for before signing with Deadite? These were books that were contracted in 2010. All were due earlier this year. In days gone by, I could have knocked them out, no problem. But these are not days gone by, for this is not the summer of my years anymore. I turned forty-four two weeks after my heart attack. On my father's side of the family (whom I take after genetically) sixty-five to seventy is a good age to die. Factor in my lifestyle these last thirty years or so, and I figure I've got twenty-five years left, tops.

Think mid-life crises are a bitch? Think standing around mulling over the eventual possibility of dying sucks? My friend, you don't know shit. Because when death suddenly comes knocking unexpectedly, you take stock of things. You do the math, and you realize that you have entered the autumn of your life without even knowing it, and then you realize just how little amount of finite time you have left.

And you slow the fuck down.

It's not like I want to slow down. Believe me, I don't. I've got more story ideas now than I've ever had, and for the first time in my life, it's starting to dawn on me that I will most certainly not live long enough to write them all down for you. But I intend to try.

Autumn is a slow season.

But take the heart attack out of the equation for a moment. Let's look at cold, hard numbers instead. In previous years, I had the luxury of writing for 10 to 12 hours a day, five days a week. Here is the schedule I've had for the last year. Monday through Thursday, I have my youngest son from approximately 8am until approximately 6:30pm. Now, I can play on Twitter during those hours, in-between Play-Doh and making him lunch and potty training and Matchbox cars. But it's impossible to write during that time, nor would I. It would be unfair to him. My time with him is my time with him, and I refuse to spend that time lost in my own head, working on a novel.

So… when he goes home, I eat a quick dinner from 6:30pm until 7:00pm. Then I go to work. Except that "work" isn't just writing the next book. It involves answering email (of which I average 120 to 200 PER DAY), looking over contracts, mailing things, etc.—and before this past summer also involved dealing with things like Dorchester. I work from 7:00pm until 11:00pm, but I only write for maybe 3 of those 4 hours. I call Mary at 11, and go to bed by 11:30.

Then I get up at 6:30am the next morning and do it all over again.

So, that gives me 12 hours of writing time per week, depending on email volume, etc. Do that math. I went from 50 hours a week to 12 hours a week. Friday—my one day off—is sometimes spent writing, but is also spent cleaning the house, buying groceries, and doing all the other things we have to do in life. Saturday and Sunday are set aside for Mary, and my parents, and my oldest son, and Mary's son, and my friends. Especially since the heart attack.

One other thing I've been doing a lot of since April is mentoring. The authors who were always there for my generation—mentors like Joe Lansdale, Jack Ketchum, F. Paul Wilson, John Skipp, Ed Gorman, Ray Garton, David Schow, Tom Monteleone, Chet Williamson, etc.—are the genre's elder statesmen now (and I say that with nothing but respect and honor). And writers like myself, J.F. Gonzalez, Tim Lebbon, Chris Golden, Jim Moore, Tom Piccirilli, Weston Ochse, etc? We're the veterans now. This was explained to me several times this summer by several of my mentors, and I wasn't the only one of my generation who was given this speech. Somewhere between our fifth and sixth beers, we became veterans, and it's time for us to start paying forward for this next generation the way those guys did for us. And we have been. Believe me, we have. And that, too, takes time out of an already busy schedule, but it is so very worth it.

So yeah, I can see how it looks like I'm apathetic lately. I can see why folks might think I no longer care. I'm late on my deadlines and the newsletter is being folded into a book and I closed down the Keenedom and I don't talk to people on Facebook anymore and the Lifetimer packages have been a few months apart, but do the math. Do the math…

The fact is, I'm still here. No, maybe we don't talk as much as we used to, you and I. Maybe I've seemed more distant. And I'm sorry for that. But rest assured, I am still here. I'm just busy trying to be a father and a boyfriend and a friend and a son and a brother and a mentor. But I am still here, and just because we don't talk as much, that doesn't mean I'm not listening.

And you're still listening, as well. Thank you for that. Thank you for your patience and support these last few years. It means a lot. I'm making the best of those 12 hours a week. I'm getting caught up. Things are in various stages of completion. And I think they will be worth the wait.

It ain't winter yet, and autumn is a nice time of year.

Hail Saten…

"DEAD AIR", OR, A RANT ABOUT ONLINE PIRACY

You'll be hard pressed to find another horror author who gives as much back to his fans as I do. That's not immodesty or braggadocio. It's a fact. The reason for that is because I genuinely like 99.9% of you. If I didn't like you, I wouldn't have written a free novel for you called *Deluge: Earthworm Gods II*, and I wouldn't have offered it here for free, with the understanding that once it was finished, I'd remove it and then sell it in book form (which is how I make my living).

Recently, I announced a second free book. It was to be called *Dead Air*. It was to feature Black Lodge in all out war against the Siqqusim. It would have also featured spot illustrations by Steve Wands. It would have been cool. And free. But I'm hesitant to do it now, because this morning, I was alerted to a digital pirated edition of *Deluge* available online. That didn't hurt. I'm used to piracy. What hurt was the pirate's identity. It's someone who has been a long-time reader. Someone who was an active and valued member of the old Keenedom forum, and indeed, who is active and valued as a reader in the genre. This person even joined in the fight against Dorchester when they were ripping many authors off. Except that he was doing the same by pirating the shit out of our books.

After I sent out the DMCA notices and contacted my attorney and did some digging, I was amazed to find that many of this thief's cronies were also fans and readers whose screen names I recognized. Some from the old forum. Some from Facebook and Twitter. Some from elsewhere. All good people, or so I thought.

Now, I know not everyone takes the same view of electronic piracy that I do. So before the comments section here gets filled up with excuses from the online piracy apologists, let me play both roles:

> ME: *Deluge* was pirated, and the print edition comes out six months from now.
>
> APOLOGISTS: Well, you did give *Deluge* away for free when it was on your site, so that's not a big deal!
>
> ME: Well, they also pirated editions of *Dark Hollow, The Rising, City of the Dead*, etc.
>
> APOLOGISTS: Well, those aren't available yet for Kindle and Nook. You're fans really want to read them bad. You can't blame them for not being able to wait.
>
> ME: They also pirated *Urban Gothic, Shades*, the *Clickers* series, *Take the Long Way Home, Castaways, Dead Sea*, and everything else that is currently available for Kindle and Nook.
>
> APOLOGISTS: "Oh… um… well… you're rich! You can afford it! You're part of the one percent! Occupy Brian Keene!"
>
> ME: I'm not rich. I make, on average, $45,000 a year. Sometimes it's a little more. Sometimes it's less. I'm able to survive on that because I live in a rural area. I have two sons,

one of whom is in college and the other of whom is in daycare. Both of them require money. So when you steal from me, you are stealing from them. I also have no health insurance, which means I'm paying the hospital bills for my heart attack out of pocket. I also have no 401K and occasionally enjoy paying for things like my house, my groceries, etc. I cannot pay for these things when you steal from me.

APOLOGISTS: "…"

2010 and 2011 have shown me betrayal from all sides—old friends, new friends, lovers, peers, and publishers. As the Year of the Hermit begins, I thought to myself, "Well, at least I can still count on my readers." But apparently, I can exclude about three dozen screen names I recognize from that list. I'm hard-pressed to understand why I should bother investing the time or energy to do *Dead Air* as a free, weekly serial here when it will just get fucking pirated by a bunch of people to whom mutual respect and appreciation are foreign concepts. If it's not appreciated, then it seems to me like it would be a lot less strain to just write it and release it the old-fashioned way.

If this upsets you, I'd tell you to take it up with the main offender, but in the last hour, he has apparently deleted both his Facebook and Twitter pages. Make of that what you will. If he's reading this, a simple apology would have been just as good.

Now, if you'll excuse me, I'm gonna get back to making Play-Doh Cthulhu with my toddler, who has been waiting patiently while Daddy dealt with this bullshit.

> UPDATE: I've now heard from several of those involved, both via the comments and via email. In fact, I just heard from the main offender via email and I believe his apology to be sincere. Like many young people, I don't think he quite understood how such a thing impacts the artist. Now he does,

and hopefully others do, as well. So, with that, I'm closing the comments discussion, which has sort of gone sideways anyway.

Disclaimers:

*I would like to point out that post-heart attack Brian avoided calling anyone out by name in this entry, or starting a flame war that would have yet again engulfed the genre.

*That is only being pointed out to a handful of people, and each of them knows who they are, and more importantly, they know why it is being pointed out to them, which is why it's here at the bottom of this post.

*A special "Hi" to those people. And here you thought I wasn't listening to you…

"GHOUL": THE AUTHOR'S PERSPECTIVE

Every bit of fiction an author ever commits to paper will be, to some extent, autobiographical. Sometimes, the author isn't even aware of this occurring until after they have finished writing the book. Usually, these autobiographical bits are just that—bits. Tiny slivers of real life experiences, mined for use in fiction. Writers are taught to do this, in fact. One of the golden rules given to authors is to "write what you know." So you do. You write about what it feels like to have your first kiss, or get your heart broken, or experience the death of a parent, or the betrayal of a friend, or that emotion that wells up inside of you the first time you make your child laugh. These are universal experiences shared by all human beings, regardless of nationality, sex, race, or religious or political creed. What makes them original is when you, as an author, put your own unique spin on them, and that's where writing what you know comes into play. You write about these things with your voice and your perspective, and thus, create a shared truth with the reader. For a writer, life itself is nothing more than fodder for the muse.

As I said, these autobiographical bits are usually minor, but occasionally, a writer will reach deeper, or perhaps cut deeper. And when they do, they bleed all over the page. That's what

Ghoul was for me. When I started the novel, I'd intended to write nothing more than a fun, scary coming-of-age novel, but as the book progressed, I recognized Timmy Graco. He was me at that age. Some of his experiences and thoughts and fears were mine. And as a result, I didn't just bleed on the page. I hemorrhaged.

Because of that, *Ghoul* has always been close to my heart. I'm not the type to look at my own work and opine on what's good and what sucks. That's for the readers and the critics to decide. But it's certainly one of my favorites, and a constant favorite among fans of my work. I hear it from folks every time I do a book signing or a convention appearance. And with that in mind, you can understand why I was justifiably a little nervous when *Ghoul* first began its journey from novel to film. For every wonderful Stephen King adaptation (T*he Mist, Stand By Me, The Shawshank Redemption*), there's a steaming cinematic turd (*The Mangler, Children of the Corn* Parts 2 through… however many of those lame sequels they made).

My apprehension soon passed when I saw the team who would be bringing my book to life. Andrew van den Houten is a dynamo of unstoppable energy. He has vision, brings people together and shares that vision with them, and then makes the vision happen—qualities that are indispensable in a producer. He's got the magic touch, and is always ready with an eleventh hour save. William Miller is not only a talented screenwriter, but a scholar of horror literature, including my own work. It's that devotion and deep knowledge that allows him to adapt an author's words into words for the screen, respectfully cutting to the meat of the story with the expert precision of a surgeon. Gregory Wilson made me a fan with his adaptation of Jack Ketchum's seminal *The Girl Next Door*—probably the most influential horror novel (along with Lansdale's *The Drive-In*) of the last 30 years. For horror fans, a movie version of *The Girl Next Door* was just as daunting a prospect as *The Lord of the Rings* adaptation was before Peter Jackson's loving adaptation finally hit theatres. And just as fantasy fans rejoiced at that faithful spectacle, so did horror fans with Greg's version of *The Girl Next Door*.

With Andrew, William, and Greg on board, I knew *Ghoul* was in good hands. That was reinforced during a set visit, when I got to meet the cast and crew and see just how invested and dedicated they were in the production.

I hope that you are, as well. I may have bled onto the page, but each and every one of them bled onto the screen. I'm proud, honored, and humbled of the work they've done.

THOUGHTS ON BEING PROLIFIC

I just finished signing the signature sheets for *Clickers vs. Zombies*.

Signing sig sheets isn't the only bit of work I've done this weekend. But before you read any further, I'd first like you to read this interview with me over at Serenity J. Banks' site.

That interview was conducted over two years ago, and while much of it remains accurate, a few things have changed. In it, I said, "The thing about writing full-time is that you're lucky enough to devote however many hours a day to it that you need to. I usually work eight to ten hours a day." For years, that was how I worked. Monday through Friday, eight to ten hours a day. And when I was younger, those were heady, intoxicating times. I used to write two books simultaneously. I'd work on one in the morning, eat lunch, and then switch over to the second book in the afternoon. Over the last fifteen years, that sort of schedule, energy, and dedication has allowed me to write well over 40 novels, short story collections, novellas, and graphic novels.

But times change and people change. Like Rush says, "Nights growing colder, children growing up, old friends growing older." At a few months shy of 45, I find myself entering Andropause, and caring for my four-year old son

Monday through Thursday, as well as making sure his twenty-one-year old brother doesn't repeat the same mistakes I made at twenty-one (and so far, he hasn't). At the end of the day, that leaves me pretty damned tired, both physically and mentally. It's hard to write in that state, and thus, I've adapted my work schedule accordingly.

These days, my work schedule is quite different. My toddler goes to his Mom on Thursday night, and that is when my work week begins. On Thursday, I write from 6pm until 4am, and then write four hours a day on Friday, Saturday, and Sunday. It was a big adjustment to go from the luxury of five eight-hour days to this new sort of hyper-compressed weekend writing burst, but I made it work because I am a writer. And so are you and so can you.

So often, new writers tell me that they can't find time to write. I've ranted about this at length, but what my advice boils down to is—stop trying to find time to write. If you look for time, you'll never find it. What you have to do instead is make time. Kids, day-jobs, significant others—these are all a part of life. You make time for all three. If you want to be a writer, you have to make time for that, as well. Maybe you get up extra early and write before heading off to your day job, the way Bev Vincent does. Or maybe you write in the evening, after you've come home from that day job, like James A. Moore does. Or maybe, like me, you're already writing full-time, and are just struggling how to balance that with your other obligations. You just have to figure out what works for you.

I'm not nearly as prolific as I once was. This gnaws at my pulp roots, but that's okay. Because what I've learned is that it doesn't matter how many books you write a year. What matters is that you write. You make the time to do it and then you sit your ass down in the chair and you write.

SOME THOUGHTS ON GENDER, GENRE, AND READING

As previously noted, I'm under some serious deadlines this month, and as a result, content has been sporadic around here. Yesterday, anticipating a lull in new announcements until *The Cage* and *The Last Zombie: Neverland* #2 go on sale, I posted this list of my 25 Favorite Writers of All Time. This led to a discussion on Twitter between myself, author Sarah Pinborough, and CONvergence's Charlotte Nickerson. Sarah and Charlotte found it curious that there were no women on my list. And after they called it to my attention, I found it curious, too.

There are a lot of fine writers who were left off that list. Some readers questioned the absence of Bentley Little, Robert R. McCammon, Richard Matheson, and others. All of them are fine writers who have written some of my very favorite books. Little's *The Store* is the crown jewel in satiric social commentary bizarro-horror, McCammon's *Boy's Life* is a coming-of-age watermark, and if there was an American Library collection focusing solely on horror, Matheson's *I Am Legend* would be the centerpiece. I enjoy reading all three (and many of the others who were mentioned) but they aren't among my absolute desert-island favorites. That's not a slight against them. That's the inherent problem with lists—no matter how expansive, somebody is always going to get left off.

But even so, I did find it curious that there wasn't one female writer on my list, so I spent much of yesterday pondering the significance of that, and what it meant. Here are my conclusions, offered as the kicking off point for a discussion amongst yourselves. As always, be polite and respectful of others.

That list is primarily compiled of genre novelists and comic book writers. More than half of them are people I grew up reading. As I've written elsewhere, it was a Steve Gerber-penned issue of *The Defenders* (along with a Jack Kirby- penned and illustrated issue of *Captain America*) that first gave me the writing bug at age six. J.M. DeMatteis, Stephen King, etc. were a huge part of my teenage years. Ditto Joe Lansdale, Skipp & Spector, etc. when I was still too young to buy a beer but old enough to know that I needed to figure out what I was going to do with my life.

But when I consider that time-period—the mid-70s to the late-80s—it occurs to me that there simply weren't as many female writers working in either the genre or in comics as there are now. I didn't discover Shirley Jackson until high school. And for whatever reason (probably the fact that my reading choices were limited to the Spring Grove Public Library—which was located in an old farmhouse—and whatever was on sale at the newsstand) I didn't discover Chelsea Quinn Yarbro or Andre Norton until then, either. In truth, the first female writers I really remember being aware of for their gender are (in prose) Poppy Z. Brite, Anne Rice, Melanie Tem, and Yvonne Navarro and (in comics) Ann Nocenti and Louise Simonson. And I had graduated high school and joined the Navy by that point.

Fact is, I simply wasn't exposed to a lot of female writers during my formative years, because work by female writers wasn't as commercially available. That's a big reason why there weren't any on my list. But that doesn't mean I don't enjoy books written by women, which brings me to thought number two.

I suspect that, to some extent, gender might influence which characters a reader identifies with, and which plot points move a reader. That's not to say I don't enjoy a story written from a female perspective or can't identify with a female protagonist. On the contrary. Some fine examples of this are Kelli Owen's *Six Days*, Stephen King's *Lisey's Story*, or Lucy Taylor's *Dancing with Demons*. And I certainly enjoy books written by women (Yvonne Navarro's *After Age* and Sarah's own *Breeding Ground* are among my Top 25 Favorite Books).

But reading is something one does primarily for enjoyment, and I think that enjoyment is increased when we identify strongly with a character or situation. Sometimes, our gender determines that. As I said on Twitter, a story about the special bond between a mother and a daughter is going to have much more of an emotional impact on a female reader than it will a male reader. The reverse is also true. I know I'm not the only male to sob uncontrollably after watching *Big Fish* or *The Wrestler*, and I also know that the female partners I watched them with were perplexed by my reaction. Unless you're a father or a son, it's hard to understand the depth of the visceral reaction many men have to *Big Fish*.

Men and women view some things differently. Read a sex scene written by a woman versus one written by a man. Most of the time, the female-written one will make use of all the human senses while the male-written one will predominantly focus only on the visual elements. It's the difference between *Gone with the Wind* and *The English Patient* versus *Braveheart* and *The Crow*. All four are romances. Two appeal more to women. Two appeal more to men.

The issue of gender and characterization is an important one, too. In the college class I used to teach, I liked using *The Sopranos'* Tony Soprano and *The Shield's* Vic Mackey as examples of great characterization. Despite some of the heinous, repugnant things they've done, we can't help rooting for them week after week. That's because the writers have created characters we can identify with on some emotional, primal level, no matter what our surface qualms about them. I identify with Tony—in enough ways that it would take me an entire Blog entry to go into with the depth required—but those reasons are certainly from a core, male perspective. I like the character of his wife, Carmella. I find her tragic and appealing and fascinating, but she's not what hooked me on the show. What drew me in week after week was seeing Tony deal with fictionalized, metaphoric versions of the very same things I was dealing with at the time (being torn between job and family, maintaining a reluctant alpha dog status and wondering where the next betrayal or challenge would come from, etc.)

So, yeah… after pondering things, that's my guess as to why there weren't any female authors on my list of all-time favorites. It does make me wonder what my list would have looked like if I was coming of age now, in an era when women have a much more prominent role in both comics and horror fiction. And that makes me simultaneously happy for how far we've progressed in our field—and impatient for how far we still have to go.

It would be great, for example, if we could get to a point where transgendered writers' books were discussed by fans online more than their sexuality is, or we didn't have to collectively groan each week about *The Walking Dead*'s treatment of T-Dog (absolutely zero characterization other than very tired racial stereotypes that should have gone out of play after Romero's *Night of the Living Dead*).

But I digress. Those are conversations for another day. It's 12:30am and I've been up since 5:00am yesterday and chased around after my toddler all day and am tired and need to get to work. But I thought Sarah and Charlotte's question was something worth examining and discussing. So now it's your turn.

Discuss.

WRITING, RELATIONSHIPS, AND "DARK HOLLOW"

Two seemingly unrelated bits of news which are more in sync than you think.

Brian Hodge asked me for one brief paragraph on writing and its impact on relationships, inspired by a comment someone made there about how their partner had given them a 'choose me or the writing' ultimatum.

I wrote six long paragraphs instead. Why did I write six admittedly raw and brutally honest paragraphs? Because I think it is important advice that I wish someone had given me twenty years ago—the kind of thing you don't find in the How-To Write books.

Which brings me to *Dark Hollow*, which is all about writing and relationships. Due to return in paperback and digital any day now from Deadite Press, and in slow development for a major motion picture. I'm happy to report that the film has been announced as part of Fantasia's first ever film market. Bloody Disgusting offers the public the first details on the film on their site today. And if you've been following the Dark Hollow Facebook page, then you've been seeing the eye-popping shots from Director Paul Campion's UK location scouting this week.

Anyway, here's what I wrote for Brian Hodge:

Writing cost me two marriages. At least, that's what I tell myself. In truth, it was really me.

My first marriage dissolved when I was trying to become a professional writer. We lived in a trailer and had about three dollars to our name. I worked all day in a foundry (and later as a truck driver) and then came home at night, and focused on my word processor, rather than my wife. I was young and dumb and it never occurred to me that my equally young wife might like me to spend some time with her rather than writing. Even when we did spend time together, we didn't really communicate. She was usually watching TV while I had my nose buried in an issue of *Deathrealm, The Horror Show, Cemetery Dance, New Blood*, or one of the other big horror lit magazines of the time. When she left, I had that word processor and those horror magazines for comfort, and not much else.

My second marriage lasted eight years (after an additional eight years of courtship), and dissolved long after I'd become a professional writer. By then, I was old enough and mature enough to have figured out that I should spend time with her and talking to her after putting in 7 or 8 hours at the computer. Despite that, communication was still the culprit in the end. There were things I was unable to properly communicate—the pressure of deadlines; the stress of fame (because even a little bit of fame can be a very fucked thing); how it felt to live under a public microscope that examined and often took issue with everything I wrote, said, thought, or did; the paranoia and self-loathing that creeps in when everyone—even your once closest friends—seem to want something from you; how utterly demoralizing it was to me that I didn't have a weekly paycheck, health insurance, or a 401K to provide for my family the way every other husband I knew did.

I should have tried harder to talk about these things, but I didn't have it in me. I didn't have it in me because after 8 hours of writing, I was emotionally and mentally exhausted at the end of the day.

I don't believe we choose to be writers (or musicians, painters or any other form of the arts). I believe we don't have a choice. To be given an ultimatum like the one that inspired this Blog—to be told 'choose me or the writing'—is no choice at all. I probably could have saved my second marriage by quitting writing and walking away from it, but doing so would have been a lie. Writing isn't like a sales job where you quit one firm and go to another. I'm a writer. I could no more quit than cut off my arms or voluntarily drag my balls across six miles of broken glass. Believe me, I thought about it. I thought about it long and hard. But in the end, quitting would have destroyed my marriage even more assuredly, because I would have been miserable, unhappy, unsettled, and eventually dead. That's not hyperbole. That's a certainty.

The key is communication. I look back now and shake my head in disbelief that a guy who made his living communicating to the general public was unable to do the same for the people he was closest to in his private life. I'm currently in a relationship with a fellow writer—somebody who has been doing this just as long as I have, and has gone through and experienced all of the same things. And while we both intimately understand each other's need for everything from solitude to the pressures of deadlines, we still make a concerted effort to communicate when we're done. Because we both know just how hard it is to be in a relationship with a writer. There really are four of us—me, her, and our muses. It's important that all four get a chance to talk.

ON IDEAS AND MAKING THEM YOURS

The following has what I think is some good advice for new writers, but it also contains spoilers for *The Damned Highway*, *Darkness On the Edge of Town*, *A Gathering of Crows*, Stephen King's *Under the Dome*, and Brad Anderson's *Vanishing on 7th Street*. Personally, if you're a new writer, I'd like you to brave the spoilers and read on, because (as I said above) I think there's some good advice here for you. Just don't say I didn't warn you in advance about the spoilers.

Earlier today, my dear friend and occasional co-writer, Nick Mamatas, linked to a Blog entry from an apparent writer and artist named Patrick Power (I say "apparent" not derogatorily, but simply because until today, I'd never heard of Patrick, and I'm unsure as to what various talents he utilizes. Judging by his Blog, I'm guessing writing and illustration). To summarize, Patrick has been working on a graphic novel that I surmise involved Lovecraft's mythos and Hunter S. Thompson. He's upset that Nick and I wrote a novel with similar themes—*The Damned Highway*.

Nick does a very good job on his Blog of addressing Patrick's assumption that we must have gotten our inspiration from his artwork, as well as recounting *The Damned Highway's* history from inception to publication, and even pointing out some examples of Hunter S. Thompson's legend overlapping with other parts of our genre. The only two things I'd add to what Nick has already said are as follows.

I remember writing the first chapter in early summer 2007. I remember this because in the summer of 2007 I was feeling all of the things that Uncle Lono is feeling in that first chapter.

In addition to the examples Nick mentioned, I'd point out Duane Swierczynski's Hunter S. Thompson versus zombies story (the title of which escapes me at the moment because I've been chasing after my four-year old all evening), the partial Hunter S. Thompson influence on *Transmetropolitan's* Spider Jerusalem, and of course, Duke in *Doonesbury* (the latter is even referenced in *The Damned Highway*).

With that out of the way, what I'd like to comment on in detail is the frustration that Patrick feels, because it's a frustration that many new writers feel at some point in their career.

I'm a firm believer that, when it comes to genre, there's no such thing as an original idea. Zombies. Werewolves. Colonizing Mars. Ghosts. Yeti Space Pirates fighting Talking Cats. They've all been done before. What matters—what's original—is your take on these old tropes and old ideas. It's your unique voice—a voice that only you possess—that makes these old ideas seem fresh and new and exciting again.

The Rising was the book that kick-started my career, but it certainly wasn't the first zombie book or zombie movie ever written. And obviously, it wasn't the last. Let's examine *The Rising's* parts. Zombies: done before. Demonically possessed corpses: done before. End of the World: done before. Military going nuts on civilians: done before. Parent looking for their child and facing incredible odds: done before. None of those things were original ideas. What attracted people to *The Rising* (as near as I can figure) is they liked my take on those old ideas and plot points. And given the plethora of zombie novels that have followed since then, I have to assume they like other authors' unique perspectives and takes on those old ideas, as well.

28 Days Later, *The Walking Dead*, and *The Rising* all came out within a few months of each other. Does that mean that Danny Boyle, Robert Kirkman, and I were ripping each other off? No. It means we all had ideas for zombie sagas at around the same time. Similar ideas, but different writers with different voices make for different stories.

There are going to be times in your career when you'll see a movie or read a book and you'll say something like, "Fuck! This is what I'm working on right now. A group of rebels fighting a galactic empire, and the bad guy is the good guy's father. Damn you, George Lucas."

I'll give you some examples. In *A Gathering of Crows*, I wrote a scene in which the Revenants construct a soul cage around Brinkley Springs. When a carload of surplus teenagers hit this invisible barrier while traveling at a high rate of speed, the result is a lot of surplus teenagers splattered all over the road. In the time between when I turned this book in to my publisher and the time it came out in paperback, Stephen King's *Under the Dome* was released. When I read *Under the Dome*, I got to a part where an airplane hits an invisible shield over a small town. The results are the same for the people in the plane, but the two books are vastly different. Similar ideas, but different writers with different voices make for different stories.

About a year after *Darkness on the Edge of Town's* release, many fans started asking me if I'd seen the film *Vanishing on 7th Street*. They claimed it was a direct rip-off of my novel. They claimed I should sue. They posted angry things on the internet. I'd planned on seeing the film anyway, because I enjoy Brad Anderson's work, but when I heard this, I added it to my Netflix queue with some trepidation. Turns out, it's not a rip-off of my book at all. He had the same idea as me—a post-apocalyptic setting, a possibly supernatural darkness, people going ape-shit, etc. but he took it in a completely different direction. Similar ideas, but different writers with different voices makes for different stories.

My sincere advice to you, Patrick (and to anyone else reading this who might be struggling with a situation similar to his) is to complete your story. You don't mention too many details on your Blog, other than that it involves Hunter S. Thompson and Cthulhu, but unless your plot is "A broken, beaten, and burned-out Hunter S. Thompson decides to reinvent himself as Uncle Lono and go in search of the American Nightmare by traveling across the country on a Greyhound bus. Along the way, he discovers that the Democratic Party are worshiping Moloch, that the Republicans are trying to summon Cthulhu, that Fungi from Yuggoth is the latest in psychedelic mushrooms, hijacks a tractor trailer, spreads hate and discontent on the Miskatonic University campus, plays both the Democrats and the Republicans against each other, and almost gets his brain transferred into a Mi-Go container by J. Edgar Hoover" then I wouldn't worry. Your graphic novel sounds like something different than this. It also sounds like something that, as a fan of both Lovecraft and Thompson, I'd dearly love to read. You've got a sale right here. So finish it!

Similar ideas, but different writers with different voices make for different stories. Tell the story that you want to tell. Make it yours, even if it's been done before. Make those tropes yours. Put your unique spin and your unique voice into it and write the story you want to read. Chances are others will want to read it, too. I know I would.

HOW TO WRITE 80,000 WORDS IN A WEEKEND

This past weekend was designated as a writing marathon, meaning all I did during my waking hours was write. This is not a normal mode of operation for me, but after a month-long and much-needed vacation, I'm behind on deadlines and had to get caught up on things.

On Friday, I wrote 40,000 words. Unfortunately, I posted about it on Twitter, and in doing so, caused a minor stir. Many people were happy for me (and I thank them). A few were skeptical. And still others were unsure of what that actually meant —"40,000 words in one day". So here's a lengthier explanation (not confined to Twitter's 140 character limit) of exactly what it means and how I did it and why you may or may not want to try it yourself sometime.

The first thing you need to understand is that this doesn't work for everybody. Writing 40,000 words in one day is really only practical for three things—pulp, porn, and first drafts. In my case, the first and last apply. I am a pulp writer. If I were of a more literary bent or a wordsmith like Peter Straub, Thomas Ligotti, Livia Llewellyn, or John Langan, we probably wouldn't be having this discussion. These are authors who labor over each and every word, and their fiction (and our enjoyment of their fiction) are richer for their efforts. But that is not one of my strengths.

It was common for the pulp writers of old to write 40,000 a day. This is because they had no choice. They wanted to eat. To earn their pay, they were required to crank out journeyman novels and stories to beat ridiculous deadlines and for a low rate. (In truth, not much has changed since then… and I see a whole bunch of mid-listers, ghost writers, and media tie-in scribes nodding silently). Michael Moorcock infamously wrote several weekend novels. And there are authors who still write like that these days. Carlton Mellick locks himself in a hotel room and writes a complete novel in three or four days. Nick Mamatas can also crank it out when he needs to. In both of their cases, the quality doesn't suffer. But it should also be noted that what they crank out is, in most cases, revised and edited later on.

And that's the case here. On Friday, Twitter went splodey with the news that I'd written 40,000 words in a day. What I didn't tell you was that over the space of three and a half days (Thursday night, Friday, Saturday, and Sunday) I wrote just a smidgen over 85,000 words—the length of a complete novel. Is that how I normally work? Of course not. If I worked regularly at that pace, we wouldn't be having this conversation because I'd be dead. Before I became a parent again, and had all day to work, I averaged between 8,000 and 10,000 words in an 8 to 9 hour day. These days, I average between 3,000 and 4,000 words per evening (I write 4 or 5 hours per night).

But when I need to (meaning I've been on vacation and now I'm fucked because everything is due) I can do more than that. Here is how.

1. NO DISTRACTIONS: My youngest son was with his mother for the weekend. My oldest son was at work and on dates. Mary and my future step-son were in New Jersey. That meant I had the house to myself (except for my cat) from Thursday night until Sunday evening. All I did for the entire

weekend was write and sleep. The only times I wasn't writing or sleeping were to check Twitter a few times a day, to call Mary once per night, and to attend my youngest son's karate class (which lasted an hour). Other than those few things, all I did was write. I didn't mow the lawn. I didn't clean the house. I ignored all incoming phone calls (sorry about that Wrath, Eryn, and all the drunks at CONvergence). I skipped out on attending events, and I declined invitations to hang out with friends. All I did was write. And when I got tired, I slept. And when I woke up, I wrote some more. Did my wrists hurt? Sure. Did I give myself carpal tunnel? It certainly seems like it. Do I feel bad that I missed out on things? Of course. But did I accomplish what I set out to do? Absolutely.

2. KNOWING WHERE I WAS GOING AHEAD OF TIME: The 40,000 words in one day constituted a complete novella (*Sundancing*) and part of a novel (*The Lost Level*). If you're curious, *Sundancing* was 20,000 words long. The other 20,000 applied to *The Lost Level*. A few of you asked me on Twitter if this writing was based on an outline. It was not. I rarely work from an outline, because I prefer a more organic, loose-knit approach to writing (that's not to say that there's anything wrong with outlining. There's not). But in both of these cases, I knew exactly where the story was going before I started the weekend's writing. *Sundancing* is a meta-fictional account of my trip to Sundance this past January (and serves as a sort of bookend to my previous meta-fictional novella *The Girl on the Glider*). *The Lost Level* is a pulp fiction homage to John Carter, *Land of the Lost*, Joe Lansdale's *The Drive-In* series, *The Warlord*, and other lost world stories.

Writing 20,000 words about my experiences at Sundance, and what going there taught me about myself and our industry, was as easy as telling a friend about it over the phone or over drinks (or both). And adding 20,000 words to *The Lost Level*, while not as easy as the former, was still a breeze because a) I knew that my characters needed to find a crashed Nazi flying saucer and then fight a giant slug, and b) it was fun as hell to write.

Had these been novels I was starting from scratch, or had the subject matter been something I didn't feel as intimate or close to (*Sundancing*), or simply frivolous and fun to write (*The Lost Level*) there's no way I would have written that many words in a day. Indeed, there have been times (*Dark Hollow*, *Ghoul*, and *Take the Long Way Home* come to mind) when the subject matter was heavy enough that I was lucky if I wrote 1,000 words a day. And you'll have novels and stories like that. But you'll also have ones that you absolutely can't wait to get down on paper (or onto a laptop screen), and it is my personal experience that those types of tales seem to write themselves a lot faster. Which brings me to…

3. QUANTITY OVER QUALITY: As I said on Twitter (but which a lot of people apparently missed) these were both first drafts. I can not stress that enough. These are first drafts. The 80,000 words I wrote this weekend are not meant to be turned in to a publisher, nor are they ready for you to read. They are the basic foundations of the books to come. I always do at least two (but usually three) drafts before I turn something in. *Sundancing* and *The Lost Level* are no exception. Consider the words I wrote this weekend to be a just-built house. Now, I'll go back and start the second draft, which is when I'll run the electrical wires and the plumbing, and hang the drywall and the vinyl siding. Then I'll do a third draft, which is when we pick out carpet and furniture, and make it ready to show to buyers. But what I did this weekend is just unpainted lumber. It is raw materials. It looks like a house, but you wouldn't want to live there… yet.

So, that's what I did and how I did it. Do I recommend doing this all the time? Absolutely not. Will it work for every writer? No. But is it something I recommend trying at least once in your career? Sure. At the very least, you might have some fun. Perhaps you will learn something about yourself as a writer. And who knows? You may even get a serviceable first draft out of it.

The important thing to remember is this—writers get too hung up on word counts. It doesn't matter if you produce 1,000 words per day or 10,000 words per day. What matters is that you produce words. Novels and stories don't write themselves. 'Ass in chair, fingers on keyboard, and repeat as necessary' is the best method I know. If you've written 1,000 words today and someone else has written twice that amount, it doesn't matter. What matters is that you've written. Be proud of what you've produced.

And now I'm off to dip my hands and wrists in a big vat of Ben Gay…

PS: And yes, I'm counting this Blog entry as part of those 80,000 words.

A GRIM, BLEAK, AND NIHILISTIC HAPPY PLACE

My contributor copies of *The Last Zombie: Before the After* #1 arrived yesterday. Mary read it last night and commented on how grim it was. I told her that was merely the set-up, and that things were about to get very bad for our characters.

In truth, this new story-arc, and the story-arc that will follow, contain what I feel is some of the bleakest and most nihilistic stuff I've ever written. Ian's continuing deterioration and the subsequent catalyst it provides for a final showdown between him and Federman, Russo and Ananti's flashbacks (which involve everything from homicide to a zombie chewing its way through a maternity ward), the loneliness expressed by Planters and Fulton in response to Johnson's new relationship, the madman who now runs Chicago—these are characters and situations with decidedly unhappy endings.

It's been a long time since I've reached down inside myself and dug for ore in the pathos mines. Those mines used to be easy to find and work. The darkness inherent in *The Rising, Dark Hollow, Take the Long Way Home*, and *Ghoul* came from personal, autobiographical experiences. I was younger then, so much of the ore was still fresh, barely buried beneath the surface, and therefore easy enough to dig up and expose. Then there were books like *City of the Dead*, *Earthworm Gods*, and *Dead Sea*, where the hopelessness on display was offered with a smile, a wink, and a nudge—"Hey kids, I know this hurts, but remember, it's just make believe." But even those wink-nudge novels, when I go back and look at them, had some very real nuggets of personal pathos at their core.

For a while, I thought the mines had gone dry. Nate Southard commented on this to me a few months ago, postulating that from *Ghost Walk* to *A Gathering of Crows*, my fiction became less personal, and almost "happier" (or as close to happy as it gets in my mythos). *Entombed* was a return to the pathos mines, although I personally feel I dug too deep with that one, something readers of the hardcover seem to have so far disagreed with (we'll see how the rest of you feel when *Entombed* comes out in paperback and digital next month).

Although, as I write this (sitting in my kitchen, drinking coffee, and musing about these things while Jamestown's acoustic cover of U2's "Red Hill Mining Town" competes in the background with the sound of crickets outside), I don't know that digging too deep was the problem I felt with *Entombed*. I think perhaps it was more, "Okay, this is it, readers. This is all I have left to offer. This shall be our final covenant."

Yes, I think that's it exactly. Because after *Entombed*, I really did think the pathos mines had gone dry, and as a result, the books I'm currently working on (*The Lost Level*, *With Teeth*, and *Hole in the World*) read much more like that happy era that Nate Southard referenced.

So when I began this latest story-arc for *The Last Zombie*, and realized what was going to happen and where it was going to go, and how I was going to have to invest you, the reader, in it and make you feel it, I returned to the mines and poked around with my shovel until I found some new veins to supply the ore.

Trust me, you will feel it. You will hurt. I certainly have, in the process of writing it. And I also know that when I'm feeling that way while writing, that's when I'm happiest.

Because that's where the best stories come from. My happy place…

"WHAT IF NOBODY LIKES IT?"
ON WRITING AND SELF-DOUBT

Last week on Twitter, Steve Melnick asked me if I had any advice regarding writer's block based on a lack of confidence. His concern that people might not like his writing was preventing him from writing. I told him I did have advice, but it wasn't something that would fit into a Tweet, so I'd write a Blog entry instead. So I have.

I should start by recapping my assertion that there is no such thing as writer's block. Writer's block is a convenient term we use simply because "I don't feel like writing" sounds less palatable.

I used to work in a foundry, back when dinosaurs roamed the Earth and books were still sold in bookstores. I held many positions at that foundry, one of which was operating a mold making machine. During my daily eight-hour shift, I was expected to make a certain number of molds. If I completed this task, I got a paycheck at the end of the week. If I didn't complete this task, then I got fired and had to find another job.

I've always approached writing the same way. Whether I've got an hour to write each day or eight hours each day, I've always envisioned my words as part of the assembly line. I have to produce X amount of them each day, or I'll get fired and have to find another job. And since I haven't had another job in over 15 years, I'm pretty sure I'd have trouble getting hired somewhere else, so it's doubly important I keep this writing gig.

That's not to say there aren't days when I don't feel like writing. Far from it. After a full day of playing with my 4-year old, the last thing I want to do is sit down and write. I'd much rather collapse onto the couch and just rest. But if I do that, then my 4-year old isn't going to eat next month. Thus, I have to produce words. To quote this wisdom from Joe R. Lansdale, "If you can't find time to write, you probably really don't want to do it."

There is no such thing as writer's block, but there are excuses for not writing. Sometimes, they're bogus. "I'd rather play video games tonight" is not a valid excuse. But there are times when the things going on in your life encroach upon your writing. Sickness. Death. Depression. Doubt. These things, and others like them, can wreak havoc on your ability to write. Below is an excerpt from my book, *Sundancing*, in which I talk about this:

> During those last three winters, I'd gone through a divorce, a year's worth of weekly visits with a shrink, absolute financial destitution at the hands of a crooked publisher, a heart attack, two devastating floods, a mudslide, a blizzard, the death of a family member, betrayal and abandonment by several once-close friends, and two nervous breakdowns. My alcohol consumption had increased in response to this, and the amount of words I wrote each day had decreased accordingly. Not that I had time to write, even if I'd had the mental strength to do so. I had my youngest son from Monday through Thursday, and by the end of the day, he left me too exhausted to work. I saw my girlfriend on the weekends, but visiting her involved a three hour commute, and again, there wasn't much time for writing. Basically, as my world fell apart, brick by brick, I kept my shit together as a father and as a boyfriend, but couldn't write for shit. In the rare moments when I did have time to write, the words I produced weren't my best, which made it even harder to write.
>
> The public didn't know this, of course. Oh, hell no. Online

and during appearances at signings and conventions, I still played the role of the hard-working writer, preaching the gospel of how there was no such thing as writer's block, and how all one had to do was make the time to write—ass in chair, fingers on keyboard. Repeat as necessary. Except that it was all hypocritical bullshit. I gave the genre what it wanted. What it needed. A pep talk in a time of crisis (and believe me, these last few years have indeed been a time of crisis for most of your favorite horror writers and publishers). But while I could rally the troops, I had no one to perk up my own sagging spirits.

So, yeah. I'm not immune. I get that life sometimes intrudes and the last thing you want to do is write. It's hard to make up stories about zombies and vampires and giant carnivorous worms when life's very real monsters are tearing you apart inside and out. And one of those monsters is doubt. Self-doubt is the worst, but it's also one of the easiest to deal with, if you know how.

The first thing you need to know, Steve (and everyone else reading this) is that you're not alone. Every single author has those moments of self doubt. It might surprise you to know that those moments don't just come early in one's career, either. You ask yourself, "What if this sucks? What if I'm just wasting my time? What if nobody likes it?" It's very easy to let those fears and uncertainties keep you from writing. But there are two things you must remember.

1. Not everybody is going to like everything.
2. You are writing for yourself. Everyone else can suck it.

Not everybody is going to like everything. I've written a metric fuck-ton of books and comic books, and every single one of them has been hated by somebody. But you know what? Other people have liked them. More importantly, I've liked them.

Write the book you want to read.

Consider this quote from Toni Morrison: *"I wrote my first*

novel because I wanted to read it." She's right. My first novel was a zombie novel. I wrote it because, at the time, nobody else was writing zombie novels, and I wanted to read one. I didn't pause to consider that nobody else might want to read about zombies. It didn't concern me that people might talk shit about it on the internet. None of these things mattered to me, because I liked what I was writing. I hoped others would, too, but if they didn't, that wasn't going to stop me from writing it. In hindsight, that worked out pretty well for me (and for anyone else who couldn't find a zombie novel to read). Some might say, given the plethora of zombie novels now available to the public, that it worked out too well. But that wasn't my concern. My only concern was writing a book that I wanted to read.

Don't worry about whether or not anybody else will like it, as long as you like it. Write a book that you'd want to read. Do that, and I think you'll find your block dissipating. Do that, and your fears and uncertainties become a lot easier to wrestle with. Do that, and you'll suddenly start producing words again.

I'd like to close with this quote from Wrath James White, because I think it ties in well with what we're talking about here: *"Whether you're writing about vampires, zombies, werewolves, demons, witches, ghosts or serial killers, the tone, the mood, the settings, the characters, and the plot should be so uniquely personal that only you could have possibly written it. That is the only reason anyone should ever write any story, ever, because you are the only person who could have written it."*

You are the only person who can write the story you're working on.

Now go do it…

AUTUMN AND THE CABAL: MUSINGS ON FRIENDSHIP, TIME, WRITING, AND COSTS

This past weekend, some friends and I flew out to Colorado to visit author Tom Piccirilli. These are the thoughts that have been bumping around in my head since returning home—some fairly lengthy musings about friendship, time, writing, and life.

Here are two pictures of authors John Urbancik, Geoff Cooper, myself, Mike Oliveri, and Michael T. Huyck. The first was taken in Seattle in 2001 by Sephera Giron. The second one was taken last weekend in Colorado by John's automatic camera. Study them for a moment.

A keen observer (see what I did there) will no doubt notice a few things when comparing these two pictures. The first is that while the passage of time has had an impact on Oliveri's hair color, my hairline, and Urbancik's waistline, it has had no discernible effect on Coop whatsoever, and Mikey's posture 12-years later is still that of a man twenty years his junior. (That is because Mikey is, in all actuality, perpetually frozen into that kneeling position. This is why you never see him at horror conventions anymore). Another thing one might notice is that we're smiling more in that original picture. Probably because writing hadn't yet broken our hearts the way it did years later.

What I notice about these pictures is something you probably don't. What I notice about these pictures are all the other people that are in them—people you can't see, but that I see as clear as day. Tom Piccirilli, Weston Ochse, Regina Mitchell, Ryan Harding, Mary SanGiovanni, Tim Lebbon, Rain Graves, J.F. Gonzalez, Wrath James White, Mehitobel Wilson, Carlton Mellick, James Newman, Mike Bracken, Drew Williams, Jack Haringa, Nicholas Kaufmann, Sephera Giron, Monica O'Rourke, James Futch, Donn Gash, Gak, Bryan Smith, Linda Addison, Michael Laimo, Alan Beatts, Matt Johnson, Seth Lindberg, Brett Savory, Darren McKeeman, Mike Marano, Brian Freeman, Chad Hensley, Holly Newstein (now Hautala), Gerard Houarner, David Niall Wilson, Vince Harper, Dave Barnett, and so many more. So very many more. An entire generation of writers. Enough for a cabal…

That was what some in our generation used to call ourselves —the Cabal. It was a tongue in cheek tag, but it gave us a sense of community and a sense of identity in the days when the Internet was still quite new, and the horror literature community was a very different thing.

We had mentors—folks like Richard Laymon, Edward Lee, Ray Garton, John Pelan, Brian Hodge, Yvonne Navarro, John Skipp, David Schow, Gene O'Neill, Joe Lansdale, Jack Ketchum, F. Paul Wilson, and Tom Monteleone. And again, many more. Veterans who took the time to offer advice and counsel, or maybe just a drink when we needed it.

It truly was all for one and one for all.

We intended to set the genre on fire. Fifteen years and some change later, it is the genre who has often burned us. Some fell by the wayside. Some folks have passed. Others have just drifted away. Some moved on to other types of writing, or quit writing altogether. Some stuck around, experienced varying degrees of success, and learned just how fucking brutal and savage and unforgiving this business can be. Some who have persevered ask themselves why, and if it was worth it.

I ask myself that quite often. I ask myself if my success has been worth the cost. And believe me, the toll has been high and there have been times when the weight was unbearable. I've sacrificed a lot, and have lost a lot more, and there have been a higher abundance of tears than there have been laughs.

But yes, it was worth it. It was absolutely worth it, and I'd do it all over again for one thing.

For the friendships I've made.

These days, there is no cabal. It's more like a collective. But the sentiment behind it still hasn't changed. All for one and one for all.

Today, my youngest son and his classmates went on their first field trip. The parents went along, which means me and all the other moms (yes, I've become a soccer mom, and I am totally okay with that. The girls give me recipes and tips on how to make jack-o-lanterns last longer and I entertain them with tips on the best cigar to smoke or how to increase your grain alcohol tolerance. It's a wonderful symbiotic relationship). But I digress…

The field trip was to a local pumpkin farm. At the end of the day, my son and his three friends climbed atop a stack of hay bales, and I took a picture of them. In a rural community such as ours, it is conceivable that these four boys will remain friends until they graduate from high school. In the seconds before I snapped the picture, they were pretending to be Iron Man,

Hulk, Thor, and Captain America. In the picture, they are smiling, arms clasped around each other, ready to conquer all that life will throw at them. All for one and one for all.

I want to warn them about what life has in store. The hurts and disappointments and heartaches that will come, but these are things they will have to learn for themselves. With luck, they will learn them together, and live them together, side-by-side. Because that's what friends do.

I have been blessed with many good friends in my life, but none like the friends I've made as a writer. So yes, it was worth it. Each and every time I got financially screwed by a publisher or criticized by some illiterate dingbat on Amazon or stalked by a lunatic who was convinced that I was the source of all his problems and also the anti-Christ—it was worth it.

You can judge a man by the friends he keeps.

And I've got some of the best god-damned friends in the world.

We went to see Tom because he is one of those friends—one of those best god-damned friends in the world, and he's fighting brain cancer, and because a friend should never be alone in a fight. A friend should be able to glance around the bar, back against the wall, and know that other friends are wading into the fray with fists and guns and knives, ready to kill motherfuckers for him.

I'm not going to speak about the details of Tom's condition. That's for Tom and Michelle to decide what they want made public and what they don't. But I will tell you that post-operation, he is most definitely still the same old Tom, still full of wry humor and sarcasm, and wonderful insights, and still a connoisseur of Asian cinema and noir paperbacks. The cancer has not beaten him, and it is my sincere belief that he will beat it in the end and emerge stronger than ever before. But the battle will not be easy, and he will need the support of friends.

Friends like you.

I'd take a bullet for Tom. So would Coop, John, Mike, and Mikey.

I'm not asking you to do that. I'm just asking you to do what you can.

All for one and one for all…

MORE THAN MAN'S BEST FRIEND

Epitaph to a Dog by Sir William Watson (with thanks to Laird Barron for sharing it with me):

> *His friends he loved. His fellest earthly foes—*
> *Cats—I believe he did but feign to hate.*
> *My hand will miss the insinuated nose,*
> *Mine eyes that tail that wagged contempt at Fate.*

Sam passed away this evening. If you've read my books, then you know him as Sanchez from *Scratch*, Samhain from *Clickers vs. Zombies*, as himself in various *Hail Saten* volumes and the metafictional *The Girl on the Glider*, and of course, his starring role in *Dark Hollow* as Big Steve.

Sam was my best friend. And that's coming from a guy who's lucky enough to have several of those. I wrote a bit about friendship a few weeks back, and I'd take a bullet for any of those guys, as well as some of my friends from my military days. But Sam was a different kind of best friend. You don't necessarily have to be a dog person or a cat person to understand that, but you do have to be a human being. People who say things like, "It's just a dog" are miscreants who deserve to be locked in a cage with Michael Vick.

Sam was a lot more than "just a dog". As I said, he was my best friend. We've shared many adventures together—exploring beaches and stirring up deer far out in the woods, hunting snakes and splashing in streams, road trips and long walks, and many, many afternoon naps. My tears fell on his muzzle countless times and deepest were the secrets and confessions I mumbled into his furry, floppy ears. He knew my fears, my joys, my failings, and my foibles. Most importantly, he knew my love.

And I knew his.

Sam was a shelter dog. My ex-wife has always said that he

chose us, rather than us choosing him, and I believe this to be true. A few years after we brought him home, another castaway showed up—Max (my cat). And although Sam occupied the spot in my office beneath my desk on a daily basis, he was more than willing to share that space with Max. That's just the kind of dog he was.

Obviously, given the time he spent at my feet while writing, and the amount of times he's shown up in my work, Sam was my muse. But he was also our family's protector. If Sam didn't like you, chances were good I didn't like you, either. Not that he was a mean dog. Far from it. He was kind and gentle—except to snakes, which he loathed as much as I do, and on one occasion, a pit bull that tried to charge me. He was a dutiful and happy playmate to Turtle, taking on the role of Doctor Doom to Turtle's Iron Man, and more recently (as Turtle has now discovered *Star Wars*) he'd been filling the role of Chewbacca.

Sam's decline was quick and sudden. In a matter of weeks, he went from his old (if older) self to a shadow of that former self. The culprit was a hemorrhagic tumor on his spleen. Luckily, he didn't suffer. We got to say our goodbyes to him, and he got to say his to us. He's buried in a special place next to another special friend, and I'm sitting here typing this with the mud from his grave still damp on my clothes, and I know what I want to say, but I fear I'm not saying it well, because last night was a long night, and today was the longest day, and I don't see tonight being any shorter. I'm grieving and I miss my friend, and I don't have the words to express it properly—which is a frustrating, heart-wrenching thing for a writer to admit.

Goodbye, Sam-dog. You were a good boy, and I love you.

SOMETIMES WRITING DOESN'T INVOLVE WRITING

Recently, I explained how my ever-changing work week is now compressed into Thursday through Sunday, essentially making it a work weekend. This weekend was no different, except for the work being done.

On Thursday, I combed over the manuscript for the Author's Preferred Edition of *Earthworm Gods*. This involved going through scenes that were cut from the original editions and deciding whether or not to include them in the new one. Most of the scenes remain cut, but I've restored a few (including a great sequence in which Kevin, Taz, Ducky, and Juan encounter their first white fuzz-infected humanoid). I also wrote a very long afterword that will be exclusive to this edition, in which I talk about the novel's origin, its publication history, and why it has a special place in my heart. Much of this is stuff I've never discussed in public before, and I think you'll dig it. The manuscript is now being picked over by trusty pre-readers Mark Sylva and Tod Clark, and Deadite Press will bring it your way later this year (probably right around the time that *Earthworm Gods II: Deluge* is released in hardcover).

Speaking of Deadite, many of you have been asking about the delay of *Dark Hollow* and wondering what's behind that.

Basically, it's the manuscript I turned in. It was formatted from a PDF rather than a Word document, which makes the production-process a little lengthier than normal. Added to that, Deadite lost a copy-editor (Troy, who has moved to New Orleans to open a voodoo shop, and we all wish him luck in that endeavor), so they've been tied up with finding a replacement for him—somebody who's freaky enough to willingly copy-edit works by myself, Bryan Smith, Edward Lee, Wrath James White, and the rest of the stable. But I'm told the delay won't be much longer, and I submitted the Deadite versions of *Ghost Walk, An Occurrence in Crazy Bear Valley*, and *Entombed* in Word, rather than PDF, so we'll catch up quick.

Anyway, Thursday and Sunday were spent working on that. Friday was spent re-tooling the synopsis for this mass-market political thriller that J.F. Gonzalez and I are writing together and aren't allowed to tell you about. You might think that spending an entire day writing and re-writing a synopsis is a bit of overkill, but it's not. When you are ghost-writing for a brand name—be it Tom Clancy or V.C. Andrews or whoever—you not only have to write in the house "style" but your plot has to be in line with the brand, as well.

On Saturday, Mary, J.F., and I checked and replenished our stock at The York Emporium (as you may recall, the three of us entered a bookselling venture earlier this year). When that was over, we had lunch in downtown York and then Mary and I headed over to the home of authors Kelli Owen and Robert Ford. Robert Swartwood and many other peers were also on hand, and of course, writing dominated the conversation— discussion of everything from alleged author con-artist Anthony Giangregorio to digital books to a history of the small press to what constitutes the bizarro genre.

A non-writer (or even a new writer) might read all of the above and think, "Well, he didn't do any actual writing." And it can certainly be perceived as such. But all of these things—edits, afterwords, creating a synopsis, catching up with peers, trading industry gossip, and even bookselling are all things that a working writer does as part of his or her living. The trick is to write more than you do these other things.

But tonight, I'll make up for it by working on *The Lost Level* and this short story for Cemetery Dance.

WIN A DATE WITH NICKOLAUS PACIONE

If you're new to the Internet, Nickolaus Pacione is a deranged man from Illinois who lives in his grandparent's basement, where he shouts at the world from a computer. He fancies himself a professional writer (he's not), a publisher (also not), and concert promoter (thrice not). He doesn't like gay people, some racial and ethnic minorities, grammar, soap, or common sense. He believes that there is a vast Illuminati-like conspiracy to keep him from being published. He has stalked, threatened, and harassed roughly four dozen professional and amateur authors and editors, including myself, Ramsey Campbell, Ray Garton, Cherie Priest, Poppy Z. Brite, Darren McKeeman, David Niall Wilson, Mary SanGiovanni, Karen Koehler, Kealan Patrick Burke, dgk goldberg, RJ Sevin, Shane Ryan Staley, Angelina Hawkes-Craig, Brian Knight, Susan Taylor, and dozens more. He has also done the same with other celebrities from music and film. His threats, while never progressing beyond his grandparent's basement, have included everything from lighting his perceived rivals on fire to murdering them with a crossbow to kidnapping their children. He has been institutionalized, locked up, and medicated a few times, but—like herpes—he always comes back.

He has recently begun stalking Mary and her son, and while her hometown police have been very helpful, their hands are tied by the law. Unfortunately, his local law enforcement are about as useful as a chancre sore, and thus, I am left having to respond myself. Keep that in mind before you deride me for "picking on the mentally ill". Yes, this man is ill, and yes, he's a violent psychotic, but he's also vile and repugnant and loathsome, and has been a source of great stress for two people I care about very much.

So fuck that noise.

Anyway, according to a listing he just posted on Craigslist, Nicky is looking for love. Since it is often difficult for the novice to understand Nicky-speak, I thought I'd translate portions of the listing as a way of providing a valuable community service. Excerpts from his listing are in italics.

It's actually been two years since I actually did a personal ad on Craigslist.org.

Nick likes to say "actually" a lot. Actually is actually his favorite word. You can make a fun drinking game out of this. Do a shot every time Nicky says "actually".

I am also published if some of you actually ask that question.
DRINK!

I am looking for that one woman who has the patience of a saint because I am...

Unemployed; spend my disability check on fixing my computer each month after I infect it with viruses from visiting unicorn-porn websites; live with my grandparents; subsist on a diet of Coke and Cheese-Doodles; shout racial, ethnic, and sexual slurs at my computer; don't own a car so I need you to drive me everywhere; think hygiene and bathing are all part of the conspiracy to keep me from being published; etc.

I end up getting women who are geographically undesirable

Translation: I don't own a car, my relatives refuse to drive me anywhere, and the bus doesn't travel to these potential suitor's neighborhoods.

I refuse to date a girl from Coal City or Morris, because they hardly leave the area in terms of going out on a Saturday or Friday night.

Who can blame them? If you went on a blind date with Nick Pacione, would you want to be seen in public with him?

I have a unique charm to me that some can't stand.

Extreme B.O. and rampant homophobia are "unique charm" in the same way that Justin Bieber is good music.

but others actually find this kind of funny

DRINK!

looking for that one lady who'd be willing to date me when I come into the city.

Translation: I need a place to crash. Can I sleep with you? If not, can I at least sleep on your couch?

person who is actually a starving artist type

DRINK!

I would run up and down the stairs of the subway for exercise when I am in Chicago.

In the paragraph before this, he said he goes to Chicago every three months. Translation: I exercise once every three months.

I am a Renaissance man.

Renaissance Man: a person whose expertise spans a significant number of different subject areas. Da Vinci was a Renaissance man. His contributions to society included numerous scientific observations, inventions, and art. Nick Pacione's contributions to society include trying to lure an underage girl into a cemetery for a "modeling session" and writing the following opening sentence: "From this that *eludes me* which I pen this—as what I say what *eludes me* is sleep, and from the sleep becomes the etchings where the dreams begin." (Excerpted from *Collectives In a Forsaken Landscape*).

Some college buddies actually coined

DRINK!

I like eating at dives and diners for the most part

Best First Date Ever!

I have the Italian looks, but got the Swedish height.

And the brain of a diseased, meth-addicted howler monkey jacking off into a razor-laced grapefruit.

I am actually a Chicago

DRINK! (Shit, I'm out of whiskey…)

The thing that the ladies are drawn the most about me is I am a photographer.

Translation: I take pictures of pigeons. And also of myself squatting on various pieces of public real estate.

I honestly really don't mind dating a BBW just as long they're height and weight balance out

As someone who has dated several BBWs, I'm not sure what this sentence means. Is he looking for a blueberry?

I want a woman I like to actually be able to carry

DRINK! I don't care that you can't stand up! You wanted to play a fun drinking game. Now drink!

I am a male hetero pig.

I am a ~~male hetero~~ pig. There. Fixed that for you, Nicky.

I don't mind if the woman actually dresses normal

DRINK! DRINK! DRINK!

I really don't look like the bookish type, I hardly drink alcohol.

Study that sentence. Repeat it aloud. Ponder its eloquence. Marvel over its structure. That shit should be hanging in a museum somewhere. Maybe he is a Renaissance Man!

I am actually a Christian believe it or not.

Drink! The power of Christ compels you to drink!

I am known in the Chicago area because of my website

I am known in the Chicago area ~~because of my website~~ as that creepy fucker who stalks and threatens people.

actually outlasted many of its hosts.

If you aren't drunk by now, you're playing the game wrong.

When at parties, my book collection is actually a conversation piece because the authors in the small press, some of them I actually worked with.

A DOUBLE SHOT OF ACTUALLY! DRINK! DRINK! DRINK!

Sometimes it grows on a person

Write your own joke here_____.

others might find this kind of sense of humor openly offensive.

In Nicky's world, saying things such as: "I want to kill all fags", "your mixed-race son is a fucking mongrel", "I'll kill you in your sleep you dyke bitch", and "I will kick you in the cunt with a steel-toed boot" are just jokes.

I love being a writer, but I wish I did make a little more money doing it.

I wish that, before I die, mankind might set foot on Mars, but we make do with what we're given, Nicky.

I might take the lovely lady with me to different events as moral support.

Translation: Carry my boxes of self-published books, pay for my way into the convention, pay for my food, pay for my taxi, and keep me from getting my ass kicked when I spew my special little brand of invective at the wrong person.

So, yeah. There you go, ladies. Form an orderly line, please…

SELF-PUBLISHING: ONE YEAR LATER

I realized this morning that it's been roughly a year since Robert Swartwood talked me into self-publishing some of my works (and thus, the teacher became the student). I thought that maybe I'd share my thoughts, one year in. What follows are some rough observations, typed out before my five-year old wakes up and we start the day.

So far, I've self-published three novellas (*Alone, Scratch,* and *The Girl on the Glider*) and one full-length short story collection (*Blood on the Page: The Complete Short Fiction of Brian Keene, Volume 1*). They've been made available on the Kindle, Nook, and Kobo platforms. I haven't yet experimented with self-publishing paperbacks, but will next month with a paperback edition of *Blood on the Page*.

My up-front costs for each book (design, cover art, etc.) have been about $400. In each case, I recouped that within the first month of sales. While I won't get into exact dollar amounts, I will say that the vast majority of my sales have come from Kindle, making up fully 85% of my monthly royalties (with Nook and Kobo sales providing the rest). I've noticed the same thing with my monthly royalties for the Deadite Press Kindle and Nook editions of my work. Clearly, Kindle is the dominant device.

Kindle is also the easiest to work with on the production side of things. Upload the file, enter the info, and usually within a few hours, the book is on sale. Kobo is also very easy to use. Uploading to Nook, however, can be a maddening and teeth-clenchingly frustrating experience. Error messages, time-outs, files not uploading, delays of up to five days for the book to go on sale—a complete cluster fuck.

But, overall, I've been very happy with the experience. Between the monthly royalties I make from self-publishing and the monthly royalties I make from Deadite Press, and the mutual respect I'm shown from Deadite, and the ease of self-publishing, I doubt there's any way I would ever go back to the Big Five mass market publishers. Oh, they want me to. They keep asking me to. But as it stands, they can't offer me a better deal than what I can offer myself. And after 15 years in this business, I'm very much enjoying that right now. I like where I am—doing a mix of indie press and self-pubbing. For me, it's perfect. Your mileage may vary.

THE MAGUS AT 45

Leaving tomorrow morning for Las Vegas and Killercon. Hope to see some of you there. I'll turn forty-five during the convention—on Saturday, in fact. I intend to celebrate by having a few drinks with Jack Ketchum, Edward Lee, F. Paul Wilson, Carlton Mellick, Wrath James White, Maurice Broaddus, and some other friends, followed by breakfast the next morning with Gene O'Neill. There are worse ways to spend the official transition into middle age.

I had a rough time with thirty, a rougher time with thirty-five, and an absolute soul-wrenching time with forty, but I'm okay with forty-five. I think once you pass the forty mark, you learn to make your peace with it and accept things.

I was reading *Fearnet's* excellent review of my novella, *Alone*, yesterday, and one line that really struck me was this:

"Keene is entering the middle age of his career, and he no longer needs to shout to be heard. He's discovered the power of restraint, and demonstrates it with his understanding of the way a silent, empty house can be just as terrifying as a horde of gut-munching zombies."

That pretty much sums things up. That is what it feels like to turn forty-five. (And thanks to Blu Gilliand for saying in a review of my book what I'm trying—and failing—to properly articulate here).

I've led a hard life, but I've also had a damn good run. I've got two happy and healthy sons, and I make a lot of people happy with the words I write. Every day I live past this point is just gravy. I'm looking forward to enjoying the time that's left.

THE CENTRE CANNOT HOLD

I meant to write a long Blog entry about yesterday's atrocity—the school shooting at Sandy Hook—and the subsequent media coverage, but I have to make a six-hour drive down to West Virginia tonight and bring my 86-year old Grandma back to visit for the holidays, so these brief musings I posted via social media will have to suffice.

What I said on Twitter: Instead of reporting the news this morning, MSNBC and FOX are simply arguing Left & Right talking points, while CNN's anchors report only how the story personally impacts them and despicably interviews little kids who survived the shooting. This country faces major problems. Unfortunately, CNN, Fox News, and MSNBC are a big part of the problems. We need to have non-partisan, factual discussions. As a nation, we should be discussing guns, mental health issues, national debt, etc. But simply echoing what you heard from Limbaugh, Maddow, Hannity, Hayes, Morgan, etc. is not a discussion.

And what I said on my friend and fellow author Mark Morris's Facebook page: Roughly two years ago, someone tried to break into my home late at night. I live in a rural area, and it would have taken police a minimum of 10-15 minutes to respond. I warned the intruder that I was armed with a .357 revolver, and then displayed it. Upon seeing this, the intruder fled. I do not know what would have happened had I not had that means of defense, nor do I want to know. As a father, and a public figure, I have a right to defend my loved ones and myself. I am responsible. My firearms (as well as anything else I don't want my toddler getting his hands on such as fireworks) are locked in a steel safe that requires both a numerical code and a key to get into. And yes, while that added a delay on the night I needed that firearm, you might also be surprised just how quickly I got that safe open and that revolver loaded.

Now, that being that, you'll notice I said .357 revolver. I didn't say Bushmaster .223 semi-automatic rifle (one of the guns used in yesterday's school shooting). I don't need a semi-automatic to defend my home and I don't need it to go deer hunting. Nobody does. We have the right to defend our homes, our property, and most importantly, our loved ones. But we don't need assault weapons to do that. A shotgun or a revolver in the hands of someone who has taught themselves to be safely proficient with it is just as effective at home defense as any automatic or semi-automatic weapon. Nor do we need assault weapons to defend ourselves from a tyrannical government (something else that is often trotted out). An assault weapon is not going to increase your odds against a drone.

And it should be noted, I say this as someone who does indeed own a Bushmaster .223, an AR-15, and several other assault style weapons. I'm not saying ban them. But we should certainly have a real conversation about them without shouting at each other.

There needs to be a factual, fair, non-partisan, and candid discussion about guns, gun culture, and gun violence in this country. Sadly, MSNBC, FOX News, CNN, talk radio pundits, lobbying groups, and politicians will not allow the American people to have that discussion, seeking instead to politicize it for their own gain. We are a nation that have regressed to rooting for political parties the way we would for football teams, forgoing logic and self-education, content instead to simply parrot the Left and Right talking points instead.

And until that stops, these atrocities will sadly continue to happen. And that is the most horrific and heartbreaking part of all.

TWENTY-FIVE YEARS IN FOUR COLORS

If you've read *Ghoul*, then you've pretty much read about how I grew up—just minus the monsters. As a kid in York County, PA, I had two options for buying comic books.

The first option was the Spring Grove newsstand. I bought my first 3 comics there at the age of five (they were *Captain America*, *The Defenders*, and *Kamandi*).

And I continued to buy them there every week, peddling my bike into town every Saturday, and spending most of my allowance on comic books, and whatever was leftover on a slice of pizza at Genova's.

My second option was our annual once-a-year trip to Baltimore, when my folks would let me visit Geppi's (who had a store dedicated just to comic books—something unheard of back then).

Time passed. I discovered girls, music, and mind-altering substances, and thus, I lost my passion for many childhood things. But I never lost my love and appreciation of comic books as a storytelling medium.

Fast forward to 1988. I was fresh out of the Navy, and had returned home to a York County, PA that I no longer recognized. Everything seemed different. Having trouble adjusting, my first week home, I decided to visit some old haunts. My hope was that I'd recapture some old magic and feel settled—or at least comfortable again. One of those haunts I visited was the old Delco Plaza mall, where my friends and I used to go see *The Rocky Horror Picture Show* together on Friday nights.

While walking through that mall and reminiscing and trying to determine if everything around me had changed or if it was just me who had changed, I came across a slim little store—almost a closet rather than an actual retail space. The store measured 100ft long by 15ft wide, and it was filled with comic books. I stared, gaping, as an angelic choir sang on high from the mall's rooftop.

It was at that moment that I felt home.

Walking inside the store, I learned that Ned Senft and Bill Wahl, two guys who used to sell comics at an indoor flea market in York City (that would later become the York Emporium) had just opened the store. I chatted for a while, and became subscriber number 19 (a box number that I kept until moving to Buffalo for a short time many years later. When I returned to York, my new number became 219).

That first visit, I gave them money, and in return they gave me comic books. And in the 25 years since then, they've given me long-lasting and valued friendship and support and made me laugh and gotten me through some damn hard times, and I've done my best to do the same for them.

Bill and Ned and the rest of the counter monkeys have become family. When my oldest son, David, was 4, I took him on his first visit to Comix Connection. Bill sent him home with a Godzilla comic and toy. David is now 22 and still enjoys Godzilla and still shops at Comix Connection. When my youngest son, Turtle, was old enough, I began taking him to Comix Connection, as well. Ned sent him home with an Iron Man comic and toy. Turtle is now 5 and wants to be Iron Man when he grows up. And I've no doubt that if, like his Daddy and his older brother, he still enjoys comics as an adult, he'll buy them at Comix Connection.

They've been a pop-culture Mecca for Central, Pennsylvania over the years, hosting signings by everyone from Joe R. Lansdale, Tim Truman, Mike Oliveri, and Duane Swierczynski to locals such as J.F. Gonzalez, Dirk Shearer, Mike Hawthorne, and myself. They give back to the community with regular food drives, toy drives, and various charitable fundraisers.

Comix Connection has gone through location changes and collapsing ceilings and expansions and a lot of growth over the years. And I know that I'm not the only long-term customer who has gone through that growth with them. Things change. To quote Rush, "Children growing up, old friends growing older. Freeze this moment a little bit longer."

During Comix Connection's first year in business, I bought the first issue of *Hellblazer*. This week, 25 years after it launched, *Hellblazer* ended with issue #300. But Comix Connection is still going strong. And it's done that without rebooting continuity, jumping from one event to the next, or having non-stop crossovers. Instead, it's done with a knowledgeable and friendly staff, brightly-lit and welcoming stores, and a genuine desire to make people happy, and share the love of a wonderful medium.

Freeze this moment a little bit longer, indeed…

Happy Anniversary, Comix Connection.

ON MARRIAGE EQUALITY

I rarely allow the public to see things on my private Facebook page (which is why I have this public page instead) but I'm copying and pasting something I wrote for my private page, because it needs to be said:

Marriage equality isn't a Conservative issue or a Liberal issue. It isn't a Republican issue or a Democrat issue. It's a human issue, and one that speaks to the very heart of Libertarian-ism. Everyone—be they straight, gay, bi, or trans-gendered—should have the freedom to marry whom they choose. Thus, I urge my fellow Libertarians to get off the couch on this one, and make your voice heard. We want less government interference in our lives, and the right to pursue the freedoms guaranteed to us under not only the Constitution and Bill of Rights, but under basic human nature, as well? Well, then, this issue is a fine place to draw the line in the sand and tell the government to butt the hell out.

I'm not a member of the Left or the Right, and once again, I stand here shaking my head while those two sides shout at each other, and all meaningful conversation gets lost in a cloying miasma of political dogma and cable news talking points. Same thing happens when we try to talk about gun violence, or the fiscal budget, or national defense, or health care, or anything else, and I'm sick of it. FOX News and MSNBC are nothing more than propaganda machines for their chosen alignments, and CNN—instead of seizing the moment and truly representing Middle America—is about as informative and effectual as an episode of *The Golden Girls*.

And I'm pissed at the dismantling of our space program, because I really want to go to Mars and get the hell away from 90% of the people on this planet.

When I am installed as World Leader Supreme, there will be some fucking changes.

End of rant.

TWENTY-FOUR HOURS AFTER KINDLE

I own somewhere between 2,000 and 3,000 books. Hardcover, paperback, trade paperback, and graphic novels. I'm a book snob. I love the smell, the feel, the experience. I like sitting in my chair, sipping bourbon and smoking a cigar and reading a book—and then looking up at all my other books. As a result, although my books are sold across digital platforms, I've always resisted taking the e-book plunge.

Twenty-four hours ago, I received a Kindle Paperwhite as a gift from my ex-wife and my youngest son …

… and I may have to reconsider this book snob thing.

I'm not a tech-guy. Ask anyone. I still type my novels using Microsoft Word 2003 because I'm afraid to upgrade. I have to call Mike Oliveri or Russell Dickerson just to post a Blog update. I've gone through four iPhones in three years. My five-year old son has to show me how to turn on my DVD player and my twenty-two year old son had to set up my X-Box avatar.

So, my first question upon un-boxing my Kindle was how hard would it be to set up? The answer: so easy, even Brian Keene could do it. I simply took the Kindle out of the box, turned it on, and it did the rest. Within five minutes I'd linked to my Wi-Fi network (which my 5-year old helped me install last year) and registered the device with Amazon.

As soon as my account was active, the Kindle gave me a quick tutorial. After that, I bought some books. Now, in the past, I got books in one of three ways: 1. Drive to a bookstore and buy them. 2. Order them online and wait for my inept mailman to deliver them. Maybe. Unless it's one of those days when he delivers them into the bottom of the river. 3. Get them as gifts from publishers or authors. All three methods are fine, but the Kindle offers a different experience. Literally, in less than five minutes, I'd purchased three books—*The Vaccinator* by Michael Marshall Smith, *Hyenas* by Joe Lansdale, and *Quicksilver* by John Urbancik. All three were easy to find. All three were simple to purchase. And all three took less than a minute to appear on my device. I can't help but mention that I have complete collections for all three of those gentlemen, so if the book is available in hardcover or paperback, it's a safe bet that sooner or later, I'll buy that edition, too.

Five minutes to shop. That gave me extra time to read. And that was when I truly fell in love with my Kindle. I wear bifocals. I am also blind as a fruit-bat. Over the last year, I've struggled with headaches that come upon me only when I'm reading. Doesn't matter if I keep my glasses on or off—anytime I read a book or comic or even a newspaper, my head hurts. With the Kindle, I was easily able to adjust the font (and remember, I'm a Luddite so when I say easily, I mean easily). By the time I'd finished Michael Marshall Smith's book (because I read it in one sitting) there was still no sign of a headache. (I did wake up with one in the middle of the night, but that was due to seasonal allergies and had nothing to do with reading).

I was halfway through *Hyenas*—just after the bit where Hap and Leonard get a love note from Smoke Stack—when I glanced at the clock and realized it was after midnight. I fell asleep, forgetting to plug in my Kindle to charge, and this morning, there was still plenty of battery life left. Unlike my laptop or my iPhone, which seem to plummet to 5% battery capacity if I leave them on for more than five minutes.

I guess none of this will be news to folks who've already taken the digital plunge, but it might be good information for those who, like me, have resisted the e-book revolution. I've had a pleasant, easy experience so far, and I can't wait to finish typing this Blog entry so I can get back to finishing that Lansdale book tonight.

TODAY'S TOM SAWYER

Turtle (my five-year old's public nickname) graduated preschool last Friday. It was a nice event. His teacher said he's "a natural leader" and one of the parents said he's "cute and a ham". I don't know where he got any of these traits from.

This was not my first preschool graduation. My oldest son had a preschool graduation, too, but that was a long time ago, as evidenced by the fact that he'll be graduating college next year.

So, while this was not my first, it will most probably be my last (unless I stick around long enough to enjoy some grandkids).

I'd done my weeping two days before, on Turtle's last official day of preschool, so I wasn't sad after the ceremony. But I was… morose. It's hard to believe my little man is starting kindergarten. And all I have to do is think back to his older brother's preschool graduation, and contrast that with the adult his older brother has now become—an adult who asks me for advice on women and who is now able to kick my ass at *Magic the Gathering* about one in every three games—and I realize just how fucking fast time really does fly. I'd always been told that time slows down as one gets older, but I think the people who told me that were lying bastards, because if anything, time is speeding up. These days, I'm all too aware of that, and I'm left wondering if I'll be able to complete everything I want to do before I die.

Filled with these thoughts, I was in no shape to write when I got back home to my mountaintop log cabin, so I decided to spend the day cutting firewood instead. After all, I reasoned, I had all day Saturday and Sunday to write. My only other plans for the weekend were for Saturday afternoon, when Geoff Cooper was stopping by to help me scout out a location on my property for us to install a shooting range (something I couldn't have when I was living in an apartment). I'd have plenty of time to write after that, I reasoned. It would do me good to chop firewood. Take my mind off things.

And it did. There is a poetry imbued in the act of chopping firewood that you probably wouldn't dig unless you've actually done it. You're standing there in the ninety-one degree heat, clad only in a pair of cutoff shorts, feeling the sun and the sweat on your shoulders, setting up a log, then swinging the ax and quartering that log, then setting up another. There's a rhythm to it—a perfect synchronicity of ax and muscle and breathing. The only sounds are of the birds and squirrels and the satisfying thunk the blade makes as it splits the logs. It's a primal, fulfilling sensation, and one I pondered as I chopped and swung.

By two in the afternoon, I'd cut enough wood for a pile eight feet long and about three feet high. The sun was beating down, and I'd run out of water and switched to the emergency bottle of bourbon I keep in the shed. Although I had the start of an impressive woodpile, I knew it wasn't nearly enough. To make it through the winter here atop the mountain, I'd need a stack at least twenty feet long and six feet high.

It then occurred to me that as poetic as this experience was, there were other author friends whom I could share it with. Laird Barron, for example. Laird used to race dogsleds in the Alaskan wilderness. He would certainly appreciate the rustic peace and camaraderie that comes with chopping wood. J.F.

Gonzalez would probably like it, too. As a former Los Angeles native who'd been transplanted here in the wilds of Pennsylvania, he was always asking me to give him rural experiences (and I was fairly certain he'd forgiven me for the last such incident, which involved cows). I thought that perhaps Nick Mamatas would enjoy it, too. The act of collectively chopping wood together so that the community can survive the hardships of winter spoke directly to the heart of Socialism. And ditto Tom Monteleone. The act of collectively chopping wood together so that the community can survive the hardships of winter spoke directly to the heart of Democracy. I figured it imbued a sense of patriotism, for it is something our forefathers had done upon coming to this country. I was pretty sure Joe Lansdale was no stranger to swinging an ax, and I figured he'd need to be on hand if only to teach *The Cage* film adaptation producer Damian Maffei how to do it properly.

Yes, I decided, sitting on a stump and now halfway into the bottle of bourbon—I would have a wood cutting party! I'd invite everyone into town for a weekend, and they could each take a turn swinging the ax while I stood in the shade and supervised.

And then, free of the mild post-graduation ceremony depression that had gripped me earlier, I forgot all about the whole scheme and came inside and wrote instead. I also decided that I'd keep this scheme in reserve in case I ever had a fence that I needed whitewashed.

Time is speeding up. But as long as I've got my sons and my work and my friends, I intend to stay on the ride until the end. To paraphrase Rush's song "Tom Sawyer, I'm always hopeful yet discontent. I know changes aren't permanent, but change is.

ON THE HOUSE

By the time you read this, I'll be on a train to New York City, where I'm taking part in a Creative Summit for a top-secret DC Comics project that I can't tell you about. Since I'll be there four days, the publisher is putting me (and others) up in the Dream New York, a midtown Manhattan luxury hotel. (I'm registered under a pseudonym, so please don't plan on dropping by). I've never stayed there before, but judging by their website, it's quite posh. Which is all very nice, but the only thing I care about is that my itinerary says my hotel room will have a 'Stocked Private Bar'.

A lifetime spent on the road will do that to you.

I've lost count of how many hotel rooms I've stayed in, how many conventions I've been a guest at, how many speaking engagements I've delivered, how many book signings I've done, and how many business trips I've taken. They all blur together after a while. I've stayed in dives and I've slept in luxury. My former assistant Big Joe and I, in the midst of a book tour, once stayed in a motel room in upstate New York that didn't even have sheets on the bed. Instead, the mattress was covered in a dusting of dried out dead cockroaches. Once at a convention in Virginia, the organizers forgot to reserve my room, and my other former assistant Tomo and I had to stay at a flea bag motel down the road whose only other tenants were a motorcycle gang. (We spent more time hanging out with the bikers than we did at the con).

I'm happy with just a clean hotel room, and I've gotten that more than not. Once in a while, the publisher or film studio or convention organizer puts me up in a penthouse suite or something similar, and that's nice, too. But no matter how high up your room is, you can always look out the penthouse window and see the roach motel just down the road.

Sometimes I've paid for my meals. Other times they've been on the house. I remember very early in my career—a movie producer once flew me out to Hollywood and took me to dinner to discuss optioning one of my books for film. We went to a nice steak joint and I had a slab of meat that cost as much as an entire cow would have cost back home. I also drank most of a bottle of Basil Hayden's because, hey, the producer was paying. It seemed silly to me that they'd spent all that money when we could have just negotiated over the phone or email. What I didn't know at the time was that the only money I'd ever see out of that deal was the air fare to and from Los Angeles, the steak, and the whiskey. The day I checked out of the hotel room, I took all the little complimentary bottles of shampoo and conditioner, and put them in my suitcase, because I was barely existing above the poverty level, and hey, the producer was paying.

These days (some fifteen plus years later) I tend to stay in nicer hotels, and I don't go to conventions as a guest unless the convention pays for my trip, and I've learned enough about business to avoid wasting my time with those who would waste my time. But there are still months when the royalties are few and far between, and thus, I still take all the little complimentary bottles of toiletries, and I still get delighted when I see the words 'Stocked Private Bar' on my itinerary.

Success and money are transitional, fleeting things, and they tend to run in cycles. My advice to writers just starting to go full time is to never get too comfortable. No matter how successful you become, never forget what it's like to eat Ramen Noodles and peanut butter sandwiches six days a week, because chances are, you'll go back to doing that off and on in your career. I know that I have. And that's okay, because at the end of the day, it's worth it if you've touched someone with something you wrote, or made their day a little better, or entertained them for a while.

People in this business promise things all the time. Sometimes, they even deliver on those promises. But in the end, the only guarantee you have are those little bottles of free shampoo.

And if you're really lucky, someone will temporarily give you a stocked private bar …

TO ALL THE GIRLS I'VE LOVED BEFORE

That's me, age nineteen, somewhere in the Mediterranean Sea.

I've been with a lot of women in my life, and by "been with" I think you all know what I mean, and by "a lot" I mean over a hundred. This is not something a man should be proud of, as

I've tried to explain to my oldest son, in the hopes that he'll do better. But it is a fact of my past, and one that informs my present, and makes up just another facet of who I am.

Out of those numbers, there have been four women in my life who I've loved unconditionally—a total and complete surrender of myself, wanting nothing more than to see them happy, attempting to move Heaven and Earth and storm the Gates of Hell to make it so, and having the courage to open myself to them, flaws and all. None of these ended well. My fault, each and every time. My flaws overwhelmed one of them. Two of them had their own flaws that exacerbated mine. And one of them loved me so unconditionally that I jeopardized the relationship myself and fled in fear. But those are musings best left to private counseling sessions. My point is this—each of those four women left an indelible stamp on my heart that also informs who I am today. And I will always be grateful for that.

There was a fifth woman who I loved, as well.

The fifth woman—she wasn't made of flesh and bone. She was made of steel and gunpowder. She was much older than I was, and as such, she taught me a lot of things about life. I met her when I was eighteen and we dated until I was twenty-one. I wasn't her first and I certainly wouldn't be her last, but I enjoyed our time together. She introduced me to some of the best friends I'd ever have in life—men who are my brothers, in every sense of the word.

She and I, we saw the world together. Literally saw the world. And in doing so, she taught this blue-collar white boy from a small town in Pennsylvania that there were other ethnicities, religions, sexual orientations, political systems, languages, cultures, and traditions. She gave me my first true glimpses of absolute poverty and absolute wealth, of true evil and pure goodness, and most importantly, that no matter how far you travel or how different the culture and people you meet—there are still common things that bind us all together as humans. There are still things we all feel and share and experience. I'm grateful to her for showing me that, because it's informed everything I've written ever since.

We had some good times together, she and I. We had some bad times, too. We didn't always get along, and when we broke up, I thought I hated her, but time has a way of healing those things. You forget the bad and remember the good.

It's been several decades since I saw her. Occasionally, my thoughts would turn to her, and I'd wonder how she was doing. I imagined she was in an exotic seaside port somewhere, perhaps in Israel or Spain or Italy. She'd always loved those places. But then I heard that she'd been sold for scrap. I felt a vague sort of disquiet at this news, but didn't really comprehend it. Nobody would ever really scrap that old girl. Then, last Saturday night, I saw a picture of how she looks now, and my heart broke.

The U.S.S. Austin, then and now.

Goodbye, old girl. You will never know how many lives you impacted. You deserved better than this, in the end.

ON WRITING FULL-TIME
(KEYNOTE SPEECH, TOWSON UNIVERSITY, BORDERLANDS BOOT CAMP 2013)

My name is Brian Keene and I am a full-time writer.

I'm honored to be here tonight. As you all know, it almost didn't happen. I was supposed to be one of your instructors this year, but due to the economy, that didn't work out. In truth, it wouldn't have worked out anyway because I would have spent all weekend sitting out there with you and sponging up knowledge from instructors F. Paul Wilson, Douglas Winter, and Tom Monteleone instead of telling you anything useful.

Seriously. I hope you know how lucky you are to have an opportunity like the one you've had this weekend. My generation didn't have a Borderlands Boot Camp. If we wanted writing advice from these guys, we had to get it the old-fashioned way— by buying them drinks at a bar. I figure that method of learning has cost me over $20,000 over the last fifteen years.

You've spent the weekend learning how to become writers, or perhaps, to be more accurate, how to become better writers. I'm here tonight, at the invitation of your instructors, to talk to you about what happens after you become a writer—how to make a living at it, what you can expect when you write for a living, and more importantly, what not to expect.

To be clear, I define writing for a living as "Writing is your main source of income." And I should also clarify that, just as there are many different ways to get published these days, there are also many different ways to make your living as a writer. This is my way, and it has worked for me. It's sort of like a VH1 Behind-the-Music special, except it has more caffeine than cocaine, and instead of Keith Richards snorting a fifth of Chivas down a guitar neck onstage, or Axl Rose getting photographed with two-dozen buxom, semi-clad groupies, there's only Tim Lebbon and I performing drunken Karaoke at some long-forgotten World Horror Convention or Joe Hill and I photographed drinking soda in a dark corner at NECON.

I have been a full-time writer—meaning writing is my only source of income, and how I provide for myself and my loved ones—for a little over a decade. My commute is great—from the bed to the coffee pot to the computer. I get paid to make up stories about zombies and giant carnivorous worms and people give me money for them. Not a bad gig. Usually. But there's a lot more to it than that. Writing is a hard way to earn a living, and the costs are high. Too high, at times. And yet, I continue to do it because the rewards are unlike those of any other profession I know. And I continue to do it because I can't do anything else. I can't not write. I've always liked my friend Tom Piccirilli's description of this condition: If you're stranded alone on a desert island, and you spend your time writing stories in the sand with a stick, then you're meant to be a writer.

I'd be one of those people. Instead of scrawling SOS in giant fucking letters on the beach, I'd be using that castaway time to finish my next novel. I'd be doing that because I write for a living, and when you write for a living, there's no time to fuck around. The only way you get paid, is to produce. The only way to produce is to sit your ass down in the chair, put your fingers on your keyboard, and type. You can't think about your books as books, because they aren't. When you write for publication, you are producing a product for public consumption. If there is no product, then the public can't consume and you can't eat. So you have to produce.

Writing for a living is a fun job, but it's still a job. If you want to do it for a living, then you have to treat it like a job. You are your own boss. Yes, you are beholden to input from editors and agents and marketing departments and readers, but at the end of the day, you answer only to yourself. So be a boss to yourself, and don't let yourself slack off.

I used to work in a foundry. I ran a mold machine. Each day, I was responsible for making X amount of molds. If I did this, I received a paycheck at the end of the week. If I didn't do this, then I was soon looking for another job. Writing for a living is the same way. You are responsible for writing X amount of words per day. Do this, and eventually you'll get a paycheck. Don't do it, and you'll soon be looking for another job.

I think it's important to write every day. Most successful writers—be they best-sellers or just genre journeymen like myself—seem to have one thing in common: they are prolific. Or, if not prolific, then they are at least dependable. A full-time writer should write full-time. This might be 2,000 words a day or 6 pages a day or 8 hours a day. It may be five days a week or seven days a week. The time clock and the production schedule are up to you. What's important is that you keep to the time clock and meet the production schedule.

If you choose to publish via traditional means (publishing companies) then understand that your pay will be sporadic. When your novel is accepted, you will receive an advance. The average advance these days, for a genre fiction novel, ranges between $2,500 and $10,000. That's right. The novel you spent a year working on only earns you between $2,500 to $10,000 at first. When the book is published a year later, that advance will have long been spent. And you probably won't see a royalty check until another year AFTER your book has been published (provided enough copies have sold to earn out your advance). So it will actually be two years from that advance check before you get paid again.

That's why being productive matters. You can't feed your family on that one advance. But if you write two books per year, and supplement that with novellas, comic books, limited collectible editions, or short stories, etc. then the money starts to add up. The more you have in print, the more money you have coming in. It's also important to try to hold on to whatever rights you can, and effectively spin them into more money. Audio-books, foreign translations, movie options, comic book adaptations, merchandising—all of this can be turned into more money for you and your family. If you have an agent, they can do this for you, but getting an agent is hard these days, and getting a good agent is next to impossible. For 14 of my 15 years as a full-time writer, I have worked without an agent. I have one now for my foreign translations, and she's excellent at what she does. But that's the only aspect in which I use one.

I should also point out that these payment factors I just mentioned are very different if you are self-publishing, particularly if you are doing it through Kindle, Nook, or Kobo. You will get paid monthly if you choose that route—but it is also harder to make a living wage with that method unless you approach it with the same business mind-set. But that's a separate discussion that we can get into during the Q&A portion of this talk.

Now, I'm going to dump some cold water on those of you who think success or best-seller status automatically equal big dollar signs. I have been prolific over the last fifteen years, and have been lucky enough to keep my work in print to the extent that I receive royalty checks for various works each and every month. I've also had books turned into film, adapted for comics, and more. I've been on CNN, Howard Stern, a documentary on the History Channel, and a trivia question answer on an ABC game show. My readers include rock stars, movie stars, stand-up comedians, professional athletes, a few politicians, a few more porno actresses, and even a daytime soap opera diva. I am one of the most popular horror writers of my generation. I say that not to brag or sound arrogant, but to set the stage for what I am about to tell you. I am one of the most popular horror writers of my generation—

—and on average, I make between $30,000 and $40,000 per year. Sometimes it's a little bit more. Sometimes, it's less. That's an average.

Not exactly big money. Many of you in this room are probably making more than that via your day jobs. But this is the vocation I've chosen, and I chose it knowing that the days of big money in publishing are gone. Several of my literary heroes, the authors whom I grew up reading, have lamented to me that I was born in the wrong era, that I came too late to the game, that had I been doing this a decade or two before I started, I'd have made a lot more.

When I was younger, I was all about the Splatterpunks. Those guys were who I wanted to be. One of them, I won't say who because I want to protect his privacy, once lamented to me that in the horror heyday of the Nineties, he'd get advances of $25,000 for a novel. Now, today, those same types of novels were earning him a $2,500 advance. Think about that—from $25,000 to $2,500.

So… stay productive. Keep creating product, and thus, creating new revenue streams for yourself.

Get a good accountant and pay ahead on your taxes. Learn to save and budget your money, as well. If you're not good with finances, become good. Attend a community college class or buy one of those For Dummies books. As a full-time writer, you never know when your financial situation will change. And it will. Often. And even when the windfalls come, they go just as quickly. For example, last year I received a five-figure check for a movie based on one of my books. But I was also left with a former publisher owing me five figures in back royalties—money that I'll never see because they went out of business. So yeah, that movie money was great, but in terms of my budget and bills, I never really saw a dime of it, because all it did was make up for the amount owed to me by others. As a full-time writer, your finances will always be in this state of flux. It can be scary and harrowing and tough, but it is part of the price you pay. As Hunter Thompson once said, buy the ticket, take the ride.

As a full-time writer, you'll have no health insurance. To get health insurance, you'll have to join a writer's organization that offers it, or get an exclusive contract with someone like DC Comics, or get it via your spouse or partner's employer. Or, if you're like me and have none of those things and can't afford monthly health insurance premiums on your own because, as a public figure, your lifestyle is well-known and health insurance companies simply laugh at you when you inquire about coverage, then you'll find yourself doing things like emailing Dr. F. Paul Wilson sitting there in the back and saying, "Hey, I saw Amoxicillin in the pet store today. It's for fish tanks. Could a human take that, and if so, in what dose? This is for a book I'm writing of course. I would never do this in real life." And Paul's response will be, "You still don't have health insurance, do you Keene?"

Seriously. When I think about how some of my favorite writers—men like Charles Grant, Poe, JN Williamson, or HP Lovecraft—have gone out, it breaks my heart. It's a cautionary tale, but it's also one that never seems to change. Writers have been dying sick and poor since the days of cave painting. The difference is that WE know this can happen. By looking at our literary heroes of the past, we can plan ahead for our own futures. Once again, you have to control your own destiny. Know your roots, and grow accordingly.

There's also no 401K. No retirement. Warren Ellis once said, "Writers don't retire. They just die..." There's a lot of truth to that. I know a writer—again, I won't mention names—who had multiple copies of everything he'd ever published. I'm talking a dozen or two dozen copies of every book, chapbook, hardcover, paperback, etc. That was his retirement plan. His life insurance policy. His work was in demand enough via the secondary and collectible market that, should something have happened to him, those editions could have been sold to cover costs. And they were. I have done something similar in my own career. Publishers will tell you that I'm notorious for demanding more author copies in my contract than most writers in my genre. There have been times when that has paid off for me. If royalty checks are light that month, and the mortgage is due, it's pretty easy to flip a first edition hardcover of The Rising for $1,000 on eBay. If I die tomorrow, my loved ones can flip the rest of them and pay for my funeral.

So, you need to plan for your health care, and your retirement. You also need to plan for your public identity. Even if you are just starting out as a writer, you should reserve a website domain in your name, and reserve every social media outlet in your name, as well. Even if you don't ever intend to use them, you should stake a claim on your name at Facebook, Twitter, Tumblr, Google+ and every other site that comes along. I don't use Reddit or Goodreads, but I've registered for them as BrianKeene simply because I don't want somebody else controlling my public identity. That's because these days, whether you are publishing traditionally or going the self-publishing route, you are primarily responsible for the marketing and promotion of your work. Yes, your publisher may get involved, but you must never, never count on that. You should take responsibility for it. Indeed, you have to take responsibility for it, if you want to do this full-time. Some of you may find marketing and promotion distasteful, but if you want to do this full-time—meaning you want to make money at it—then you will have to engage in them.

More importantly, you are responsible for growing and communicating with your audience. How and to what extent you do that is up to you, but understand something—the days of Bentley Little are gone. Bentley Little, who has a large readership but maintains no web presence himself and has done only three signings throughout his career, is an exception to the rule. Thanks to the Internet and social marketing, readers these days have an expectation to interact with their favorite author in some way. Again, how you do that and to what extent is up to you, but if you choose to write full-time, then you will have to do it. This is as vitally important as staying productive and writing every day. It is the second part of the writing for a living equation.

Hand-in-hand with that is how much of yourself you put out there. Some professional writers keep it simple, and confine their public musings to their work. Others might talk politics or pop culture. This can be a double-edged sword. Yes, Paul, Tom, and Chet Williamson might occasionally post something from their respective Libertarian, Conservative, or Liberal perspectives, which is fine, but I bet each and every one of you can think of other authors on Facebook or elsewhere whom you've considered un-following simply because it's all they talk about. You probably haven't un-followed them, because you're a writer and you want to keep that professional association. But readers have no such qualms, and they will turn away if you offend them.

You've got to decide who you want them to see you as. Maybe you'll just be yourself. Perhaps you'll choose a caricature of yourself. Maybe you'll be the joker, like Jeff Strand, or the Peacemaker, like Christopher Golden, or the Strong Independent, like Sarah Pinborough. For years, Nick Mamatas and I got away with being the genre's Angry Young Men, willing to speak bluntly—perhaps too bluntly at times—about what we thought and saw. These days, you'll no doubt notice that we speak softer. That's because you can't be Angry Young Men when you're in your Forties. But our audience still know we'll speak bluntly, because our audience has come to expect that from us. Decide what your audience will expect from you, and then give it to them.

Perhaps more important than deciding how much of yourself to put out there is deciding what parts of you not to put out there. Writing is a solitary act, but publishing is public. We're part of the entertainment industry, albeit the entertainment industry's red-headed mutant stepchild. And just like any other entertainer, we attract our share of crazies. My own encounters with stalkers are well-documented. I'm sure you all know about the guy who mailed me a dead bird or the gentleman from Illinois who is convinced that Ray Garton, Poppy Z. Brite, and I (among others) are psychically stealing his story ideas. These people exist, and the Internet and social media make it easier for them than ever before to fulfill their unhealthy obsessions with you. As a result, you have to be mindful of what information is out there.

If you plan on becoming a full-time writer, get yourself a PO Box now. I recommend that you get it in a nearby town—one that's easy for you to get to but not the one in which you live. That address, and only that address, should be given to the public. You should also stop posting pictures of your children or loved ones online. If you want to continue to do that, then create a private Facebook account for yourself, and don't let readers or fans on it. The public knows that I have two sons—one of whom is 22 and the other of whom is 5. But I have never mentioned my 5-year olds' name in public. To my readers and fans, he is known as "Turtle"—the nickname I use to refer to him in public (and not even his real nickname, truth be told). I did this because I live in a small town, and I don't want someone finding my son or my other loved ones or myself through public grade school listings or any of the other ways people can find this info online. If I sound like a paranoid alarmist, well… I have reason to be. And so should you. The world is a dangerous and strange place, and if you become a full-time writer, if you are creating a product for mass consumption by the public, then you will have no choice but to interact with that dangerous and strange place.

But it's also important to remember that ninety-nine percent of your audience are kind, gracious, genuine people just like yourself. You'll find that—on days when the royalty checks haven't shown and you have to go to the free clinic because you don't have health insurance—that they keep you going. Fans and readers can be a source of strength and solace. It's a nice, symbiotic relationship. They get you through the long hours spent writing. You get them through study hall or their lunch hour or their commute or their bad marriage or incarceration or tour of duty or abusive relationship or their loneliness. And that is a noble thing.

That is a very noble thing.

Focus on them. Focus on that audience. Don't make the mistake of only marketing your work to other authors. That's the dumbest thing a writer can do, yet I see them do it every day. Don't post a link to your book on places like the Shocklines message board or a writer's group on Facebook. The only people who will see it are people posting links to their own books, and all of you are writers, and none of you can afford to buy the fucking things. You have to go to where the readers are, or better yet, create a place where the readers can come to you, via Facebook, Twitter, your website, etc. Letting them come to you is less spammy and more sincere, and it also creates long-lasting loyalty.

Don't get wrapped up in Stokers and ITW awards and all these other awards and honors. Don't get wrapped up in HWA politics or who fondled who at a convention or any of the other bullshit we distract ourselves with. Yes, like any other job, interacting with your co-workers is important. And a little bit of industry gossip can be useful. So go to conventions. Be a part of organizations if you wish.

But never let talking about writing become more important than the writing itself.

Also be mindful of the toll full-time writing can have on your relationships. I spend my time alone and spend my alone time writing. Writing is a solitary act, and it makes for a solitary existence. Hell, I should know. Writing is the reason I'm alone. I'm good at it—writing, I mean. I'm not so good at being alone, despite the fact that it's how I spend my life. But I'm good at writing, or at least, that's what my editors and publishers tell me. I sometimes suspect they only tell me that because I make them lots of money. People will tell you whatever they think you want to hear when you're making them a lot of money. I've often wanted to purposely write a bad book, just so I can see their false praise for what it is, but I wouldn't do that to my fans and readers. And I wouldn't do it to myself. Because other than cooking, sex, surviving outdoors, and being a father—writing is the only thing I'm good at. It's the only constant in my life. The only thing I can always count on.

And all it cost me was everything else. Let me tell you some of the costs, so that you can avoid them in your own career.

Writing cost me two marriages. At least, that's what I tell myself. In truth, it was really me.

My first marriage dissolved when I was trying to become a professional writer. We lived in a trailer and had about three dollars to our name. I worked all day in a foundry (and later as a truck driver) and then came home at night, and focused on my word processor, rather than my wife. I was young and dumb and it never occurred to me that my equally young wife might like me to spend some time with her rather than writing. Even when we did spend time together, we didn't really communicate. She was usually watching TV while I had my nose buried in an issue of *Deathrealm, The Horror Show, Cemetery Dance, New Blood*, or one of the other big horror lit magazines of the time. When she left, I had that word processor and those horror magazines for comfort, and not much else.

My second marriage lasted eight years (after an additional eight years of courtship), and dissolved long after I'd become a professional writer. By then, I was old enough and mature enough to have figured out that I should spend time with her and talking to her after putting in 7 or 8 hours at the computer. Despite that, communication was still the culprit in the end. There were things I was unable to properly communicate—the pressure of deadlines; the stress of fame (because even a little bit of fame can be a very fucked thing); how it felt to live under a public microscope that examined and often took issue with everything I wrote, said, thought, or did; the paranoia and self-loathing that creeps in when everyone—even your once closest friends—seem to want something from you; how utterly demoralizing it was to me that I didn't have a weekly paycheck, health insurance, or a 401K to provide for my family the way every other husband I knew did. I should have tried harder to talk about these things, but I didn't have it in me. I didn't have it in me because after 8 hours of writing, I was emotionally and mentally exhausted at the end of the day.

I don't believe we choose to be writers (or musicians, painters or any other form of the arts). I believe we don't have a choice. I probably could have saved my second marriage by quitting writing and walking away from it, but doing so would have been a lie. Writing isn't like a sales job where you quit one firm and go to another. I'm a writer. I could no more quit than cut off my arms or voluntarily drag my balls across six miles of broken glass. Believe me, I thought about it. I thought about it long and hard. But in the end, quitting would have destroyed my marriage even more assuredly, because I would have been miserable, unhappy, unsettled, and eventually dead. That's not hyperbole. That's a certainty.

The key is communication. I look back now and shake my head in disbelief that a guy who made his living communicating to the general public was unable to do the same for the people he was closest to in his private life. So—before you set out to become a full-time writer, sit down with your partner or spouse and communicate with them. Make sure they intimately understand your needs for everything from solitude to the pressures of deadlines, and make a concerted effort to communicate with them and meet their needs when you are done. And if you don't know what their needs are, you better ask. Because your spouse or partner are making just as many sacrifices as you are to see you become a successful full-time writer, and you'd better damn well appreciate it.

Writing has also cost me friends—both from before I became a writer and after. Childhood chums, pissed off that I mined so much of our lives for fiction. Friends from High School and old Navy buddies who I no longer had anything in common with, who assumed that just because they saw my books in stores or my movies on television that I must somehow be wealthy and hey, could I lend them a few dollars or help them get published or be the dancing monkey and star attraction to impress all their friends and family members with at their next Christmas party. Fellow writers and peers, people I'd come up with, promised to do it together with, only to have them lose touch with me when I got successful.

Or maybe it was me who lost touch with them. Maybe it was my own insecurities—my own guilt at achieving everything we'd all hoped for, while they still hadn't. And maybe that applied to those old High School friends, as well. Maybe they were just proud of me, and I mistook that pride for something else. And maybe those childhood chums were right to be angry. Perhaps not all of our personal demons needed to end up as grist for my fiction mill. And maybe—just maybe—my two ex-wives had been right to expect me to choose a healthy relationship with them instead of fifteen hours at a keyboard living inside my own head seven days a week instead of talking to them or living with them.

These are the thoughts that keep me awake some nights, and on those nights, I write. It's a self-perpetuating vicious cycle. Lose everything because of writing until the only thing you have left is the writing itself. Rinse and repeat.

But this is what I do. This is the life I've chosen.

My name is Brian Keene and I am a full-time writer.

HOW LONG, OH LORD, HOW LONG: HUNTER S. THOMPSON AND HORROR

When *The Damned Highway* was first published, a lot of the reviews and articles in the press expressed some variation of wondering how Nick and I got the idea to mash-up Hunter S. Thompson and H.P. Lovecraft. Our response was always, "How could we not? And how is it that nobody thought of it before us?" To us, gonzo journalism and horror fiction seemed to go hand in hand. As Brendan Moody wrote in his review of the novel (published in *The Stars At Noonday*): "…a hybrid of the gonzo journalism of Hunter S. Thompson with the horror fiction of H. P. Lovecraft, of radical political critique with cosmic horror, is eminently natural. They have in common a conviction that dark forces are moving behind the scenes, an exclusion from mainstream society, a paranoid intensity that is, under the circumstances, justified and saner than the usual variety of sanity."

Despite the fact that Hunter S. Thompson was a voracious reader, a hyper-prolific journalist and author (with over fifteen books, thousands of essays and articles, and other miscellany in print), and both a counter-culture and pop-culture icon, we do not know for certain if he was a fan of horror fiction. There are a small handful of scattered reference to the works of Edgar Allan

Poe and H.P. Lovecraft in some of Thompson's essays and rants, as well as a brief nod to Lovecraft's eldritch pantheon, but not much else. We know that Thompson was a fan of Joseph Conrad's novella *Heart of Darkness*—not a horror story per se, but nevertheless a tale fraught with horrific elements and imagery. But other than these meager and somewhat iffy signposts, there isn't much to suggest that Thompson was a fan of the genre.

And yet, he knew horror. He knew it well and wrote it well. It is perhaps most prominent in one of his most popular catchphrases: "fear and loathing", which he first used to describe his thoughts regarding the assassination of President John F. Kennedy, and which would go on to be used in book titles (*Fear and Loathing in Las Vegas*, *Fear and Loathing on the Campaign Trail*), articles ("Fear and Loathing in Elko"), and other writings.

Thompson was taught about fear at an early age. About his formative years, he wrote (in *Kingdom of Fear*): "Never turn your back on Fear. It should always be in front of you, like a thing that might have to be killed. My Father taught me that." He goes on to say that his father told him there is no such thing as paranoia, advising the young Thompson that, "Even your worst fears will come true if you chase them long enough. Beware, son. There is Trouble lurking out there in that darkness…"

Is it any wonder, then, that so much of Thompson's career was spent journeying into that darkness, looking for the Trouble, exposing it to the light, and chasing our nation's worst fears so that they could be conquered?

From early in his career until his final days freelancing for ESPN, Thompson's work often captured the daily horrors of real life—political corruption, police brutality, drug abuse, bigotry, racism, bestiality, sexual perversion, sadism, abrupt and shocking violence, war, murder, pedophilia, etc.—detailing and presenting them in a way that put them on par with the fictional horrors of zombies, vampires, werewolves, serial killers, and the like. Sometimes these horrors were ones he personally witnessed, such as his savage beating at the hands of the Hells Angels motorcycle gang, the garish excesses of the elite at the Kentucky Derby, or the violent clashes between police, protestors, and journalists at the 1968 Democratic Convention in Chicago. Other times, such as his ill-fated trip to Vietnam to cover the end of the war, or his coverage of the Muhammad Ali and Joe Frazier fight, the horrors he wrote about were second-hand (often because Thompson was too drunk or stoned to experience them first-hand).

Consider his commentary on organized religion (again from *Kingdom of Fear*): "I have seen thousands of priests and bishops and even the Pope himself transmogrified in front of our eyes into a worldwide network of thieves and perverts who relentlessly penetrate children of all genders ... I have seen the Jews run amok in Palestine like bloodthirsty beasts with no shame, and six million brainless Baptists demanding the death penalty for pagans and foreigners and people like me who won't pray with them in those filthy little shacks they call churches."

Or this missive on Autumn which descends into a madcap litany of modern America's suburbanite horrors (from *The New Dumb*): "Autumn is... a time of strong Rituals and the celebrating of strange annual holidays like Halloween and Satanism... a time of Fear and Greed and Hoarding for the winter coming on. Debt collectors are active on old people and fleece the weak and helpless... There is always a rash of kidnappings and abductions of schoolchildren in the football months... these things are obviously Wrong and Evil and Ugly, but at least they are Traditional. They will happen. Your driveway *will* ice up, your furnace *will* explode, and you *will* be rammed in traffic by an uninsured driver in a stolen car."

Then there is his eerily uncanny and prescient examination of the War on Terror ("Fear and Loathing in America: Beginning of the End", published in *Hey Rube*), written exactly one day after the September 11th terror attacks of 2001, which predicted with astounding accuracy the events of the past decade—from the wars in Afghanistan and Iraq, the erosion of our civil liberties via the Patriot Act and contains such lines as, "The towers are gone now, reduced to bloody rubble, along with all hopes for peace in our time..." or his warnings about what would happen next: "Coming of age in a fascist police state will not be a barrel of fun for anybody, much less for people like me, who are not inclined to suffer Nazis gladly and feel only contempt for the cowardly flag-suckers who would gladly give up their outdated freedom for what they have been conned into believing will be freedom from fear..."

Hunter S. Thompson knew all about horror, and he mastered it just as he did every other obstacle or adversary he ever encountered. It was part of his work, part of his life, and part of his destiny—all the way to his final act of defiance and control, when he took his own life rather than face the horror of debilitating pain and the steady decline of old age (something he'd warned friends he'd do some thirty years beforehand). From the alleys of Watts and Compton to the jungles of Vietnam and the shadowed halls of Washington D.C., be it demons and devils like Richard Nixon, Idi Amin, or Osama Bin Laden, the vampires involved in the Roxanne Pulitzer divorce case, or a potential succubus in the form of the former porn director whose unfounded charges and allegations led to his infamous "lifestyle bust", Hunter S. Thompson boldly charged forward, ready to battle the monsters, exposing them to us all.

Selah!

ON PROFESSIONALISM, ELITISM, AND THINGS MORE IMPORTANT

In which we talk about chasing dreams, walking away from dreams, what it means to be professional, what it means to be elitist, and things far more important than your goddamned writing.

If you follow this Blog regularly, then you know that for the last two and a half months, I've been doing preliminary work on several projects for DC Comics. I'd dreamed of this gig since I was six-years old, and while I'd occasionally moonlighted with them before, I was now being offered the opportunity to write for them full-time.

This type of thing is a far more involved process than you might think. It doesn't just involve sitting down with your laptop and typing 'Corporate IP-Man crashes through the wall of the Council of Ten's secret hideout'. Before you even get to that phase, there are meetings, and meetings about those meetings, and meetings to talk about that meeting, and then meetings that cancel all of the previous meetings, and then meetings to decide upon new meeting, and then more meetings.

I've been heavily engaged in that for the last two months, taking several trips to New York City and participating in weekly phone calls and email chains and research and pitch sessions.

And as a result, my other work obligations began to suffer. There were novels and novellas to finish, manuscripts to critique, things to mail, Lifetimer Packages to finalize, and a metric fuckton of emails to answer, and while I was still making an effort to work on all of those things, the time I could devote to them shrank more and more with each passing week.

Worse, I could see a point coming where it would begin to impact time spent with my youngest son (whom I identify in public as 'Turtle' because he doesn't need his real name out there among the crazies until he turns eighteen and then, like his older brother before him, can decide if he wants people to know who his Dad is or not). I have Turtle Monday through Thursday, which means I have Friday, Saturday and Sunday to write, go on dates with my girlfriend, do laundry, clean house, and all the other things grown-ups and writers do.

But giant New York-based multimedia companies don't work on that schedule, and those weekly phone calls and other things were happening while Turtle was here in the house. Now, he's old enough that he can play by himself for an hour or two, and he's also enough of a fan of the corporate characters that he thought it was neat to eavesdrop on conference calls about them. But it still felt, to me at least, that I was giving up precious time with him. I don't know many divorced dads who have as much time with their children as I've had, and I'm very grateful to have a profession that allows that, and a wonderful co-parent who was agreeable to it. These last few years have been truly special. In just a few weeks, Turtle will start big boy school, which means this time comes to an end, and the time I have with him in the future will be even more precious.

Unfortunately, things didn't work out with DC Comics. Last Wednesday, when it came time to become officially married, I made a professional decision not to move forward with it. The reasons why are unimportant, and it would be unprofessional of me to go into them publicly. Suffice to say, it wasn't anybody's fault in particular. They weren't cruel and terrible people who wanted me to sign away my soul. If anything, I just looked at how my other professional and personal obligations had already been impacted, and calculated how they'd be impacted going forward, and then I calculated the dollar amount of that impact, and made the professional decision that everything would be impacted in a way that I wasn't comfortable with if I continued. And so, I chose to not continue with something I've wanted to do since I was six-years old. And I'm totally okay with that, because I know I could have done it if I wanted to. And I still could, at a later date. It was an amicable enough decision on both sides. But right now, there are things that are more important, and they take precedence. The folks at DC Comics understood because they are professionals. And I made my decision because I am a professional.

So, that was on Wednesday. I got home Wednesday night, picked up Turtle Thursday morning, and a few hours into our day, his former pre-school burned to the ground.

If you're a parent, then you know as well as I do that special kind of fear that only parents live with. You get twinges of it every time your child climbs a tree unassisted, or rides their bike without training wheels for the first time, or gets their first high fever, or lets go of your hand while crossing the parking lot, or chases their ball toward the street, or walks up to you in the backyard clutching a live, thrashing, pissed off snake in each fist and saying, "Daddy, look what I found. Can we keep them?" Children seem to exist in a perpetual state of wonder and fearlessness about the world, and I sometimes think that we parents must exist in a perpetual state of caution and wariness, because we know that the world has teeth. Sometimes, the world likes to bare those teeth at you when you least expect it.

According to officials, there were several explosions and the fire spread rapidly. Ninety-percent of the building was absolutely destroyed. They stopped it before the classroom was engulfed, but the heat and smoke rendered that unusable, as well. Had it not been summer, and had school been in session …

Well, there are no words. I'm a writer, and there are no words. I was allowed to go inside the building hours after the fire had been extinguished, and I have no words to describe what I saw. The table where Turtle sat each and every day was buried beneath a ton of debris. The roof had collapsed on it. The chair my son sat in every day was a twisted, melted lump of plastic. He graduated pre-school just a few short months ago. Had this happened earlier…well, as I said, there are no words.

So, if you tell me that I made the wrong decision, and that as a professional, I should have opted for a business arrangement with DC Comics that that would have been great for my career but that I suspected would impact my time with my kid, I'm gonna refer you back to that image and invite you to shut the fuck up.

There are things that are more important.

Which brings me to the recent article by the HWA's Lisa Morton, which appears on the Los Angeles chapter of the HWA's Blog. The article is on "Professionalism" and it is a load of horseshit.

Don't misunderstand. I don't have an issue with Lisa, personally. The few times I've interacted with her socially, I've found her to be quite pleasant. Nor do I have an issue with her fiction (I've enjoyed what I've read of it). But I've got big problems with what was communicated in this article, and I'm not the only one. There's a great discussion about it over on Laird Barron's Facebook page. I don't even have a problem with the HWA, per se, other than that, like any other organization or group entity, it is only as good as the people in charge. It's sort of like the government. When you've got Lincoln or Kennedy in charge, you get advancements in human rights, and when you've got Bush or Obama in charge, you get the erosion of the Constitution. But I digress …

The HWA is only as good as the people guiding it, and public perception of the HWA is shaped and formed by the public's perception of those same stewards. There have been great administrations (Dean Koontz, Charles Grant, Craig Shaw-Gardner, Richard Laymon) and not-so-great administrations (S.P. Somtow, for example). Since around 2005, the public perception of the HWA has been that it's nothing more than a life-support system for the Bram Stoker Awards. It's not uncommon to hear horror writers refer to it as the Hardly Writing Association rather than the Horror Writers Association (the sense being that the members focus more on the awards and spend more time talking about writing than they do actually writing).

To his credit, current HWA President Rocky Wood has made great strides to right the ship again, and change the public's perception. And, for the most part, he's got a great team in place to help make that happen—folks like Linda Addison, Ellen Datlow, Joe McKinney, John Palisano, and Ron Breznay, all of whom are dedicated to seeing that vision come to fruition.

Which is what makes Lisa's article all the more vexing. Imagine you're striving to become a horror writer. You've made a few sales, and managed to stick with it while juggling family and day job obligations. You made a little extra money this year, maybe from a sale to an anthology, and you decide to join the HWA. Then you run across this condescending article written by the Vice-President of the HWA and published on an HWA-affiliated website, and it's telling you that, despite all of your hard work, you're not a professional. You're a hobbyist. At that point, you might ask yourself, "Why the hell would I want to join this organization?" And you'd be absolutely right to do so.

As Laird Barron said in regards to it, "The distinction between pro and non pro writer is mainly useful if one wants to join a club with particular membership requirements, or when engaging in pissing contests."

Or, as Tim Waggoner said, "No one gets to define someone else. You only get to define you."

A professional writer can be defined as "you make enough money to support yourself and your loved ones from writing that you don't need to work a day job", and while that works in the broadest, most general of terms, it doesn't really hold up under scrutiny. I'm lucky enough to support myself and my loved ones off my writing. I haven't had a day job in well over a decade. But does that make me more professional than James A. Moore, who moonlights as a barista? Or the legendary Ramsey Campbell, who, a few years ago, had to take up employment in a bookstore? Or Bev Vincent, who gets up a few hours early and writes before he goes to work? Or Michael Laimo, who manages to write two or three novels a year during his morning and evening commute from home to day job? Does that make them "hobbyists"?

In the article, Lisa states that she stumbled into a discussion group of professional writers, and bemoaned the fact that, in her opinion, they were hobbyists because they, quote "chatted about health and told jokes and moaned about personal problems… anything, in other words, but writing careers."

I'm lucky enough to have a pretty broad local social circle composed of writers, editors, and illustrators. When I have a barbecue in my backyard, and the music is playing, and burgers are grilling, and I'm standing around with Tom and Elizabeth Monteleone, Chet Williamson, J.F. Gonzalez, Robert Swartwood, Kelli Owen, Geoff Cooper, Mary SanGiovanni, Mike Hawthorne, etc., you know what we talk about? Our health. Our personal problems. We tell jokes. We talk about our kids. Sure, we talk about writing, too, because we're writers, but our lives extend beyond that. Nobody wants to go to the foundry worker company picnic on their day off and sit there and talk about work. Fuck that noise. The last thing you want to talk about is work. But apparently, such a mindset marks one as unprofessional.

And then we come to the part of the article that really left me scratching my head—the ten questions you must answer yes to in order for Lisa Morton (and presumably the HWA) to consider you a professional. Complete with the disclaimer that, quote, "If you've already glanced at these questions and scoffed, you are a hobbyist."

Well then, let's see what I am, shall we?

1. Is your home/work place messy because that time you'd put into cleaning it is better spent writing?

No. I have two sons whom I'd prefer didn't have to sleep in spider webs or eat cat hair in their spaghetti, so I clean the house every Sunday.

2. Do you routinely turn down evenings out with friends because you need to be home writing instead?

No. I do occasionally, if there's a pressing deadline, but not "routinely". Writing is primarily a solitary endeavor, but there's a danger involved in living and existing inside your own head. A writer needs to get out and socialize, if only to experience real life and real people so that they can then imbue their stories and characters with more realism. But also because if you spend all your time alone, you'll turn into a drooling, gibbering mushroom.

3. Do you turn off the television in order to write?

No. I always write with the television (or music) on in the background.

4. Would you rather receive useful criticism than praise?

Yes.

5. Do you plan vacations around writing opportunites (sic) (either research or networking potential)?

No. When I'm on vacation with my loved ones, the last thing I'm thinking about is "networking potential" I'm instead thinking about what an awesome day it was on the beach, and I wish we didn't have to go back home tomorrow, and that seafood restaurant we ate at last night was really good. Now, in the course of these events, a story idea might present itself to me (in fact, that happens often) and I may, in fact, begin working on it after everyone else has gone to sleep, but the primary goal of a family vacation should be just that—family.

6. Would you rather be chatting about the business of

writing with another writer than exchanging small talk with a good friend?

No. In fact, I often want to stab people like that in the eyes.

7. Have you ever taken a day job that paid less money because it would give you more time/energy/material to write?

Sort of. Until I began writing full time, I worked a dozen different jobs: foundry, stockroom, truck driver, telemarketer, daycare, janitor, data entry, etc. All of them were a means to an end—something to pay the bills until I could pay those same bills with what I earned as a writer.

8. Are you willing to give up the nice home you know you could have if you devoted that time you spend writing to a more lucrative career?

No. And in truth, I don't really understand this question. What defines a "nice home"? Are we talking about material things like new kitchen cabinets and a perfectly landscaped lawn? Or are we talking about warmth and comfort and safety? I like to think I have a nice home. I enjoy it and my children do, too. I guess there are some who might look at it and say, "You live in a fucking cabin on top of a mountain. You have to burn firewood for heat! What are you, Darryl Dixon from Walking Dead?" But it works for me. It's a nice home because it's where the people I love gather—even if it doesn't have vinyl siding.

9. Have you done all these things for at least five years?

No, because so far, I've only answered yes to one of your questions. But I have been writing full time for closing in on fifteen years. Does that qualify me as a professional, or am I still considered a hobbyist?

10. Are you willing to live knowing that you will likely never meet your ambitions, but you hold to those ambitions nonetheless?

Well sure, but that's just human nature, isn't it? Everyone has dreams. Everyone has things they strive for and aspire to. Earlier this week, I made a professional decision to walk away from mine, because it was the right thing to do for both my loved ones and my career.

But I guess I'm just a hobbyist.

Here's the thing, kids. A professional writer is not deemed so by how much they get paid per word, or how many words they produce, or how many awards they've won, or what position they hold in a writer's organization, or how much networking they do at conventions. A professional writer does one thing—they treat their writing professionally. They produce. They edit. They constantly strive to get better. They sit their ass down in a chair and put their fingers on a keyboard and they type.

A professional writer spends more time writing than they do talking about writing.

Now, it's almost 11am. I need to get a few thousand words done on this novella. Then I'm going to clean the house, play cards with my oldest son, call my girlfriend, and perhaps finish the evening off by reading a good book. My name is Brian Keene, and I am a hobbyist. So far, that's worked pretty well for me. As always, your mileage may vary.

MORE ON PROFESSIONALISM AND ELITISM

There are a lot of website, Blog, Facebook, Google+, and Twitter discussions on this now. I'm not going to link to all of them, because there are just so many. But I will point you to John Scalzi's post, because it sums up a lot of the others, but probably in a more polite tone than I used.

I also want to take a moment to post an addendum, and address some things I see popping up elsewhere.

One or two people have said that I must be personally attacking Lisa because I don't like her. This is nonsense. I like Lisa just fine. I said so in the original article above. I like her as a person. I enjoy her fiction. I once toured the KNB FX facilities with Lisa, her husband, and J.F. Gonzalez. I wasn't taking issue with Lisa. I was taking issue with the message she conveyed in that particular article.

One or two people have said that I must be personally attacking the HWA. Again, this is nonsense. I took great lengths in the article above to point out that I think the organization is going in the right direction again, under the stewardship of Rocky Wood. I wasn't taking issue with HWA as a whole. I was taking issue with the message conveyed on an HWA-affiliated website by a current HWA-officer.

It is being said a) that this didn't appear on an HWA-affiliated website, and that b) it was one person's opinion, and that c) those rebutting it are somehow engaged in censorship. Nonsense, nonsense, and nonsense. A) It appears on the website of the Los Angeles Chapter of the HWA. B) It was written by the current VP of the HWA. If it had appeared on Lisa's own personal website or Blog, I don't think there would have been any outcry from anyone. The point is that it was inappropriate content for a website affiliated to a professional writer's organization. And as for C) Freedom of speech means people get to say things, and other people get to say things in return.

It's being said that I took things out of context, and that Lisa meant this to be a sarcastic, tongue-in-cheek satire that would get folks talking about professionalism. Okay, let's examine that a little more in detail, because that's what I really want to address here.

I didn't take anything out of context. I linked to the article in question. I wasn't even the first person to comment on the article in question. I discovered it via Laird Barron, who apparently discovered it via Geoff Brown, who—incidentally—is one of the key figures in the Australian HWA. So forget your conspiracy theories. I wasn't the first person to comment on this, and I wasn't the last. I was one of many. Those many did so on their own Blogs and social media platforms (or in the comments sections of others platforms). Those many included, among others, John Scalzi, Neil Gaiman, Christopher Golden, Rose O'Keefe, Lee Thomas, and many, many more.

I'm perfectly willing to accept that Lisa meant this as a satire. Like I said above, I have nothing against her personally. It's entirely conceivable that was indeed her intent. But it's an intent that was simply not conveyed to the vast majority of people who read the article in question. I mean, when Neil Gaiman or Chuck Wendig, two men who are as kind and gentle as LOLcats are funny, takes issue with what you've written, then it's time to look at the words you chose, what they conveyed, the medium you conveyed them from, and how the audience perceived them. Again, I don't think this would have been commented on at all had it not been on an HWA Chapter-affiliated website.

I see some folks on other social platforms commenting on Lisa's article about small towns as settings for horror fiction, and how she can't relate because she lived in a city all her life, and how that further brands her as an elitist. With no offense to the people who brought this up, I have to disagree. I live in the country. My friend Nick Kaufmann lives in the city. He thinks I'm crazy because he can't identify with living in a place where it's conceivable you will be eaten by a black bear if you walk outside, and I think he's crazy because I can't identify with living in a place where it's conceivable you will be stabbed by a mugger if you walk outside. That doesn't make me elitist against city folks, and it doesn't make Nick elitist against country folks. Different strokes is what makes the world go round. If someone doesn't like books set in small towns, they don't have to read them. And the same could be said of vampires, zombies, werewolves, giant space walruses, or sentient genital warts. A trope is a trope, and a matter or personal preference. The genre is rife with them. Always has been. Always will be. The best thing to do, as writers, is to put your own unique spin on those old tropes, and come up with something new as a result.

So… hopefully that clears a few things up. Now, professional, hobbyist, other… we probably all have writing to do. We should go do that.

WHY I STILL DO THIS SHIT
(KEYNOTE SPEECH, C3 WRITER'S CONFERENCE 2013)

Hi. I was asked to fill-in for Christopher Golden. I know what many of you are thinking. "He's not as pretty as Christopher Golden." Well, you're right. I'm not. I don't know anyone who is as pretty as Chris Golden, except for maybe GI Joe with Kung Fu Grip or Bob Villa—both of whom Chris has a striking physical resemblance to.

Regretfully, Chris couldn't be here tonight because he's got a case of the gout. I didn't even know people could get the gout anymore. That's like an old people's disease. It's 2013. We've mapped the human genome and landed a robot on Mars. We still have gout?

I'm not Christopher Golden. My name is Brian Keene and I am a full-time writer, by which I mean that writing is my main source of income and how I provide for myself and my loved ones. I've been doing that for about thirteen years now. My commute is great—from the bed to the coffee pot to the computer. I get paid to make up stories about zombies and giant carnivorous worms and people give me money for them. Not a bad gig. Usually. But there's a lot more to it than that. Writing is a hard way to earn a living, and the costs are high.

I'd like to lay some of those costs out for you.

I have been prolific to the point of just over forty books, and have been lucky enough to keep my work in print to the extent that I receive royalty checks for various works each and every month. I've also had books turned into film, adapted for comics, and more. I've been on CNN, Howard Stern, a documentary on the History Channel, and a trivia question answer on an ABC game show. Several heavy metal and hip-hop bands have recorded songs or albums inspired by my work. My readers include rock stars, movie stars, stand-up comedians, professional athletes, a few politicians, a few more porno actresses, and even a daytime soap opera diva. I am one of the most popular horror writers of my generation. I say that not to brag or sound arrogant, but to set the stage for what I am about to tell you. I am one of the most popular horror writers of my generation—and on average, I make between $30,000 and $50,000 per year. Sometimes it's a little bit more. Sometimes, it's less. That's an average. Not exactly big money. Many of you in this room are probably making more than that via your day jobs.

As a full-time writer, I never know when my financial situation will change, but it does. Often. And even when the windfalls come, they go just as quickly. For example, two years ago I received a five-figure check for a movie based on one of my books. But I was also left with a former publisher owing me five figures in back royalties—money that I'll never see because they went out of business. So yeah, that movie money was great, but in terms of my budget and bills, I never really saw a dime of it, because all it did was make up for the amount owed to me by others. As a full-time writer, my finances will always be in this state of flux. It can be scary and harrowing and tough, but it is part of the price we pay for this gig.

As a full-time writer, I have no health insurance, and I can't afford monthly health insurance premiums on my own because, as a public figure, my lifestyle is well-known and health insurance companies simply laugh at me when you inquire about coverage. So I resort to buying Amoxicillin for tropical fish tanks at the pet store and calculating the dosage for a human. It's a cautionary tale, but it's also one that never seems to change. Writers have been dying sick and poor since the days of cave painting. There's also no 401K. No retirement. Warren Ellis once said, "Writers don't retire. They just die…" There's a lot of truth to that.

I'd like to think that I'll die in my sleep, surrounded by loved ones rather than gunned down at a book signing by my very own Annie Wilkes. Writing is a solitary act, but publishing is public. We're part of the entertainment industry, albeit the entertainment industry's red-headed mutant stepchild. And just like any other entertainer, we attract our share of crazies. My own encounters with stalkers are well-documented. Perhaps the best known examples are the guy who mailed me a dead bird or the gentleman from Illinois who was convinced that Ray Garton, Poppy Z. Brite, and I were psychically stealing his story ideas. These people exist, and the Internet and social media make it easier for them than ever before to fulfill their unhealthy obsessions with us. As a result, you have to be mindful of what information is out there. I know I am.

I'm also mindful of the toll full-time writing can have on your relationships. Writing cost me two marriages. My first marriage dissolved when I was trying to become a professional writer. We lived in a trailer and had about three dollars to our name. I worked all day in a foundry (and later as a truck driver) and then came home at night, and focused on my word processor, rather than my wife. I was young and dumb and it never occurred to me that my equally young wife might like me to spend some time with her rather than writing. Even when we did spend time together, we didn't really communicate. She was usually watching TV while I had my nose buried in a book. When she left, I had that word processor and those horror magazines for comfort, and not much else. My second marriage lasted eight years (after an additional eight years of courtship), and dissolved long after I'd become a professional writer. By then, I was old enough and mature enough to have figured out that I should spend time with her and talking to her after putting in 7 or 8 hours at the computer. Despite that, communication was still the culprit in the end. There were things I was unable to properly communicate—the pressure of deadlines; the stress of fame (because even a little bit of fame can be a very fucked thing); how it felt to live under a public microscope that examined and often took issue with everything I wrote, said, thought, or did; the paranoia and self-loathing that creeps in when everyone—even your once closest friends—seem to want something from you; how utterly demoralizing it was to me that I didn't have a weekly paycheck, health insurance, or a 401K to provide for my family the way every other husband I knew did. I should have tried harder to talk about these things, but I didn't have it in me. I didn't have it in me because after 8 hours of writing, I was emotionally and mentally exhausted at the end of the day.

Writing has also cost me friends—both from before I became a writer and after. Childhood chums, pissed off that I mined so much of our lives for fiction. Friends from High School and old Navy buddies who I no longer had anything in common with, who assumed that just because they saw my books in stores or my movies on television that I must somehow be wealthy and hey, could I lend them a few dollars or help them get published or be the dancing monkey and star attraction to impress all their friends and family members with at their next Christmas party. Fellow writers and peers, people I'd come up with, promised to do it together with, only to have them lose touch with me when I got successful.

So, that's what writing for a living is like. I hope I've painted a romantic picture for you all.

Good night.

What's that? Why do I do it? Why do I still put up with this shit, rather than getting a proper job as an IT professional or an HVAC technician?

Well, there are a couple reasons.

I continue to do it because the rewards are unlike those of any other profession I know. And I continue to do it because I can't do anything else. I can't not write. I've always liked my friend Tom Piccirilli's description of this condition: If you're stranded alone on a desert island, and you spend your time writing stories in the sand with a stick, then you're meant to be a writer. I'd be one of those people. Instead of scrawling SOS in giant fucking letters on the beach, I'd be using that castaway time to finish my next novel.

And I do it for the young mother who contacted me on Twitter, and told me that her infant son had a brain tumor, and she was living at the hospital with him, and the only thing that kept her going in those long dark hours were my books. Apparently, she read through my entire backlist during that time.

I do it for the men and women serving in Iraq and Afghanistan and elsewhere who get so excited when a new book comes out. The squad who named themselves after a character in my books. The battalion who started a Brian Keene book club. The airmen of Whiteman Air Force Base's 509th Logistics who pooled their own money together and had a beautiful award fashioned for me simply because my book donations had boosted their morale.

And for the dozens of parents who've lost children and told me how *Dark Hollow* helped them grieve, and talk to their significant others about that grief.

And the dozens of others who told me how *Ghoul* helped them come to terms with their abusive childhoods.

And the dozens of single or divorced fathers who told me that *The Rising* made them rededicate themselves to their kids.

And the dozens of people who told me that after reading *The Girl on the Glider*, they made sure their spouse or partner knew how much they loved them.

And the dozens of inmates who write me letters saying they

never liked to read until they got to prison and discovered my books.

I put up with this shit because somebody has to do it. We are here to communicate truths that everyone already knows on some instinctual level but are unable to voice. It is our job to give words to those truths. We've been doing that since cave paintings. Our job, regardless of whether we are writing crime or horror or science fiction or westerns or romance or any other genre, is to examine the human condition. To say to the reader, "Hey? What you're feeling right now? It's okay. We all feel it." As writers, we must go beyond Conservative or Liberal, Republican or Democrat, Christian or Muslim, Jew or Hindu, Black or White. We must transcend politics, religion, race, sexual orientation, nationalism, patriotism, and every other fucking ism and communicate the one thing we all have in common—our humanity. What it is to be human.

Can people really remember every contextual detail of their first kiss—how it felt physically and emotionally? Can they really remember the sound of the voice of a long-dead relative? Can they remember what it's like to be five years old, and your entire world rests in your mother's arms? They might think they do, but they don't. The details get blurred. That's just the way the human mind works. The details are lost—until we bring them back again. This is what we do. This is why we put up with this shit.

The vast majority of the people who read our books are kind, gracious, genuine people just like ourselves. On days when the royalty checks haven't shown and another publisher has screwed me and another critic has savaged me and I have to go to the free clinic because I don't have health insurance—that it is the readers who keep me going. Fans and readers can be a source of strength and solace. It's a nice, symbiotic relationship. They get us through the long hours spent writing. We get them through study hall or their lunch hour or their commute or their bad marriage or incarceration or tour of duty or abusive relationship or their loneliness. And that is a noble thing.

That is a very noble thing.

I don't believe we choose to be writers (or musicians, painters or any other form of the arts). I believe we don't have a choice.

But if we can touch one reader, enrich their lives, entertain them, distract them, or help them articulate something they've desperately wanted to say for themselves but didn't know how, then we've done our jobs and done them well. And that is so very worth it. It's worth more than all the costs I mentioned before combined.

Thank you.

HOW PAUL CAMPION BECAME THE FRANK DARABONT TO MY STEPHEN KING

Fearnet has an extensive interview with Paul Campion about the success of his film *The Devil's Rock*, its sequel, how he and I became friends, and the latest on his adaptations of my works *Dark Hollow, Kill Whitey*, and *The Siqqusim Who Stole Christmas*.

Film-making is an even stranger and more cutthroat business than writing and publishing, and I learned long ago not to trust ninety-percent of the people involved in it. My advice to authors about to sign their first option is usually "get paid a lot up front" because all-too-often that's the only money you will see. Even if the film is made, and even if it's successful, and even if you managed to negotiate a contract that says you'll continue to get paid, Hollywood has all sorts of creative accounting tricks to show how a profitable film actually isn't, and therefore they don't owe you money. Then there are the yahoos who option your work and tie it up for years with no intention of making the movie, but simply to have it in their portfolio because you're considered "hot" or "edgy".

There are all sorts of other pitfalls and soul-sucks, too. I've written about much of this at length in *Sundancing*, which is out of print, but usually available on the secondary market.

Long ago, I decided my rule when dealing with anyone

involved with film-making was to get as many steak dinners and first class flights and up-front money as I could, because things often never progress beyond that, and not get close to anyone other than business-friendly.

Paul is one of the few exceptions to my rule (along with a handful of others such as William Miller, Damien Maffei, Mike Lombardo, etc.). I've known Paul for a decade. He's become a dear friend, and I trust him implicitly. Further, I trust his vision for my books. It took Frank Darabont over a decade to make *The Mist*. As Paul says in the *Fearnet* interview, it took twenty years for *Dallas Buyers Club* to get made. I don't care how long it takes—Paul Campion is the only person I trust to make *Dark Hollow* and *Kill Whitey*. You'll see them when he's done.

CRAWLING FROM THE WRECKAGE

I've been out of touch because the Polar Vortex came to town. After two months of ice storms, blizzards, power outages, burst pipes, fallen trees, sporadic internet access, school cancellations, HN1 death flu, near-bankruptcy (again), PTSD, and very little writing, I made it back to civilization in time for yesterday's appearance with Kasey Lansdale at Comix Connection (as well as a nice lunch with J.F. Gonzalez, Robert Swartwood, Chet Williamson, and Laurie Williamson).

The National Weather Service was calling for another six to ten inches of snow, but despite that, you folks showed up and made the signing a big success. Shout out to Chris who drove four hours from Poughkeepsie, NY, and the other Chris who drove up from College Park, MD, and Kevin who made the trek from Hagerstown, MD. Thanks to Deena for the cookies, and Paul for the *Dead Sea*-inspired painting. Special thanks to Tim Truman and Beth Truman for their kindness. And, as always, to Bill, Ned, Jared, Steve, and the rest of the Comix Connection crew for being such excellent hosts.

This morning I awoke to a pleasant surprise. Instead of the forecast six to ten inches, it looks like we'll get far less. Maybe this long, cold, dark winter is finally on the wane. That would be okay with me.

Things will remain sporadic here for the foreseeable future. After much careful thought and consideration, I'm abandoning this mountaintop cabin that I've lived in for the last two years and moving back to civilization. Yes, it was my dream home, and yes, I'm a prepper, but this situation has been tough on my youngest son. He deserves to live in a more comfortable setting where falling trees don't smash your emergency generator and where you don't have to pour river water into the toilet to flush it.

So, we're moving back to town. I'll find a different wilderness retreat when he's eighteen (and this time, I'll protect the generator better).

Thanks in advance for your continued patience during this —yet another—delay and transition.

THE SOUND OF ONE MAN GIVING UP

The more I explore Tumblr, the more I loathe it. Tumblr's the worst thing to happen to civil public discourse since CNN/FOX/MSNBC.

Being a white male doesn't mean I don't want to learn more on issues of gender or race. I just don't want to learn from the Tumblr crowd.

Me: Help me understand white male privilege?

Tumblr: No you're a white male and therefore hijacking the discussion so fuck you rarrrgghh!!!

I didn't want to sign up for Tumblr, but when you're a public figure, you have to reserve your name every time some new social media platform pops up. Otherwise, someone else gets it and then you've got some chump using your name and posting porn to Pinterest.

I've toyed and experimented with Tumblr, first by bringing back *Jobs In Hell*, and then, hoping for a bit more interaction other than just people clicking 'Like" and "ReBlog", switching it to essays. But, in preparation for those essays to come, I've been exploring Tumblr in-depth, and I still just don't dig it. Maybe I'm old, or maybe it's unrealistic of me to expect people to exchange ideas and viewpoints and knowledge civilly, regardless of which political affiliation, religion, gender, race, or sexual persuasion they might be.

But that seems to be the way of things now. Everything is like a sporting event, and you have to root for your home team. Conservatives versus Liberals. Christians versus Muslims. Heteros versus the LGBT community. Black versus White. Pre-52 fans versus the New52. There seems to be no room for us independent thinkers. No place to continue asking questions and testing our own boundaries and learning more about the world around us and the people living in it. I don't know. Call me old-fashioned, but in a world where female circumcision is still forced in some barbaric backwoods nations, shouldn't we be talking about that rather than the fucking cover to *Catwoman*? Republican, Democrat, Socialist, or Libertarian—shouldn't we all be concerned over the NSA's reach, and the Patriot Act's expansion under both Bush and Obama? Or do we have to wait until it directly impacts our next game of Candy Crush Saga?

I'd been told Tumblr was a place for such discussion, but it occurs to me that I should hunt down whoever told me that and punch them in the face. It's my impression that Tumblr is good for funny cat pics and porn and Benedict Cumberbatch fan clubs. I've found a few pages of note (Rachel Edidin's *Postcards From Space* and Greg Rucka's *Front Toward Enemy*). But if the type of discourse I'm looking for (the type that used to be found on Livejournal and Blogger, many years ago when we still had to live with the possibility of dinosaurs eating our dial-up routers) doesn't seem to exist here, overall. And to be honest, I don't feel like spending the time it will take to create it here—not when so many people already come to Brian Keene dot com for it anyway. It had been my hope to get those people to start coming here, and begin using my website more for breaking news and not much else, but—it occurs to me that maybe the best idea is to just keep things the way they were before.

So, yeah, look for this Tumblr page to turn into something else. Maybe funny Cthulhu pics or Cthulhu porn…

NICKOLAUS PACIONE: CONCERT PROMOTER

Nickolaus Pacione is a mentally-ill man from Illinois who fancies himself a writer and publisher. Over the past decade, he has stalked, harassed, or threatened over four dozen professional authors including (but not limited to) myself, Cherie Priest, Ramsey Campbell, Mary SanGiovanni, Kealan Patrick Burke, Angelina Hawkes-Craig, Darren McKeeman, Poppy Brite, Ray Garton, Christine Morgan, David Niall Wilson, and many more.

In recent years, he has also begun to target minors. Although his threats never progress beyond his basement, they are a source of annoyance and aggravation for many of his victims, and have earned him numerous visits from various law enforcement agencies, as well as several involuntary stays in mental health facilities. Unfortunately, like herpes, he always comes back. And also unfortunately, there is always some well-meaning or kind-hearted person who is not aware of Pacione's abusiveness, which is why I run these quarterly public service announcements (given his penchant for befriending people on social media and then stalking or harassing people from their friend lists).

And now, having utterly failed as a writer and being exposed as a publisher who doesn't pay his contributors and prints work without the author's permission, Pacione has decided to reinvent himself as a concert promoter.

His official announcement:

MC'ing Heavy Metal Shows: My Rider

Those of you who are promoters in Chicago want me to host a live show—I do have a rider this is rather easy too if you can get everything together. I ask for a $190 guarantee for out of state gigs and if you bring a Chicago band in and have me host—you must have someone help me get to the area because I can't drive. Don't offer me any alcohol during the show—I refuse to drink on stage when hosting a band or introducing them. When I hosted my friends Neutral Red—I was puking my guts up because my nerves were off the scale. One thing to keep around is a coffee maker; and a lot of coffee. If you can get Tourniquet's coffee for the show I never had this and those who knew me back when I was 18-19 years old I was drinking as much coffee as Metallica when they drank vodka. The coffee mug if you can grab one—try find a mug based upon H. P. Lovecraft or Edgar Allan Poe, if you can't get the coffee then two six packs of 24 oz Coke and six cans of Monster Java. I drink the latter on stage when I am introducing a band and helps me relax when I am nervous for friends who never played Chicago. The guarantee pays for both me and the out of state's food bill and in some ways pays for my hostel dorm in the city. The guarantee have that sent to my paypal.com account and I will get things going—I would sign a few anthologies during the meet and greet so keep room for me to bring in anthologies and what not or if the anthology is pre-signed I will be happy to do a Q&A. Italian Beef or Gyros (this is a Chicago era that is,) if outside of Illinois—find a fast food Italian place so I can have a plate of spaghetti. If you know anywhere you can get street food that's ideal for me because that's what I live on when I am traveling around. I am kind of like Anthony from No Reservations in this sense. I don't go to tourist traps. If you have me in for a few days—please tell me where I can get easy access to *a movie theater (if outside of Chicago that is. In the City I would go to The Showplace on the South Side.)*

And my official translation:

If you manage a club or concert hall featuring live heavy metal music, and would like a misogynistic, racist, homophobic, deranged squirrel with a voice like Alvin the chipmunk after a tracheotomy to introduce the bands, here are the terms.

1. It's free if your club is in Chicago. Anywhere else, there is an appearance fee of $190.

2. Plus travel fare because he doesn't drive.

3. Plus Tourniquet coffee, because he's never tried it and would like you to pay for it.

4. Plus a coffee mug featuring the likeness of either H.P. Lovecraft or Edgar Allan Poe.

5. Plus two six-packs of 24oz Coke and six cans of Monster Java **because these help him relax**.

6. But you don't have to buy his food or the band's food, because the $190 appearance fee is paying for that.

7. But you do have to provide a place that serves Italian Beef, Gyros, or "a plate of spaghetti" in which he can spend that $190.

8. And also provide a place to sign anthologies.

9. And also provide directions to the nearest movie theater.

Act now, because you want him careening around on stage before the band plays.

In his announcement, Pacione mentions "hosting his friends Neutral Red". What this means is he conned his way onstage before the band played. Thanks to the internet, we have two eyewitness accounts of what happened next.

An audience member reported (sic): "*it was pretty quick yet painful last night. in the minute or so he was up there he rambled on about something so fucking fast you could hear the crowd going "huh?" he moved one of his arms up at one point causing his concert shirt to pull up over his fat gut which made half the people cheer the other yell "ew" and gross. some chick laughed at that point loud enough to make others and it made him stutter a little more before he finished his spiel and got off the stage. didnt see them attack him though. oh someone yelled that he got the wrong size shirt which made people laugh too but I think he missed it. he was pretty nervous and shakey. and short and fat."*

And a band member from Neutral Red added (sic): "*pacione did some screaming into the mic (something we asked him to not do —he responded with something about "pumping the crowd up"), which clipped the board, promptly pissing the sound guy off. we then had to quickly explain that it was not us doing the screaming in an attempt to keep the sound guy from giving us the "P.A. fuck" as to which it is somtimes referred."*

So, there you go.

(Special thanks to "L", "Al Uylik", and our friends at *The Rusty Nail*, who helped with this report)

MISS MANNERS GUIDE TO BEING NOMINATED FOR A BRAM STOKER AWARD

Note: The Polar Vortex is about to dump a bunch more snow on us (apparently in an effort to drive me insane), school is cancelled, and I'm going to be busy with my son all day, so this won't be a long and thoughtful post. Bram Stoker season is upon us again, which always leads to sniping, arguing, and fighting, especially among authors who are HWA members versus authors who aren't. Every year, someone asks for my thoughts on the matter. So here they are, excerpted from a discussion this morning on my private Facebook page between myself, J.F. Gonzalez, *Ginger Nuts of Horror's* Jim McLeod, and others.

I've got two Stokers, and I think I still hold the record for most nominations in a year (nominations, not preliminary) but that being said—it's a popularity contest among other writers. Does it feel nice? Sure. But it's rarely representative of the larger readership or community, and instead, is a snapshot of who the HWA's cool kids are that particular year. Sometimes, deserving works make it onto the ballot, and sometimes, those deserving works even win ... but there's also a lot of blatant nepotism and nonsense on the ballot and in the process itself. Winning one feels nice. Of course it does. It's nice to win things. But the larger public doesn't care, and a win isn't going to do shit for your career. (Mike Oliveri can speak to that).

And therein lies my problem with the awards. If the nominees would just be gracious and humble and handle it with dignity and good grace, it'd be one thing. And most do. But... you also have the contingent of nominees who campaign relentlessly and annoy the fuck out of everyone else. And those people are usually the ones who landed on the ballot via nepotism in the first place. And they are the ones who taint the process for everyone else, including their fellow HWA members.

And understand, I'm only speaking about the campaigning for votes. I'm not even a member and already I'm getting spammed with "Hey, will you read this and consider voting?" That happens every year, and it's annoying and unseemly.

My only point was if you're nominated, conduct yourself with dignity and grace. And the flip side is also true. While it's okay to express your misgivings about the awards or the process (and many do) it's a dick move to disparage those nominated. Treat them with dignity and grace, as well.

ON RAPE AND REPUGNANCE

While I was offline dealing with a weather system that destroyed my new home, Janelle Asselin, one of my former editors at DC Comics, wrote an article for *CBR* critiquing the T&A aspects of the cover to the forthcoming *Teen Titans* #1. Some readers liked the article. Some didn't.

And some of those who didn't decided to anonymously threaten her with rape.

Think about that for a minute. Multiple individuals were so incensed over an article pointing out the sexual objectification of a teenage female superhero that they felt their only recourse was to threaten the writer of the article with rape. Sadly, this isn't the first time this has happened in the comic book section of publishing, nor is it only in comic books that it happens. I know of it happening in both the horror fiction and science fiction sectors, as well.

Too often, this is brushed aside or excused or ignored. In our own section of the industry, Nickolaus Pacione regularly threatens to rape various females, but too many of our peers shrug and say, "Well, he's mentally ill so it's okay" and then continue to follow him on Twitter for the comedic value of watching a train wreck.

Or we often hear the excuse, "Well, it was probably just some dumb kid making a dumb joke." That's horseshit. My oldest son is 24, and while I love him and am immensely proud of him, there are times he is the living embodiment of "all-the-dumb-things-we-all-did-at-24" (and I can't holler at him for it because I did many of the same things at that age). But no matter how many times he acts without thinking, he's not out threatening to rape people. It's disingenuous to excuse such transgressions as simply youth saying something stupid.

Another excuse I often see thrown around is "well, even if they threaten it, they'll never act on it". Which is, again, horseshit and misanthropic idiocy.

During my time offline, I was so incensed by what had happened to Janelle that I hopped online via my ex-wife's computer and posted to Facebook about it, promising that this essay you're now reading would be forthcoming once I'd finished my move. Loyal reader Thomas Clark shared the post on his wall. And then, something that calls itself Tim Bruzdzinski (I say 'something' because the individual in question is certainly not a man, and in my opinion, doesn't qualify as human) offers pearls of wisdom in the comments like *"idiot threats don't matter. Nobody is getting raped, this happens eleventy billion times every day and nothing ever comes of it."*

(Incidentally, Little Timmy is the front-man for a Syracuse-based bar band called Nails In The Pulpit, so yeah, fuck them.).

I've always had more female friends than male friends. Looking back, I'd say three out of every five women I've known has been directly impacted in some way by rape. I also know men who have been impacted by it, and not just indirectly. Rape happens. It's not a sexual crime. It's a violent crime—a crime of force and will and blood and pain and control. It is absolutely one of the most repugnant, heinous things a human being can perpetrate on another human being, and it leaves scars that never wholly heal no matter how much therapy you undergo or how much vodka you drink. To threaten another human being with rape makes you just as repugnant as the act itself.

We have spoken up about this within the horror fiction section of the industry before, and now, as a result of what has happened to Janelle, we see comic professionals beginning to speak out against it, as well. But that is not enough. I encourage professionals from all sectors and ghettos of publishing to speak up. Let your audience know that this type of behavior is unacceptable, regardless of race, creed, or gender. Whether you read comics or horror novels or science-fiction tie-ins or true crime or westerns, whether you're a socialist, libertarian, conservative, progressive, liberal, anarchist, or apolitical—you should agree that people should be treated equally and not threatened with fucking violence just because they wrote something you disagree with. If you can't agree to that, then quite frankly, I don't want you as a fan, or a reader, and I don't want you in my genre (and since they're giving me the Grand Master Award in Portland next week, it *is* my fucking genre).

And if you're a fellow professional, don't think "Well, my fans would never do this" or "I don't have an audience as large as Brian Keene or Joe Hill or Jeff Lemire or John Scalzi or Greg Rucka or Chuck Wendig so it's not worth it for me to speak up". Because that's horseshit, too. This is a problem that impacts us all, and it is your duty to speak up. If you make art, if you create entertainment, if you examine the world via words or pictures and offer folks a few hours of escapism and release, then you have a responsibility to get involved.

Which brings me to part two of this rant.

Amid the legitimate and justified outcry I've seen over this issue, I've also seen a secondary narrative decrying the usage of rape in comic books, television, horror novels, and other forms of the medium, and the suggestion that such works should be banned, and that there is something wrong with the people who create them or read them. This is also horseshit.

I'm a horror novelist. Just as it is a science-fiction writer's job to invoke a sense of wonder (or perhaps dread) about the future, it is my job to invoke unease and fear. All writers, regardless of what genre they work in, act as a mirror of sorts. We examine life and humanity and we write about those things. You may remember your first kiss, but do you really remember the actual emotions that came with it? Can you still articulate how it felt the first time you encountered death or love? How it felt the first time you realized your parents weren't infallible? What it was actually like to be six-years old, and the unique worldview that comes with that age? You may think you do, but you don't. Not really. Memories dim over time, leaving us with impressions, but nothing more. A writer's job is to make you feel those things again. We observe the world around us and we mine our observations into prose, and thus, make the reader feel them once again. As a horror writer, I'm meant to make you feel scared, uneasy, horrified, uncomfortable, etc. I'm supposed to examine what's out there in the darkness. There's nothing wrong with that. People have been examining the darkness since primitive man first drew comic books on cave walls. The Bible, the Koran, the Epic of Gilgamesh, the Vedas—all of our earliest texts contained elements of horror.

Rape is a horrific act. But to call for banning it from film or literature (and when I say literature, I'm including comics) is chilling, as well. Instead, perhaps a call should go out to use it responsibly, rather than gratuitously, but even then, that's a slippery slope. One person's porn is another person's art. One person reads an Edward Lee novel and is repulsed by the grotesqueness within. Another reads an Edward Lee novel and sees the clever social commentary nestled between the excess bodily fluids. Some people think *Crossed* is vile. Others think it is delightfully horrific. Personally, I'm repulsed by the so-called "rape porn", in which adult film stars act out scenes of violent rape, but as long as nothing illegal is occurring, I'm not going to tell someone else they can't watch it. There's a difference between two actors and a film crew in a studio following a fantasy script versus a victim and group of thugs armed with a cell phone camera in a back alley somewhere. Comics, film, and books have featured murder, cannibalism, and other atrocities (and not just in the horror genre). Why should rape be an exception?

An example I see offered again and again is *The Killing Joke*, a Batman graphic novel written by Alan Moore. There is a scene in which the Joker shoots and seemingly rapes Batgirl. The shooting is shown. The rape is suggested. But there's no doubt in the minds of most readers that it happened. Putting aside for the moment that Alan Moore is a horror writer (even his non-horror work such as *Watchmen* and *V For Vendetta* contain elements of the horror genre and influence from Lovecraft, Machen, Hodgson, and others) let's examine what Moore, as a writer, intended to do with that scene. He wanted to show just how violent and dangerously unhinged the Joker was. Furthermore, he wanted to shock and terrify the reader. As someone who read *The Killing Joke* upon its initial release in 1988, I can tell you he succeeded. Before that, the Joker has always been sort of a neat villain. With *The Killing Joke*, and specifically that particular scene, he became absolutely terrifying.

Moore used rape to a similar effect in the pages of *Swamp Thing*, when Abby Holland has sex with a man who she thinks is her husband, but in reality is her husband's corpse, possessed and reanimated by her uncle, Anton Arcane. Disgusting? Sure. Horrifying? Absolutely. Gratuitous? No, not in my opinion. Moore's goal in *Swamp Thing* was to scare the reader, and that scene was scary to the point that I remember it clearly, some three decades later.

I don't think the problem is using rape (or murder or cannibalism). I think it's *how* you use rape (or murder or cannibalism). And I think that awareness only comes with time, because you see others discussing it and then you look back and examine your own work.

I have two friends named Amanda and Eryn. If I ever had daughters, I'd want my daughters to be like Amanda and Eryn.

They are very much involved in geek culture, and unapologetic in their fight for equal standing at the comic book shop. They make me so proud and fill me with hope for this next generation (and I've never told them that before now). A few years ago, I signed a copy of *Castaways* for Amanda at a convention. Admittedly, she doesn't read much horror, preferring superheroes and sci-fi instead, but she read *Castaways*, and when she was finished, I asked her what she thought.

"It was okay," she responded, "but have you written anything without giant rape monsters in it?"

I explained my stance that rape made sense in the context of the book—the tribe of cryptids are dying out because of inbreeding, and they need new mates, and I pointed out the afterword I'd included at the book's conclusion, discussing rape and its usage and how it made me uncomfortable but it was necessary for the plot. But because I respect Amanda, and because she and Eryn teach me things without them even knowing it, I went back and examined the rest of my books. I've written a lot of them. I can happily say that not all of them include rape. But some do.

In the case of *Ghoul* and *Dark Hollow*, I'd argue that it was as necessary as it was in *Castaways*. But *The Rising*? Gratuitous. I didn't think so at the time. The man who wrote *The Rising* was a much younger man, and not as well-informed, and he thought he was showing how cruel humanity could be to one another after society collapses, but in going back and re-reading that old manuscript a decade later in advance of the publication of the anniversary edition? I cringed. I cringed and I thought, "Jesus fucking Christ, Brian. What the fuck were you thinking?" I was tempted to edit the scene down, but ultimately I didn't, because there are a bazillion other copies out there already. But I can tell you this—I don't like that scene, and I wish I'd written it differently.

And if we'd been having this discussion back in 1998, I

probably *would* have written it differently, *because I would have been more aware*.

And that, in a nutshell, is why it's important for creators to speak up now. I've done my part.

Now it's your turn.

Discuss. You have your own Blogs and social media outlets. It is not okay to threaten people with rape, and that shit stops now, but it only stops if you do your part.

CHILDREN PLAYING WITH GUNS

There is an early scene in the film version of *Battle Royale*, in which a shotgun-wielding Kawada confronts Shuya and Noriko and demands to know what kind of weapons they've received. Shuya sheepishly displays an innocuous pot lid, and Noriko is armed with a simple pair of binoculars. Kawada shakes his head, obviously bemused.

Battle Royale is full of weapons—automatic submachine guns, double-barrel shotguns, axes, hatchets, stun guns, bombs, and even a ludicrous paper fan. Most of these weapons are used at some point throughout the film, but it is the scenes depicting the non-gun violence that are among the most graphic and disturbing. Killing a fellow student with an Intratec TEC-DC9 or a Hi-Point 995 carbine can be done from a distance, thus allowing the killer to somewhat disassociate themselves from the act. Murdering a classmate with a machete or an ice pick requires a more personal involvement—the bloodying of one's hands, in a very literal sense. Shooting someone from seventy-five yards away keeps the brain matter off your boots. Stabbing them up close with a knife means you're close enough to smell the very particular stench that wafts from a fresh gut wound.

In the hands of a determined killer, anything can be a

weapon. The adults in *Battle Royale* knew this, as evidenced by the selection of weaponry they bestowed upon the unlucky students of class 3-B. And I knew it myself as a teenager in the early Eighties, when Frank Miller's seminal run on Marvel Comics' *Daredevil* introduced an entire generation to the ways of the ninja. My friends and I spent an entire summer obsessed with ninjas—saving money from our paper routes and allowances to order books and pamphlets offering 'The Secrets of Ninjitsu' from the backs of our fathers' copies of *Soldier of Fortune* magazines. Because ninjas supposedly had the ability to turn anything into a weapon, we would often play a game, pointing out innocuous, common household items to each other, and asking how we'd turn it into a weapon. (My pals thought they had me when they suggested a sheet of typing paper, until I decided that you could use it to deliver a paper-cut to someone's jugular vein).

My friends and I, it should be noted, were all normal (if somewhat hormonal) teenage kids. We may have listened to too much Iron Maiden and Black Flag, but none of us ever embarked on a shooting spree. Instead, we grew up to be parents and doctors and steelworkers, and, in my case, a writer.

It should also be noted that each of us knew our guns. I grew up in a small Pennsylvania paper mill town. Most years, it seemed like the union was on strike, which meant that funds were tight. Almost all of the families I knew supplemented their groceries and their government cheese handouts by hunting, and we were no strangers to venison, rabbit, or wild turkey on the table instead of Ballpark Franks. Hamburger Helper, it turns out, goes just as well with squirrel as it does with hamburger.

I learned to hunt when I was fourteen, and when I shot my first deer, I learned that I didn't have the stomach or conscience to be a hunter. Some of my friends discovered the same thing about themselves. Others took to hunting with zeal. But all of us knew how to shoot. More importantly, we knew how to safely handle a firearm. Hunting was so widespread in our community that we had classes in middle school on firearm training and safety. The first, and most important, safety tip was this—lock your guns up so your kids don't have access to them. And our parents did just that. In our households, we only handled those weapons with direct parental supervision. We played with toy guns, but we never played with real guns.

In today's culture, according to the plethora of gun laws on the books in most states, it is supposed to be harder for teenagers to gain access to firearms, and yet, in case after disturbing case, we hear of them obtaining such weapons with ease. Seung-Hui Cho, the college student who killed thirty-two people at Virginia Polytechnic Institute and State University, was able to legally purchase a number of firearms despite being diagnosed with several psychiatric disorders as far back as middle school, two previous stalking complaints by female students, and a history of abnormal behavior that concerned both family and friends. Sandy Hook Elementary shooter Adam Lanza obtained his guns at home, many of which were gifts from his mother, who encouraged his firearms training during trips to the local shooting range, despite a similar background to Cho's. Eric Harris and Dylan Klebold, the infamous teenaged Columbine gunmen, were able to obtain their weapons through straw purchases made by adult friends, paid for with money Harris earned working part-time at a local pizza shop.

So, obviously, the common denominator is guns. Except that it isn't. Just like the class of 3-B in *Battle Royale*, the arsenal of Columbine's Harris and Klebold's wasn't limited to firearms. The two had manufactured several different kinds of homemade bombs and pyrotechnics, as well as amassing a collection of knives and other non-explosive weapons. The pre-teen killer in Japan's Sasebo elementary school used a common utility knife to butcher his victims. The juvenile murderer in Japan's Kobe slayings used a hammer and a hacksaw on his targets. When Charles Carl Roberts besieged an Amish schoolhouse in rural Pennsylvania, his auxiliary weapons included chains, plastic ties, and a tube of K-Y sexual lubricant. And in the case of the Bath School massacre, a bomb and other improvised explosives killed thirty-six children and two adults.

In all of these cases except for the latter two, the massacres involved youth killing other youth. In *Battle Royale*, it is former teacher Kitano and his military cohorts who arm the students prior to turning them on each other. Can the same be said of these real-life cases of child-on-child murder? Perhaps not maliciously, but does gross parental irresponsibility (such as in the case of Adam Lanza's mother, Nancy) not equate the same thing? In some cases, possibly. It's natural for us to wonder what Nancy Lanza was thinking, encouraging her emotionally disturbed teen to take up firearms and go target-shooting with her. We can't ask her, since she was Lanza's first victim, shot in the head four times while lying in bed. But we can wonder. Was she aware that she was arming him for a massacre to come? Or was she simply a stressed-out single mother, trying to do the best for her special needs child, a child who had trouble connecting with others? Did she find that connection through target shooting, a pastime enjoyed by hundreds of thousands of responsible parents and teens throughout America?

Or what of Eric Harris, whose basement bedroom was filled with explosives, detonators, ammunition, and bomb-making equipment? Were his parents culpable in arming him, simply by not going into his bedroom and finding such materials? Was the local sheriff's department equally responsible by preparing a draft search warrant for his home after learning Harris and Klebold had been fashioning pipe bombs and threatening their classmates—but never formally filing the search warrant or following up on the claims?

Perhaps not. No parent wants to consider the possibility that their child is a murderous psychopath. Indeed, few parents even know what warning signs to look for. Focusing on greater mental health care and awareness is a good start. But so many of those "warning signs" are behaviors seen as normal in our everyday teen society. A fascination with violent video games, comic books, movies, or literature? Lock up ninety-percent of our youth. A fondness for heavy metal or gangsta rap? Ditto. Weaponry? What about those kids like me and my friends, hunting with our fathers or playing with ninja throwing stars we bought at a flea market for a buck a piece? We didn't take those throwing stars to school and begin puncturing our classmates with them. At worst, we impaled a few trees.

Despite the plethora of plain sight evidence against Harris, most of his classmates and teachers described him as bright, friendly, and outgoing. His accomplice, Klebold seemed "nice, but shy. Kind of quiet." To many of their victims, they seemed like normal kids, until the killing started—just like the children of class 3-B. Sure, we learn early on that Mitsoku is a sociopath. (In an extended-cut version of the film, it is revealed that murderous tendencies are rooted in an earlier attempted molestation at the hands of her mother's boyfriend, whom Mitsoku pushes to his death down a flight of stairs.) And sadistic transfer student Kazuo Kiriyama is certainly no stranger to killing. Indeed, he seems to revel in it. But the vast majority of the kids in *Battle Royale* are just that—kids, normal teenagers who are suddenly armed by adults and told to slaughter each other.

Because it's the law.

It is easy to point to America's gun laws, and argue for more restrictions. But the fact remains that in almost every case, the culprits obtained their guns either by circumventing the very laws designed to safeguard against such atrocities or through the adults in their lives. While an argument for stricter gun laws can certainly be made (and should be discussed—calmly, rationally, and without the hyperbole from both the Left and the Right)— the fact remains that such laws would not have prevented these massacres from occurring. Nor would they have stopped the culprits in the Kobe murders or the Bath bombing or so many other cases.

So, what then, are we to do? If enforcement of current gun laws or the passage of yet stricter laws won't help, and if parents can't responsibly access and identify if their child may be at risk of committing such heinous atrocities, then what are we to do?

Is it possible that *Battle Royale*, like the best dystopian science fiction, is a dark precursor to what's to come—a prediction of what lies ahead for our children and our society? Could it be the antithesis to The Who's statement that "the kids are all right"?

During *Battle Royale's* climax, a mortally wounded Kitano tells his daughter, Shiori that "If you hate someone, you take the consequences". As a parent, I've taught my children to always stand up for themselves and those they care about, and to never, ever tolerate a bully, be it a classmate or some aspect of the system itself. But I've also taught them not to hate. I like to think I've succeeded—that they don't view others in terms of race or gender or faith or sexual preference. I've tried to teach them that love is the answer to all things, and that the only things that deserve hate are ignorance and oppression. I hope that I have armed them, not with machine guns or axes or pot lids, but with compassion and reason.

But every morning, when I drop my son off for another full day of kindergarten, and I watch until he goes inside and disappears from my sight, I'm left wondering what lessons his classmates are learning at home, or from each other, or from our society, and what the consequences of those lessons might one day be. I wonder what they're being armed with, and what weapons are in their arsenals, and if compassion and reason and love are an equal match.

And then, I wait for the school day to be over so I can hold him again.

GRAND-MASTER AWARD ACCEPTANCE SPEECH
(WORLD HORROR CONVENTION 2014)

Thank you, Don, for that wonderful introduction, and thank all of you for being here. I stand before you today expressing two things you probably didn't expect from me—humbleness and humility.

It's impossible to not be humble when you consider the previous winners of this award. Before writing this speech, I went back and perused the list, just to freshen my memory. Previous winners are (in order) Robert Bloch, Stephen King, Richard Matheson, Anne Rice, Clive Barker, Dean Koontz, Peter Straub, Brian Lumley, Ramsey Campbell, Harlan Ellison, Ray Bradbury, Charles Grant, Chelsea Quinn Yarbro, Jack Williamson, F. Paul Wilson, Ray Garton, Joe Lansdale, Robert McCammon, Tanith Lee, James Herbert, Jack Ketchum, T.E.D. Klein, and Dan Simmons.

And now me.

You know what that's like? It's like you go to the Rock and Roll Hall of Fame induction ceremony and you're looking at all of the previous winners—The Beatles, The Rolling Stones, George Clinton and the Parliament, Jimi Hendrix, Black Sabbath, Led Zeppelin, Metallica, NWA, Guns n Roses… and then you find out tonight's honoree is Justin Bieber.

My name is Brian Keene and I am the Justin Bieber of the horror genre.

It's impossible to accept this award without humbleness and humility. I feel those things very deeply today. And those aren't the only things I feel. In the months leading up to this, it's been a struggle for me to feel that I was worthy of this honor, and to feel like I belonged to the canon of authors who received it before me.

I remember the very first World Horror Convention I ever attended. This was back in 1999, when the Internet was still relatively new and most of us were still sending submissions via snail mail with the required Self Addressed Stamped Envelope. Before attending that convention, the only author I'd ever met in person was Joe Lansdale, who I met during a signing he and Tim Truman were doing at a local comic book store. And that meeting didn't count because my conversation with him was limited to, "Holy shit. You're Joe fucking Lansdale" and "Could you make that out to Brian", and finally, "Holy shit. You're Joe fucking Lansdale."

So, prior to World Horror Convention, most of my interactions with my peers had been conducted solely online, using Windows 3.0 and a very primitive chat room that took approximately twenty minutes to refresh every time you typed a response. On the airport shuttle, I met Gak, an artist whose name I recognized because we'd been appearing in the same fanzines together, and whose art, years later, is now indelibly inked across much of my back in the form of a large tattoo.

When we got to the hotel, Gak disappeared. My room wasn't ready yet, and I found myself standing in the lobby, not sure what to do next. There was a guy dressed all in black sprawled across one of the sofas in the lobby. He looked like the love child of Rob Zombie and Blue Oyster Cult's Buck Dharma. There's no one else around. And then this guy, maybe sensing that I'm lost or unsure, calls me over and shows me something he'd just bought in the dealer's room. To this day, I can't tell you what the item was, because it quickly dawned on me that the guy was John Shirley. He's trying to show it to me and have an intelligent conversation with me about it, and meanwhile, I'm standing there with my mouth clamped shut because I know if I open it, I'm going to shout things like "Dude, you wrote *A Splendid Chaos*! You're John fucking Shirley!"

Most of the weekend was like that. I quickly discovered just how open and welcoming this community of ours is, and in moments—be it having dinner with Brian Hodge and Yvonne Navarro, or socializing at a party with folks like Neil Gaiman or getting high with Ramsey Campbell—I repeatedly resisted the urge to shout at them about who they were and what they'd written and then melt down into a quivering puddle of fan boy goo.

It is fair to say that particular WHC changed the course of my life. It was at that con that I also met most of the peers I'd been talking with online. We all quickly became friends—and in the decade and a half that have followed, they remain some of the best friends I have ever had in life. Indeed, one of them (Mary) eventually went from being one of my best friends to the woman I love.

But it also changed the course of my life for another reason. Before attending that convention, I'd approached writing as a past time—a hobby. I'd write things occasionally and send them out to zines, and sometimes they'd get published and more often they got rejected. Coming home from that first WHC, I was driven to write. Compelled to write. It changed my entire outlook and approach to this vocation. I began writing every evening, no matter how tired I was at the end of the day. The publication versus rejection ratio changed. I became more involved with our community. I finally began to view myself as a writer, rather than as a blue collar guy who worked a succession of various jobs and wrote occasionally on weekends.

I'd always dreamed of writing for a living. Attending that

first WHC was what finally gave me the gumption to actually strive towards it.

At my second World Horror Convention, Richard Laymon introduced me to his editor, Don D'Auria, and told him about a little zombie novel I was working on. Don talked about that in the introduction to this event. At my third World Horror Convention, Jack Ketchum sat down with me at the hotel bar and went over the contract for that zombie novel with a red pen and taught me everything I'd ever need to know about negotiating a publishing contract. I still have that red-penned original at home, and I still have the receipt for the bottle of scotch I bought him in return.

I've been coming to World Horror ever since. It's done a lot for me, and I hope I've done a lot for it.

World Horror is not a fan convention. It's a professional gathering—a trade show for those of us who are involved in dark fiction and publishing. But it's also a family reunion. Like any family, we don't always get along the rest of the year. But the drama seems to fall by the wayside when the family gathers here. As horror writers, we're used to having to defend ourselves from attacks. Writers from other genres belittle us, the media often excoriates us, our friends and family and agents wonder aloud when we're going to write something serious—we're used to having our backs against the wall. It has been my experience that when that happens, our family—our tribe—invariably bands together and stands firm. We have each other's backs.

As a full time writer, I can't count on retirement or a 401K or health insurance or even a steady paycheck. But I can always count on you, my tribe, and I'd like to think I've shown that you can always count on me. Trends change, publishers go under, and readers can be fickle, but at the end of the day, we still have each other, and we still have this wonderful genre for which we all share a deep and abiding love and appreciation.

Due to the bidding nature of the con, some WHCs are deservedly legendary. Others are unmitigated disasters. I think we all know by now which this year's con is. And if this is your first WHC, you might be justifiably scratching your head and wondering WTF. But here's the thing, folks. It doesn't matter who is putting on that year's WHC. They're competence or incompetence doesn't matter. What matters is that you are among friends. You are among family. Horror writers have always been welcoming of anyone, regardless of race, creed, gender, or sexual orientation. Indeed, we've often been the first to do so. You will never find a more welcoming, friendly, and good-humored group than the people in this tribe.

And even though I still don't think I deserve it, the people of this tribe have decided that I should receive this award, and thus I do so with great humility and humbleness and honor.

In closing, I'd like to do one thing, and then I'll be happy to answer questions. Bookseller Alan Beatts used to throw an awesome party every year at WHC. During the party, he would get everyone's attention and have them look around the room and find one person that they did not know. Then he'd invite everyone to go introduce themselves to that person. I'd like to ask you to do that now.

As Robert DeNiro says in *Brazil*, "we're all in this together."

Look around this ballroom. Find someone you don't know, and go welcome them to the family.

Thank you.

WHAT WAS I THINKING?

Dark Fantasy author John Urbancik, who is one of my closest friends, took this pic of me one morning in Portland six weeks ago. A few hours after it was taken, I was presented with the Grand Master Award. John told me I could use it for my new publicity photo, and I will, since my last official publicity photo was taken when the movie version of *Ghoul* came out, and I've changed a bit since then (the beard for starters).

I posted the pic on social media yesterday, and a number of people on Facebook, Twitter, Whosay, and elsewhere asked me what I was thinking when John snapped the shot.

Well, I'll tell you what I was thinking…

I was thinking about money, and how it fluctuates, and how royalty checks and advances are like dipping your hands in a mountain stream. I was thinking about how your cupped hands are initially full, and so is your belly as you take a deep drink, but very quickly, the water slips between your fingers, leaving your hands empty. And soon enough, your belly is empty, too. I was thinking about how writers get paid, and how financial security seems to elude the vast majority of us. I was thinking about whether or not I could afford to take my girlfriend out to eat after I got the award that night. I was thinking that it was time to re-think how I'm doing business, and actually start doing business again.

I was thinking about the group of writers I started out with, and who was still around, and who wasn't, and who had made it, and who hadn't, and if there was anything else I could do to help those who hadn't, and if so, what. I was thinking about the peculiar form of guilt that comes with success, and how you can pull for others until your fingers bleed, but at the end of the day, it's up to them and luck. I was thinking that you cannot control luck and you cannot control others, but you can control your own misplaced guilt, and decide that you're allowed to be happy with what you've accomplished.

I was thinking about those accomplishments, and how my son and his mother and my peers and my friends and my girlfriend and my girlfriend's family had all said how proud they were of my accomplishments, and the award, but that the people who I'd wanted to hear it from the most made their indifference clear, and how that sucked. And then I thought about how I'm 46-years old, and I've already written *Ghoul*, so fuck that noise. I was thinking you can be a disappointment to others, as long as you're not a disappointment to yourself.

I was thinking about how it had been a very long time since I'd written a full novel. I was thinking about how the last full novel was *Entombed*, and that was written in 2009. I was thinking about how *Clickers vs. Zombies*, *The Damned Highway*, and *Sixty-Five Stirrup Iron Road* didn't count, because I didn't write them by myself. I was thinking about how five-years' worth of nonsense, starting with a heart attack, a divorce, and the epic Dorchester clusterfuck and ending most recently with more health problems and an uninhabitable post-storm mountaintop home and a very-real case of PTSD, had really wreaked havoc on not only my ability to write, but on my confidence overall. I was thinking about how I'd focused for the last five years on getting the backlist back into print again, and tried my hand at producing a movie, and writing comic books, all in an effort to lie to myself that I was busy with other things, when the truth was, I was meant to be writing novels. I was thinking about how I'd failed to heed my own advice, given time and time again, about writer's block, and how it's nothing more than an excuse, and yeah, maybe the excuse was I felt washed up and tired and didn't have the drive to do it anymore, but fuck that noise, they're giving me a Grand Master Award, and a few moments ago I was thinking about how it would be nice to not be broke for a change, so maybe I'd better face down my fucking fears and start typing some shit again. I was thinking about getting home, and tackling things realistically, and getting out from under a few deadlines (done), and then taking care of manuscripts and Lifetimers (now), and then mailing packages to people who are owed packages and sorting out the technical issues with the forum that prevent me from joining you (next) and then nailing the rest of the deadlines (after next).

I was thinking about how I'm almost fifty, and that's actually pretty cool, and about what a long, fucked-up trip it's been, and about how that trip isn't near finished yet, and about how, yeah, maybe I did pull into a Rest Stop for five years and fell asleep in the bathroom as an excuse not to write, but it was time to get back on the bike and see the rest of the road.

So I did. And have been doing so for the last six weeks.

That's what I was thinking when John took the picture.

Thanks for asking.

NOT DEAD YET

Well, that was fun, wasn't it?

Maybe for you. Not so much for me.

I'm typing this on a cool morning in September 2014, after having spent the last week compiling and editing the material in this book you've just read. Much of it was as new to me as it probably was to you. I don't often go back and re-read Blog entries, essays, or other things I've written. When I write them, they're usually borne out of some desperate desire to get something off my chest, or vent, or try to impart my perspectives on various matters in a timely fashion.

In going back through this book, and re-reading the material, I got to relive my second divorce, the long and protracted Dorchester war, the downfall of Borders, my personal financial ruin (twice), the death of my grandfather, the death of my dog, my heart attack, a serious case of bronchitis, the bullshit I went through with a comic company I'd wanted to write for my entire life, two hurricanes, a tropical storm, several blizzards courtesy of the Polar Vortex, and two houses and two apartments (the moves to which were necessitated either by bankruptcy or the weather).

And those are just the things the public knows about. There's a whole bunch of shit that I never even mentioned here.

I thought about calling this book *Brian Keene's Country Songs*, but decided against it (the joke being that nothing good ever happens to the protagonists in country songs). If this book was fiction, you'd tell me that above laundry list of calamities and setbacks were too unbelievable. But they are all-too-real. They happened, one after the other. They happened to me.

And despite that, I'm still standing. Bloody, certainly. Beaten, for sure. But definitely not broken.

This book spans the years 2009 to 2014. I can honestly say, without hyperbole or exaggeration, that those six years have been the most difficult, trying, demoralizing years of my life. There have been several times where I almost gave up, and a full year of counseling sessions with a shrink, and at least one possibly subconscious suicide attempt, which involved me falling off a cliff into rushing, hurricane-swollen waters that smashed me into rocks and almost drowned me and ultimately concluded in me hiking through the wilderness while bleeding, and then having a nifty new scar and a fun story to tell people when they ask why my iPhone is shattered and held together with clear packing tape.

See? I told you there were other things that happened to me in the past few years that you didn't know about.

But I digress.

When I think about it a bit more, I also realize that the last six years have brought me one of the highest honors in our industry, and (for a while) awesome times with an awesome girlfriend to whom I will always be indebted (even though we eventually parted), and wonderful days spent with my youngest son, and a deep and profound post-divorce friendship with his mother, and the certainty of knowing who really cares about me and who is just along for the ride. So I guess it hasn't been all bad.

It's just life. Good. Bad. The universe is indifferent. The

universe doesn't care about your trials, triumphs, or tribulations. The universe just is.

As I write this, my heart gave me some trouble again yesterday, and I'm still broke, and still getting used to having downsized from a mountaintop cabin to an apartment, and way behind on deadlines. But I also had a nice day with my son, and some quality time with my cat, and this weekend I'm going to do some writing.

The universe just is.

If there's one thing the last six years have taught me, it's that anything can happen at any time. It doesn't matter how prepared you are, how confident you are, or how ready you think you are. Things turn on a dime. Changes aren't permanent, but change is (to quote Rush). Enjoy every good moment, be it something as simple as playing Legos with your child or a hug from your partner or a walk with your dog. Never think that things can't get worse, because they most certainly can.

Just like in a Brian Keene novel.

But I'm still standing.

And I intend to go on enjoying the little things.

And I intend to keep fighting back against the bad things.

And I'm not dead yet.

Brian Keene
September 2014

ABOUT THE AUTHOR

BRIAN KEENE writes novels, comic books, stories, journalism, and other words for money. He is the author of over fifty books, mostly in the horror, crime, and dark fantasy genres.

His 2003 novel, *The Rising*, is credited (along with Robert Kirkman's *The Walking Dead* comic and Danny Boyle's *28 Days Later* film) with inspiring pop culture's recurrent interest in zombies. Keene's books have been translated into German, Spanish, Russian, Polish, Italian, French, Taiwanese, and many other languages. He oversees Maelstrom, a small press publishing imprint specializing in collectible limited editions, via Thunderstorm Books.

He has written for such Marvel and DC properties as *Thor, Doom Patrol, Justice League, Harley Quinn, Devil-Slayer, Superman, and Masters of the Universe*, as well as his own critically acclaimed creator-owned comic series *The Last Zombie*. Keene has also written for media properties such as *Doctor Who, The X-Files, Hellboy,* and *Aliens.*

Keene also hosts the popular podcasts *The Horror Show with Brian Keene* and *Defenders Dialogue,* both of which air weekly on iTunes, Spotify, Stitcher, YouTube, and elsewhere.

Several of Keene's novels and stories have been adapted for film, including *Ghoul, The Naughty List, The Ties That Bind,* and *Fast Zombies Suck.* Several more are in-development. Keene also served as Executive Producer for the feature length film *I'm Dreaming of a White Doomsday.*

Keene's work has been praised by *The New York Times, The History Channel, The Howard Stern Show, CNN, The Huffington Post, Bleeding Cool, Publisher's Weekly, Fangoria, Bloody Disgusting,* and *Rue Morgue.*

His numerous awards and honors include the 2014 World Horror Grandmaster Award, 2001 Bram Stoker Award for Nonfiction, 2003 Bram Stoker Award for First Novel, the 2016 Imadjinn Award for Best Fantasy Novel, the 2015 Imaginarium Film Festival Awards for Best Screenplay, Best Short Film Genre, and Best Short Film Overall, the 2004 Shocker Award for Book of the Year, and Honors from United States Army International Security Assistance Force in Afghanistan and Whiteman A.F.B. (home of the B-2 Stealth Bomber) 509th Logistics Fuels Flight. A prolific public speaker, Keene has delivered talks at conventions, college campuses, theaters, and inside Central Intelligence Agency headquarters in Langley, VA.

Keene serves on the Board of Directors for the Scares That Care 501c charity organization.

The father of two sons, Keene lives in rural Pennsylvania with author Mary SanGiovanni.

Printed in Great Britain
by Amazon